Praise for Carla Neggers' *New York Times* bestselling Swift River Valley novels

Also by Carla Neggers

Swift River Valley

RED CLOVER INN
THE SPRING AT MOSS HILL
A KNIGHTS BRIDGE CHRISTMAS
ECHO LAKE
CHRISTMAS AT CARRIAGE HILL
    (novella)
CIDER BROOK
THAT NIGHT ON THISTLE LANE
SECRETS OF THE LOST SUMMER

Sharpe & Donovan

THIEF'S MARK
LIAR'S KEY
KEEPER'S REACH
HARBOR ISLAND
DECLAN'S CROSS
ROCK POINT (novella)
HERON'S COVE
SAINT'S GATE

The Ireland Series

THE WHISPER
THE MIST
THE ANGEL
THE WIDOW

Black Falls

COLD DAWN
COLD RIVER
COLD PURSUIT

Cold Ridge

ABANDON
BREAKWATER
DARK SKY
THE RAPIDS
NIGHT'S LANDING
COLD RIDGE

Carriage House

THE HARBOR
STONEBROOK COTTAGE
THE CABIN
THE CARRIAGE HOUSE

Stand-Alone Novels

THE WATERFALL
ON FIRE
KISS THE MOON
TEMPTING FATE
CUT AND RUN
BETRAYALS
CLAIM THE CROWN

Look for Carla Neggers' next novel
in the Sharpe & Donovan series
IMPOSTOR'S LURE
available soon from MIRA Books.

CARLA NEGGERS

the RIVER HOUSE

mira

mira

ISBN-13: 978-0-7783-3083-7

The River House

Recycling programs
for this product may
not exist in your area.

For questions and comments about the quality of this book, please contact us at CustomerService@Harlequin.com.

www.Harlequin.com

Printed in U.S.A.

To the memory of my cousin
Mary Ann Harrell Domingos,
always in our hearts

the
RIVER HOUSE

One

"We have to have badgers at your party."

Felicity MacGregor knew her comment would raise most people's eyebrows, but she also knew Kylie Shaw would be fine with it.

"Absolutely," Kylie said. "Russ and I had a badger couple on our wedding cake."

That spring, Kylie's whirlwind romance with Russ Colton, a security consultant, had taken them both by surprise, never mind everyone else in their small town of Knights Bridge, Massachusetts. Felicity smiled. "Of course you did." They were seated across from each other at the table on the balcony of Kylie and Russ's second-floor apartment in a renovated nineteenth-century hat factory. The balcony overlooked the river, flowing gently on the warm summer afternoon. Russ had spent the past two weeks in Southern California, wrapping up his life and work there now that he and Kylie had decided to settle in Knights Bridge. They'd bought a house a mile or so farther up the river and were having work done on it before moving in later in the summer.

Kylie reached for her iced tea. "Russ let Sherlock

Badger oversee security for the wedding," she said, matter-of-fact.

Sherlock was one of her popular fictional characters. "I'm sure Sherlock did a fine job," Felicity said.

"He's the best. Russ likes to say we'll be fine provided I don't confuse my Middle Branch badgers with real badgers."

"Who says your Middle Branch badgers aren't real?"

Kylie beamed. "Exactly what I tell him!"

Felicity wouldn't be surprised if Kylie was only half kidding. Under her pseudonym of Morwenna Mills, she was the creator of the Badgers of Middle Branch, a popular series of children's books. Felicity, an event planner, was helping Kylie with a party to celebrate the newest installment in the series, set in an idyllic village on a river. The mom and dad badgers were veterinarians, modeled after Kylie's own family. A tiny version of Sherlock Badger occupied a spot on Kylie's worktable. She'd made the mini badger herself with scraps of fabric and tufts of dryer lint.

Unlike Felicity, Kylie hadn't grown up in Knights Bridge. They'd hit it off upon Felicity's return to her hometown in May, when she'd bought a house farther up on the river, just down from the site of Kylie and Russ's new house. Felicity loved her house despite her complicated personal history with it, seeing how she'd lost her virginity there. Not in the house itself. It hadn't been built yet. But on a blanket in front of the outdoor fireplace that still stood there...

"Knights Bridge is keeping you busy, Felicity," Kylie said.

She yanked herself out of her thoughts. "Works for me. I'm having a blast."

Kylie studied her a moment, as if guessing Felicity's mind had wandered to someplace forbidden. They were both wearing dresses, given the warm weather, Kylie in a casual maxi, Felicity in a knee-length tunic. Kylie had her hair pulled back, its pale blond making her blue eyes stand out. Felicity had never been good with hair. Hers was dark blond, shoulder-length and unruly unless she fussed with it, which she rarely did.

"My book party is just a week after the launch of the entrepreneurial boot camp," Kylie said. "That won't stretch you too thin?"

"Not at all." The one-day boot camp, the brainchild of Dylan McCaffrey, another Knights Bridge newcomer, was Felicity's biggest event yet in her hometown. "I did corporate event planning in Boston for three years. I love being on my own, having the chance to do more fun events. Baby showers, bridal showers— your book party. I have a Jane Austen tea party on Sunday at the local assisted-living residence."

"The aptly named Rivendell. There's a lot of knowledge in that place."

"No question," Felicity said. "The tea includes a literary lecture and Regency period costumes."

"You must know almost everyone there." Kylie drank some of her tea and returned the glass to the table. Lunch had been simple—salads from the local country store, chocolate, iced tea. "I'm still fairly new to Knights Bridge. I'm doing better with names and faces, but I still get lost in the connections between the locals. Russ does, too, but he figures sometimes the less he knows, the better. He doesn't want to know who slept with whom as teenagers, that's for sure."

Felicity wondered if her cheeks had reddened, given the turn her mind had taken a few minutes ago. "I don't, either, but since I *did* grow up here…" She picked up her iced tea. "I'll leave it at that."

"Now that's a tease! Not you and Mark Flanagan—"

"No," Felicity said. "Absolutely not. Never."

But Mark, the architect who'd renovated and owned the old mill, had a brother, and he was another story altogether.

Felicity shook off *that* thought, gulped her tea and returned to planning Kylie's book-launch party. They'd chosen the Knights Bridge Free Public Library as the venue. Written before Kylie had met Russ, this latest installment featured a lonely badger aunt who helps the mice and the badger kids with their fairy-house dilemma and in so doing reunites with her own family and friends. Felicity could sort of identify with Auntie Badger. Kylie was also illustrating a series of classic fairy tales that would launch over the winter with *Hansel and Gretel*. Then came *Sleeping Beauty* and *Little Red Riding Hood*. She was working on *Beauty and the Beast*. Felicity assumed there'd be a launch party for the series, but she and Kylie hadn't gotten that far in their discussions.

"I've been holed up here working for weeks," Kylie said with a contented sigh. "It'll be good to be around people again."

"Going from solitude to a launch party is a big change."

"It is, for sure. I've kept up with my children's story

hour at the library, and I sometimes run into people when I'm out for a walk."

Felicity had come to realize Kylie wasn't the least bit antisocial. She just had protracted periods of deep work. Felicity thought she understood, but her own work as an event manager was quite different. For one thing, the events she organized were never *her* parties, meetings or conferences. Kylie's books were very much hers. She was dedicated to her work. Felicity liked running her own business, but she'd expected to have a career in finance. When that didn't pan out, she'd ventured into event planning. She'd learned the ropes working with a small, high-end business in Boston and struck out on her own nine months ago, finally returning to Knights Bridge.

In Boston, she'd never known her clients on a personal level. These days she found herself planning events with clients who were friends and neighbors. She still had a handful of out-of-town corporate clients, but her small hometown was bursting at the seams with all sorts of parties and events. Weddings, milestone birthdays, babies, retirements, new jobs, housewarming parties. She didn't plan every get-together in town, and she didn't focus on weddings—they were a particular specialty—but with an experienced event manager right there on the river, why not hire her?

"We need to throw a party for *you* one day," Kylie said, breaking into Felicity's thoughts.

"Me? I'd need something to celebrate."

"Pick something. It doesn't have to be big. Paint the kitchen. We'll celebrate."

Felicity didn't for a moment doubt Kylie's sincerity. Kylie was incredibly genuine, with none of the maneuvering and artificial niceties Felicity had too often witnessed in her work. "Cake it is," she said lightly. "In the meantime, I'm enjoying your badgers."

"If anyone can make badgers work at a party, it's you, Felicity."

"Thanks, I appreciate that. I have some ideas I want to explore. Feel free to let me know if you have any suggestions," Felicity said as they wrapped up the party plans.

"It'll be a fun evening. Thanks for stopping by."

Kylie started to get up, but Felicity stopped her. "I'll see myself out. Enjoy the perfect summer day."

"It is perfect, isn't it?" Kylie sighed, the sunlight catching her eyes. "I came to Knights Bridge never thinking I'd stay. Now it's home." She shifted her gaze back to Felicity, who was on her feet, collecting lunch dishes. "I'll get those. Sometimes I'm tempted to throw my dirty dishes in the river, but the ducks would have my head if Mark didn't. Oh, wait. That reminds me. He asked me to tell you that his brother is a last-minute addition to the boot camp speaker lineup and is hiring you to organize a party at the end of the day."

"Mark—Mark Flanagan's brother?"

"Right. Only Mark I know here."

The only one Felicity knew, too, but she'd needed to cover for her shock.

Kylie frowned. "You know his brother, don't you? Gabe, isn't it? Short for Gabriel?"

Oh, she knew him, all right. She'd just been thinking about him. That night before they'd set off for college. He'd been working construction and had been tanned and muscular, eager to get out of Knights

Bridge and make something of himself. She'd been working at her father's bank in the village and restless.

Felicity nodded. "Gabe is Mark's younger brother." She tried not to sound too stiff. Keep it casual. Matter-of-fact. "It's just the two of them."

"That's what I thought." Kylie swooped up her tea glass, no sign she knew she'd stepped on a hornets' nest. "Mark had to be out of town this morning on business and wasn't sure when he'd return. It must be late in the game to add a party, but if anyone can swing it, it's you, although I suppose you could always say no."

"Thanks for letting me know." Felicity reminded herself she'd been hired to do a job, and if Gabe had been added as a speaker and wanted to sponsor a party, she would have to manage. Even if her stomach was churning. "It's short notice, but the boot camp is straightforward as events go—sort of an open house with speakers. It'll be fine."

The one-day event was meant to provide a taste of what Dylan had in mind for the periodic entrepreneurial boot camps he planned to host in Knights Bridge throughout the year. He was an ex-professional hockey player and a multimillionaire businessman from California who'd fallen in love with Olivia Frost, a graphic designer who'd returned to her hometown last year to open an inn. They were married on Christmas Eve. A few months earlier, Olivia's sister, Jessica, had married Mark Flanagan. That was just one of the many connections that were part of life in their small town.

Felicity smiled, trying to take any shock and dread out of her expression. She was a pro. She needed to act like one. She swallowed, breathed. "Gabe isn't in town yet, is he?"

"I don't think so," Kylie said. "Mark didn't say."

Felicity gathered dishes and started toward the glass doors into the apartment. "I assume Gabe will be staying with him. Doesn't matter. Thanks for the information."

"Mark will be back soon if you want to talk to him."

Felicity thanked her again and headed into the apartment. She dropped off her dishes in the kitchen. The mill's dozen apartments were spacious, sleek and modern, with an industrial feel to them—Mark hadn't fought the building's origins—given their tall, arched windows, cement floors and brick walls. Felicity loved the views of the winding, shallow river. Kylie had added her own touches to her apartment, now shared with her husband. Sherlock Badger, propped next to a task lamp on her worktable, oversaw her sketches and scribblings, as she liked to call them.

"Wish me luck, Sherlock," Felicity said under her breath as she headed out.

When she reached the parking lot in front of the mill, Felicity forced herself not to break into a run. She had no reason to run. She wasn't late for anything. She wasn't being chased by a bear. She had her workload under control. She was letting herself get freaked out for no reason. So what if Gabe Flanagan was speaking on Saturday and wanted to throw a party? Despite that night between high school and college, they'd never been an item. They'd been friends. They'd had a falling-out and hadn't seen each other in three years, and it was natural that would be on her mind. The trick now was to put it out of her mind.

She took in a breath, releasing some of her tension. She'd walked to the mill, enjoying the mid-summer day before heat and humidity had a chance to build in over the next few days. Nestled on the river, the Mill at Moss Hill had started its life in 1870 as a manufacturer of straw hats, immensely popular at the time. They hadn't been made here since the first years after World War I. The mill had enjoyed a few short-lived incarnations before giving up life as a factory—well before Mark had seen its potential for a new century and got to work. Felicity remembered the sprawling, abandoned property he'd gotten hold of, with its boarded-up brick-and-cement buildings, Do Not Enter and Danger signs and overgrown grounds.

She looked across the quiet road to woods that rose steeply to the top of Moss Hill itself. The trees with their lush foliage and evergreen needles were unmoving under the blue summer sky. As teenagers, Mark and Gabe both had vowed to get out of Knights Bridge and never return. They'd been ambitious and driven, determined not to repeat their father's mistakes and drift through life, dreaming and complaining about what might have been. Mark's vow never to return hadn't stuck. After a few years in Boston, he moved back to his hometown, launched a successful business as an architect and married Jessica Frost, who'd never lived anywhere else.

Gabe had never returned to Knights Bridge to live.

Felicity hadn't expected to return, either, but she had never made any vows to the contrary. Her hometown *was* small and a bit off the beaten track, changed forever with the construction of the sprawling Quabbin Reservoir early last century. Felicity's own family had been displaced from Prescott, the smallest of the four small towns lost to history in the now-flooded Swift River Valley. They'd been bankers, accountants and bookkeepers, never farmers and factory workers. She had to be the first MacGregor event planner…now with a party to plan for Gabe Flanagan.

Mark trotted out from the main building and caught up with her before she started up to the road to her house. He was tawny-haired, blue-eyed and lanky, dressed in a polo shirt and khakis. He and his younger brother bore a strong resemblance to each other, but Gabe's eyes were a deeper marine blue, his build naturally more muscular.

"Hey, Felicity," Mark said. "I just got back from meetings in Worcester. Did Kylie tell you about Gabe?"

"She did, yes."

"Great. I hope it's not a problem."

"No problem. Did he give you a budget?"

"I'd spend what you need to make it nice and hand him the bill. You know what you're doing."

"Will do." Felicity hesitated but decided to ask the question gnawing at her. "Does Gabe know I bought the river house?"

"I might have mentioned it. He knows I sold it."

Not the same thing but Felicity didn't pursue the subject. She motioned up the road. "I should get going."

"You walked? Do you need a ride? I can drop you off."

"It's a great day for a walk."

Mark didn't look convinced, but he simply said goodbye and returned to his office.

Felicity heaved a sigh and crossed the parking lot to the road. She had known Gabe's name would come up now that she was living in Knights Bridge, and she anticipated she'd run into him at some point. He'd attended Mark and Jess's wedding last September. Felicity had been invited but had been on the road for a major conference that weekend, her last before giving notice. She doubted she'd have attended even without a conflict. She hadn't wanted to risk any unresolved, long-buried emotions rising to the surface. Mark's wedding wouldn't have been the right time or place for her and Gabe to see each other again.

The entrepreneurial boot camp wasn't the right time or place, either, but there was nothing she could do about it.

She came to a narrow bend in the river and crossed a red-painted covered bridge, a plaque noting it had been built in 1845. She veered off onto a one-lane paved road that wound through open fields then toward the river. It looped back to the river road, but Felicity's house was located on the curve, tucked among evergreens, oaks, maples and birches on the edge of the steep, wooded riverbank. It was contemporary in style but blended with the landscape, a hallmark of Mark Flanagan's work. He'd designed and built the house two years ago on land his paternal grandfather had purchased decades ago as a campsite. Mark had lived there for a short time, but he and Jess had opted to restore an old house in the village.

Felicity turned onto the driveway, which led to a detached garage. Given its connection to the Flanagans, she'd thought twice before she'd toured the house. Then she'd thought more than twice before making an offer.

And now here she was.

She'd grown up on a quiet residential street near the high school, but she'd loved to ride her bike out along the river. Her parents still lived in town but were visiting friends in Virginia. They'd retired a year ago. Her father had presided over the local bank, and her mother had been a CPA in town. They'd loved their work and now they loved retirement. Felicity's older brother—her only sibling—had followed their father into banking and lived outside Amherst with his wife, a hospital administrator, and their two small children. The little ones—a boy and a girl—*loved* to visit their aunt Felicity and get into her supply closet. Stickers, ribbons, balloons, streamers, markers, paints, colored pencils, paper of all types and sizes. Kid heaven. She'd finally had to lay down a few rules after they'd decorated her house one time too many.

Her parents had never trusted Gabe. Not that they'd ever said so outright. Not their style, but Felicity was adept at reading between the lines. "Driven, ambitious, not ready to settle down." Those and many similar comments had been code for "stay away."

If only she'd listened.

Restless and on the verge of being out of sorts, she bypassed the front door and went up the stairs to the back deck. The views of the river, the sounds of the water coursing over rocks and the potential for a variety of gardens had sold her on the house. It was perfect for days such as today. Its history was just part of the deal. She'd weighed the pros and cons of buying the house. There were many pros. Convenience, size, cost, quality, landscaping, layout, proximity to friends and family. The only serious drawback: her history with the property.

Gabe.

She sat at her square wood table, shaded by oak, hemlocks and white pine at the back of the house, above the river. People often said Knights Bridge had the feel of a place where time had stopped. Since moving back to her hometown, Felicity sometimes felt as if time had gone backward for her, but she hoped that would pass once she finished decorating and made the place completely hers. Gabe's unexpected appearance at the boot camp wouldn't help. She could be a professional about it. They weren't teenagers anymore. They weren't even friends.

Today was Wednesday and the boot camp was Saturday.

It'd be done and dusted in no time, and he'd be gone to wherever he was hanging his hat these days.

Feeling calmer, Felicity listened to the rustle of leaves in a light breeze, stirring the stillness of the summer afternoon. Through high school, she and Gabe would come out to his grandfather's "camp" on the river to sneak down to their personal swimming hole, play cards by a campfire, meet up with friends. They were in the same class, but as an October baby, he was almost a year older than she was.

They'd been tight. Good friends. He'd been a reluctant student with big ambitions after high school. She'd been a good student with no real focus for after graduation. She figured she'd get a degree in finance. Something like that. She'd put a lot of her energy into encouraging Gabe.

She chewed on her lower lip, pushing back the flood

of memories the news about Gabe's impending return to town had triggered.

One memory in particular, of a night much like last night had been. Warm, still, starlit. She and Gabe had a fire going in the outdoor fire pit, the only permanent structure then on the Flanagans' riverfront campsite. They hadn't needed the fire's heat. The flames were atmosphere, creating a glow that encompassed just her and Gabe, as if they were in their own little world. They'd been getting ready to leave for separate colleges hundreds of miles apart, feeling the mixed emotions of what lay ahead of them. Fear, uncertainty, excitement, resolve. They'd all bubbled up that night. Neither of them had lived anywhere but Knights Bridge. What would life be like outside their small town?

"We'll stay friends," she'd said, half to herself. "We'll always be friends, won't we, Gabe?"

"Always, Felicity. Always."

He hadn't hesitated. She'd believed him, had needed to hear—wanted to hear—those words.

Later, with the fire dying and stars glistening overhead, they'd gotten carried away.

Felicity let out a long breath. It'd been a wild night. No question. She wondered if Gabe even remembered it.

She put it out of her mind. Her life in Knights Bridge was good. Fun, energizing, busy. It was different from where she thought she'd end up when she'd left for college in upstate New York, and maybe it wasn't what her friends and family or anyone else had expected.

No maybe about it. It was *definitely* not what anyone had expected.

"Except Gabe."

The words were out before she could stop them.

She could hear him now, on a cold February morning three years ago—the last time she'd seen him. "You have to do what you *want* to do, Felicity. You're doing what everyone *expects* you to do."

"What if what everyone expects and what I want are the same thing?"

"They aren't."

That was Gabe. Always so certain.

No way had he changed in three years.

Sometimes she wished he'd fought harder to maintain their friendship, but he hadn't fought at all. If he had? Would she have taken that first event management job, or with him breathing down her neck would she have tried again as a financial analyst—to prove to him she could do the work, *wanted* to do the work? Giving up fit right into his ideas about her, but would he have approved of her alternate career? Would he have encouraged her, or would he have told her not to "settle" as a party planner?

She checked her phone for an email, text or voice mail from Gabe about the boot camp party, but there was nothing. He wouldn't have understood her choice of new career. He'd have wanted it both ways. She'd face her failure as a financial analyst *and* come out on the other end in a stable, high-paying job.

She did fine as a party planner. She'd paid down her debt, reined in her spending and bought a house.

She sent Saturday's caterer—a friend from town—a quick email to set up a time to discuss Gabe's addition to the day.

She let that be enough for now. She'd work on Kylie's party and tackle Gabe's party later.

She brought all eight books in the Badgers of Middle Branch series out to the deck and set them on the table for inspiration. She grabbed her brainstorming colored pencils and a pad of lined yellow paper and a pad of plain white paper.

Badgers. She'd think about badgers.

But she was positive when he'd told her she was hacking away in the wrong jungle and needed to get out of finance that Gabe Flanagan hadn't envisioned her figuring out how to incorporate badgers into a party at the Knights Bridge public library.

Two

Gabe Flanagan looked out at Boston from the living room of his twelfth-floor condo in the heart of Back Bay. He gripped his phone. "Say that again, Mark."

His brother didn't answer at once. Gabe had been home for ten hours after two months in California, working his way down the coast from Sonoma to San Diego on a mix of business and pleasure. He didn't know whether Mark's call was business or pleasure. Some of both, maybe.

"You hired Felicity to handle the party after Dylan's boot camp," Mark said.

"Felicity MacGregor."

"None other."

"Why didn't you tell me?"

"I just did."

Gabe sighed. Felicity. Mark had no idea what he'd stepped into, but still. "I should throw you in the river when I get there."

"You and what army," his brother said, teasing, as if they were kids again. "I did you a favor. The party's on. You're the host. Everyone will be thrilled. You'll have a great time, and you don't have to lift a finger."

Gabe could see his reflection in the window. His jaw was tight, his angular features and tall, lean frame giving away that he and Mark were brothers. Gabe had put on muscle now that he'd been doing CrossFit for two years, dropping into studios when he was on the road. He'd gone to one yesterday in LA, before his overnight flight to Boston.

"You told Felicity it was my idea to hire her?" Gabe asked.

"Yeah. It was simpler. I don't need to be the middleman."

"You *are* the middleman. I didn't know anything about it."

"Now you do. Why are you jumping down my throat? You should be thanking me. You said you wanted help. I helped."

"Do I need to do anything for this party?"

"Just show up. It's not much notice, but Felicity's good at what she does."

Mark had mentioned in passing she was an event planner now. She'd started shortly after she and Gabe had fallen out. He'd figured it was something she'd do to make ends meet while she tried to find another finance job, if only to spite him. But she'd stuck with it, obviously. Mark didn't know the ins and outs of his younger brother's relationship with Knights Bridge's own party planner. They were close, but not that kind of close.

"Okay, thanks," Gabe said finally.

"You're not regretting saying yes to speaking at the boot camp, are you?"

"It's a day and then it's done."

A few minutes ago, Gabe would have said he was

looking forward to the boot camp. Dylan McCaffrey had invited him when they'd met briefly in San Diego before Gabe had returned to Los Angeles and then flown onto Boston. Mark, who'd designed Dylan and Olivia's new home in Knights Bridge, had put them in touch with each other. Gabe had accepted the invitation without a second's thought. A panel discussion on start-ups for an audience of aspiring entrepreneurs? What was there to think about? He was on his way back to Boston, anyway, and he owed his brother in Knights Bridge a visit.

But he changed the subject. "How's Jess?" he asked.

"Puking."

"Fun call, Mark. Real fun call. She sick?"

There was a slight hesitation. "She's pregnant. I was going to wait until you got here to tell you. Morning sickness came on fast and strong. You're going to want to rethink staying with us."

"Mark…" Gabe stared out at the blend of old and new that was Back Bay, but he found himself picturing Knights Bridge on a warm summer evening. He hadn't been to the Colonial Revival house Mark and Jess were restoring off Knights Bridge common, but he knew it. Mark specialized in older buildings as an architect and it had made sense—felt right—when he and Jess had bought one of their own. Now they had a baby on the way. "That's wonderful news, Mark. I'm happy for you."

"Thanks, Gabe. We're thrilled."

"I'll find somewhere else to stay."

"Your call. That reminds me. There's one more thing you should know before you get here. I've been meaning to mention it. I know you and Felicity haven't been close the past few years but thought you'd want to know she bought the house."

"What house?"

"The house we built on the river at the old campsite."

Gabe had known Mark had sold the house, but he'd never identified the buyer. Gabe hadn't asked. He hadn't wanted to know. He'd contributed ideas and cash to the building of the house but had left everything else to Mark. "Felicity bought it," he said, trying to keep his tone neutral. "Thanks for letting me know."

"I'm happy it sold to someone who remembers the property as a campsite."

Oh, she'd remember it, all right, Gabe thought. "A lot of changes in town."

"Tons. It'll be good to have you back here. See you soon."

After he and Mark hung up, Gabe didn't move from the windows. He watched the city lights twinkling in the fading light. He was going to be an uncle. His brother had a wife, and they were expecting their first child.

It was a lot. It was the best.

He could see himself on a lazy summer afternoon fishing with Mark on the river, in a beat-up canoe they'd discovered buried in their father's shed. Their mother had just been diagnosed with the breast cancer that would eventually kill her. "We're going to get out of here, Gabe," Mark had said, not for the first time. "We're not going to get stuck here dreaming about a different life. We're going to get out and never come back except to visit."

Mark had stayed away for a while, but he'd returned

and now had offices out on the river where he and Gabe had grown up. Things hadn't worked out the way he'd meant them to when he'd set off for college. They'd worked out even better.

"They worked out perfectly, brother," Gabe said, turning from his city view.

A few minutes later, his phone buzzed and he saw he had a text from Mark: Felicity expects you to get in touch with her about the party.

What's there to get in touch about? Place settings?

Ask her. Ball's in your court.

How did the ball get in his court? Gabe gave up. How's Jess?

Eating a pastrami sandwich. I don't know if I can take nine months of this.

But he could and he would, and he looked forward to it. Mark and Jessica's wedding announcement last summer hadn't been a total surprise to Gabe, but earlier in the year he'd wondered if they'd make it. Mark had taken Jess for granted, and she'd shown signs of serious impatience.

She'd gotten his workaholic brother to take her to Paris. That was something.

Gabe typed his response: Good thing you like pastrami.

He received a smile emoji from Mark, and they were done. Gabe set his phone aside. He was adept at taking in new information, processing it, making a decision and moving forward—but he needed a moment to process Mark's call. He hadn't expected Felicity to be involved in the entrepreneurial boot camp, and he sure as hell hadn't expected her to be living in the house on the river. To *own* it. He loved that place.

"Should have bought it yourself, then," he muttered. Instead he'd let Mark buy out his interest.

He'd had no plans then, and he had none now ever to spend much time in his hometown. He'd gone in with Mark to buy the property in order to help their grandfather afford assisted living. They'd have paid his way, but that wasn't what the old guy had wanted. The property had been in Flanagan hands for decades. Mark had designed the house—with Gabe's input—and eventually bought Gabe out...which had made sense at the time. Mark was living in Knights Bridge. Gabe wasn't. He'd never considered it might not stay in the family. If there was one spot in Knights Bridge he could get nostalgic about, it was that one.

Of all the places for Felicity to end up.

He took in the state of his condo. When he'd arrived that morning, he'd collapsed for a few hours' sleep and had barely noticed the drop cloths, the covered furnishings, the smell of fresh paint. Workers had arrived mid-morning. The condo was undergoing cosmetic work ahead of going on the market. It would sell in a heartbeat, at a profit. Gabe had bought it two years ago more as an investment than as a place to live. It wasn't home, not in the sense of Mark and Jess's Colonial Revival. Gabe was young, unattached, didn't have a baby on the way—and he liked to travel. He'd had top-notch employees and freelancers, all of whom worked remotely. He could work from anywhere that had an internet connection.

His company's new owners had kept on most of his employees and freelancers. Together, they'd take the company and its specialty in product development to the next level. Gabe liked starting businesses. He was good at it, although sometimes they didn't work out. He'd had a few going when he'd launched the one he'd just sold. He liked being nimble, moving fast, and when that newest start-up had taken off, he'd focused on it. As it grew, he discovered digging in and building a company didn't interest him as much as getting one off the ground, and he wasn't particularly good at it. It'd been time to move on. Three years of intense work and focus had made his start-up attractive to a buyer who would do what he didn't want to—couldn't—do. As the founder, Gabe had done his best to make a clean exit.

Clean from a business perspective, anyway. One of his freelancers, a customer development specialist who'd been with him from the start, happened to be in the process of divorcing the man who'd bought the company. She was out of a job *and* a marriage. Gabe had met with her in Los Angeles to reassure her he'd be in touch with any new venture.

Everything had revolved around him during those intense years getting his business off the ground. Friends who'd been in his position advised him to have a post-sale plan in place, and he'd listened, at least to a degree. The boot camp had cropped up while he was still twiddling his thumbs in California, trying to figure out what was next.

What was next was Knights Bridge and Felicity MacGregor.

He hadn't been to his hometown in months and he hadn't seen Felicity in three years.

He needed a reentry plan.

Gabe went into the master bedroom. The painters had taped off the windows and trim, but otherwise it was untouched. It was just the bed and a sheepskin he'd picked up in Ireland. He sat on the edge of his king-size bed and dug a small photo album out of his night-stand. His mother had put it together for him before her death. She'd done one for Mark, too. It contained pictures of their childhood, and hers, in Knights Bridge. Tucked inside was a sheet of Rhodia notepaper he'd folded in half three years ago that past February and hadn't looked at since. He opened it now and wondered why he'd kept it. A cautionary tale? Hell if he knew.

The note was in two parts, one he'd written, one Felicity had written. He'd written his portion in black Sharpie pen. They were the only pens he used. He was tidy, and he had his rituals. Felicity had resisted anything smacking of order, at least back then.

Felicity,
Meetings in Boston. Back at 5 p.m. Company arrives at 6 p.m. Hint.
Gabe
P.S. You know I'm right

Then her scrawl in blue Sharpie pen:

I made brownies for you and your "company."
They're in the freezer. Enjoy.
Felicity, financial analyst
P.S. We'll see who's right

He'd left her that morning scowling at him in his bathroom doorway, wrapped in a wet, threadbare towel. He could have afforded new towels even then, but he hadn't seen the need. It'd been her fifth day sleeping on his couch, nursing her wounds after getting fired from yet another finance job. She had degrees and knew her stuff, but her heart wasn't in the work. He'd told her so, not mincing words. Then he'd jotted the note and was on his way. By the time he returned, she'd cleared out of his apartment. She'd cleaned up her pizza boxes, collected her dirty dishes, folded the blankets she'd borrowed, put her sheets and towels in the washing machine and tidied up the bathroom.

His "company" had been a woman he'd invited over to watch a movie. She'd promptly discovered a stray pair of lacy bikini underpants Felicity had missed in the couch cushions, refused to believe his explanation and stormed out of his apartment before he'd had a chance to pour wine. He'd thrown out Felicity's underpants—damned if he'd mail them to her—and opened the freezer. He'd figured he'd microwave a couple of brownies, drink the wine by himself and put the lousy day behind him. But there'd been no brownies, and he'd realized Felicity had never had any intention of making him brownies. She'd *wanted* him to open the freezer and not find any brownies.

Spite. Pure spite.

Seemed a bit childish now, but he supposed he'd had it coming.

He'd drunk the wine without brownies, without a date for the evening, without Felicity camped out on his couch with take-out pad thai or another pizza delivery. The next morning, he'd decided the ball was in her court. She was the one whose life was a mess, and he needed to respect what she wanted to do—needed to do. He'd had what he wanted and needed to do, too. He didn't have time to hold Felicity's hand through another mess. Nearly a week on his couch had proven that to him. She was a distraction, and he couldn't afford distractions. Since she didn't want or appreciate his advice, why push it with her?

And so he hadn't. He'd let her go.

He reread the note. Yeah. She'd been furious with him.

He folded the note and returned it to the photo album. He'd be lying if he tried to tell himself or anyone else that he hadn't missed her. Didn't still, at times, miss her. Especially in those first few months, he would reach for his phone to send her a text or email her a cute puppy video, but he never had.

He *had* been right about her hacking away in the wrong jungle. Who was planning parties in Knights Bridge now instead of scratching out a living in a career to which she was unsuited?

"Didn't matter you were right, pal."

If there was one thing he knew about Felicity, it was that she wouldn't thank him for being right. She wouldn't credit him with helping steer her onto a better course for herself.

Assuming it *was* better.

Gabe grabbed his laptop and sat on his bed, his back against several insanely expensive down pillows, and drafted an email to Felicity about the boot camp party. It took him thirty minutes to write the damn thing. Forever by his standards. Normally he was in, out, done. He didn't angst, especially over something as trivial as planning a ninety-minute open house. He had limited experience hosting parties. In fact, no experience. He'd always delegated that sort of detail. He was good at delegating.

He was delegating now, if only because of Mark.

Wording the email was tricky in part because he didn't want to get Mark in trouble, never mind he was the one who'd created this situation by sticking his nose in with Felicity in the first place.

Gabe gave an inward groan. This wasn't an email to a Fortune 500 CEO. It was an email to a Knights Bridge party planner. To *Felicity.*

He read it over:

Dear Felicity,
Mark tells me you're able to put together the open house after the boot camp talks. Let me know if you need anything from me.
Best,
Gabriel

It didn't sound too stiff to him. Professional. This was a business arrangement. He read the email once more and changed *Gabriel* to *Gabe.* Using his full first name struck him as too formal and might make Felicity think he was feeling awkward and self-conscious. Whatever the case, it hit the wrong note with him.

They were no longer friends, but they weren't enemies, either. They'd drifted apart. She'd moved on; he'd moved on. That was all there was to it, and *Gabriel* suggested there was more to it.

There was, but whatever.

He hit Send and got up and found a bottle of Scotch he'd bought in Edinburgh to celebrate some milestone in his business. He didn't remember the details, but he did remember the Scotch. He splashed some into his glass and found his way back to his bedroom.

He glanced at his in-box but Felicity hadn't yet responded.

He drank his Scotch and headed out for a late dinner on his own. By the time he returned to his condo, he was marginally less preoccupied with his ex-friend in Knights Bridge.

Gabe slept late but was awake before his assistant, Shannon Rivera, arrived. She was his last remaining employee. She'd lived next door to him at his first house and only ventured into the city if she had no other option. She'd arranged for the workers at his condo. He figured she knew most of them. Thirty-four, married to a police officer and mother of three, she had finely honed instincts about what he should do in any given situation.

Probably should ask her what to do about Felicity.

He checked his email, still in bed, which wasn't a great habit but since he was alone, who cared?

He had a reply from Felicity:

Dear Gabe,
Thank you for your email. I'm sure I can manage with-

out involving you in any details. Please don't hesitate to get in touch if you have any questions.
Best wishes,
Felicity MacGregor

He kicked off his duvet and sat up straight. He read the email again. No second thoughts on her part about being self-consciously stuffy and awkwardly formal, obviously.

So much for bygones being bygones.

He grinned and rolled out of bed. Sort of appropriate he was in the buff while dealing with a snotty email from Felicity MacGregor. Was he misinterpreting her email? Was she actually self-conscious and awkward?

"Hell, yeah."

He contemplated his response for a good thirty seconds. Then he typed it:

Great, my one request is to have brownies on the menu.
Gabe

He hit Send before he could change his mind. She'd know the mention of brownies was deliberate, a reminder of their past—their abrupt parting of ways three years ago.

By the time he made coffee and let in the painters, Felicity had responded:

I already had brownies on the menu. Everything's well in hand. Enjoy your stay in Knights Bridge. I might not see you since there's a good chance I'll be in Wyoming.

Gabe stared at the email. No signature. Just those dashed-off words, striking back at him for his own dashed-off words.

It was the gut punch Felicity had intended it to be.

Back in high school, they would sit out on the rocks by their favorite swimming hole on the river and plan trips to Paris, London, Vienna, Vancouver, Sonoma— they'd had a long list. But the place that had captured their teenage imaginations and gripped their teenage souls had been Wyoming. It became their default getaway. Whenever anything happened, they'd say, *I'm going to Wyoming now.*

And they would go together.

Always together.

"Start packing," one or the other of them would say. "I'm not going without you."

As much as he'd traveled, Gabe had yet to visit Wyoming. He wondered if Felicity had, but the crack about going now—it'd been the slap in the face she'd meant it to be, a reminder of innocent times when their futures had been filled with possibilities. Failure, dashed hopes, tragedies, mistakes and all the other ups and downs of a normal life had seemed avoidable or at least distant.

Less so these days.

Gabe greeted Shannon when she arrived. She handed him a doughnut. "The best in Boston," she said.

"I've no doubts."

"Good. Never doubt me when it comes to doughnuts."

He bit into it, and it was so good he knew he'd have another before he left for Knights Bridge. Shannon helped herself to the gooiest doughnut in the box and updated him on the condo work, his schedule, messages, things he needed to sign and possible itineraries for a trip to Australia and New Zealand he wanted to move off his someday/maybe list onto his calendar. "Take a look at Wyoming, too, would you?" he asked her.

She frowned. She was dark-haired, blue-eyed and casually dressed in capris pants, a tunic top and sandals. "Wyoming. Sure."

She retreated to the foyer with her doughnut to let in more workers.

Gabe stood at the living room windows. The last of the early-morning fog was burning off. It'd be another beautiful summer day in Boston. Where was Felicity now? Out on her deck above the river? Counting plastic champagne glasses? Picking out party favors?

He winced at his condescension. What an ass he was being. Good, professional, creative event planners made the lives of hosts easier and helped ensure guests had a wonderful time.

But this was Felicity.

"My entire family is involved in finance," she'd told him. "I'll make my own mark, but I'm a MacGregor. Money is what we do."

Had she given up her dreams because of him?

Never mind he'd had good reason to lecture her, given her string of firings, her out-of-control debt and her days camped out on his couch. He'd seen so clearly then, that cold February morning, that being a financial analyst wasn't working for her, and trying to make it work was making her miserable. But had it been his place to tell her so?

He gritted his teeth. Probably not.

He read her email again.

Wyoming.

He had no idea how to respond. His reentry plan was going to take more work than he'd thought, and probably more out of him than he wanted to admit.

Gabe spent the day doing what Shannon needed him to do, packing for Knights Bridge and resisting the temptation to look up Felicity's party-planning website. By mid-afternoon, he was on his way to Logan Airport in his BMW SUV. It was an indulgence, but he was no longer that struggling kid, putting every dime to work, determined to make his mark and not drift through life. A fancy new car wasn't a good investment, and he just didn't care. Who would give a damn what kind of car he drove?

He picked up Dylan McCaffrey and Russ Colton at the airport. They were clearly more eager to get to Knights Bridge than he was. Dylan had Olivia waiting for him. Russ had his new wife waiting for him. Gabe looked forward to seeing family and friends, but it wasn't the same as having a woman in his life—and he didn't, not in Knights Bridge or anywhere else.

Both men were strongly built. Russ was ex-navy, Dylan a former professional hockey player. Gabe got along with them. As they hit the tunnel to head west, Dylan articulated his misgivings about being away from Olivia. "I know it's irrational," he said. "She has her parents there, her sister, friends. She's independent. She can handle herself."

"She's a Frost," Gabe said, as if that explained everything.

"A year and a half ago, I wouldn't have had any idea what that means," Dylan said.

Gabe had difficulty imagining Olivia married and expecting a baby, but, contrary to his prejudices about his hometown, time hadn't stood still in Knights Bridge since he'd lived there. The conversation shifted to basic security procedures for the entrepreneurial boot camp. Dylan and Russ both looked relieved at the change in subject from personal to professional matters. Gabe felt his relief right to his bones. He was the only one of the three who'd grown up in Knights Bridge and remembered Olivia and Jessica Frost as kids leaping into cold brooks and piles of raked leaves. He remembered Felicity, too, but she was another matter. Definitely more complicated.

Dylan finally turned to Gabe. "We'll make time to continue the conversation we started in San Diego."

Gabe nodded. "Looking forward to it."

A conversation about a new venture with Dylan and his friend and business partner, Noah Kendrick, the founder of NAK, the high-tech entertainment company they'd shepherded to immense success. With NAK sold to new owners, Dylan and Noah were turning their attention to fresh projects. Like Dylan, Noah had found himself falling in love with a Knights Bridge woman, Phoebe O'Dunn, the former Knights Bridge town librarian. Gabe remembered her, too. Quiet Phoebe, engaged to a California billionaire. They'd be arriving separately from Noah's central California winery. Noah would be presenting at the entrepreneurial boot camp. Gabe could feel in his gut this trip was different from when he'd blown in and out of Knights Bridge last fall for his brother's wedding.

As he jumped on Storrow Drive, heading west out of the city, Knights Bridge might as well have been another world. Tired, preoccupied, Gabe had to admit he liked being behind the wheel of his BMW rather than his last car, a heap he'd bought off his mechanic father. "Years and years left in this sweetheart," he'd told Gabe. His father wasn't right about much, but he did know his cars. Gabe had donated the heap to the son of Mark's assistant. As far as he knew, it was still running.

He smiled. It'd be good to see his father, too. The guy was a mess, but he was a happy mess—an incurable optimist. It was one thing he, Mark and Gabe all had in common.

"Felicity MacGregor is also organizing a party for Kylie next week," Russ said from the back seat, matter-of-fact. "It's at Knights Bridge Free Public Library. She's celebrating the publication of her latest badger book."

Gabe frowned. "Badger book?"

Dylan grinned next to him. "We've got to get you caught up on Knights Bridge's goings-on."

Russ explained the badgers. Gabe supposed Mark would get into the series now that he and Jess were having a baby. "I knew your wife was a children's author, but I didn't know about the badgers."

"It's a good thing Felicity's in town," Russ said. "Kylie's sister volunteered to organize the party, but Kylie wisely turned her down. Lila's a vet—she can splint a broken leg on a dog, but if it was up to her, she'd leave the party to the last minute and open up cans of peaches and a box of vanilla wafers. Kylie wouldn't mind, but it's good Felicity is on board. Kylie says she's taken on the badgers."

Gabe kept his hands firmly on the wheel. Badgers. Felicity. "Parties galore in Knights Bridge these days," he said, leaving it at that.

He, Russ and Dylan fell into silence. Gabe hadn't figured out where he'd stay that night—he'd camp out on his father's couch if he had to—but as Boston gave way to the Massachusetts countryside, he suddenly knew exactly where he would stay.

It was irresistible, and it was long overdue.

Three

Felicity was sitting at her table on her deck fantasizing about absconding to Wyoming when a client in Boston phoned to reschedule a conference call. "I might have to go to Wyoming," she said.

But there were phones in Wyoming, and she set a date for next week.

After she hung up, she opened her laptop and saved the updated files on the entrepreneurial boot camp. Organizing Gabe's party, even on short notice, would be simple enough. She already had a venue, a caterer and a confirmed guest list. She doubted he'd care what she came up with. He was a master delegator, and he'd delegated her to handle his party. She could have kangaroos in pink tutus there, and he'd trust they were appropriate because she was the professional he'd hired to do the job.

She regretted her comment about Wyoming in her email to Gabe but not much. It had felt good to say it out loud to her Boston client and act as if she was serious about clearing out of Knights Bridge while he was there.

"Maybe I am serious," she said.

She looked up flights, hotels, camps and itineraries. She wanted to see Jackson Hole, the Grand Tetons, Yellowstone. She'd wanted to see them forever. Why *not* go now?

Because she'd never imagined going to Wyoming without Gabe.

She shook off that uncomfortable thought. She wished he'd cancel his appearance at the entrepreneurial boot camp, but she knew he wouldn't. This was Gabriel Flanagan. He would keep his commitment.

She'd manage. She knew she would, even as she checked out the sites in Jackson Hole. She'd been mad at him after his blunt lecture about her situation, but that anger was behind her. He had no role in her life. He wasn't a positive or a negative. His visit to Knights Bridge for the boot camp and hiring her to handle the party weren't anything out of the ordinary. Last-minute adjustments were part of her job as an event planner.

She flipped through the photo gallery for a quality Jackson Hole hotel. "I can afford a suite," she said.

Well, two nights in a suite.

The sun hit her laptop screen, and she gave up on absconding for the moment and went inside. The house had one main living area, where she often worked despite having taken over one of the three bedrooms for an office. She sat in her living room and switched to working on a final list of possibilities to present to Kylie for how to handle the badgers at next week's launch party. The boot camp would be past her by then. Gabe would almost certainly have left town. It'd be a fun, relaxing evening.

"Do *not* let Gabe worm his way back into your life," Felicity said aloud. "Just don't."

Not that he had that in mind. He'd had a lot going on the past few years with his work as a digital start-up whiz. She didn't ask questions about him around town, but she'd pieced together the casual tidbits she'd heard, especially from Mark. After she'd stalked out of Gabe's apartment three years ago, she'd resisted spying on him on social media. At first it'd been a struggle. Now she was never tempted.

She sighed. "Well. Seldom tempted."

Sometimes she'd overhear a tidbit about him in town, and she'd feel the urge to find out what he was up to. She'd been tempted to ask Mark or Jessica, but she knew she couldn't go backward—she had to keep moving forward. She and Gabe had made the break with each other three years ago. She'd decided it wasn't in her interest or his interest for her to be a crutch for him or for him to be a crutch for her. That wasn't what a real friendship was, and they knew—they couldn't deny it any longer—that they couldn't have a real friendship. Friendship would get in the way of *relationships*. Men for her. Women for him.

"More like women for him."

Men and her...

The truth was, there were no men and her. A dinner or a movie here and there but that was it. At first she'd blamed necessity. She'd had to focus on getting a roof over her head, paying bills, getting out of debt, learning the ropes of how to throw a wide range of meetings, conferences, parties and other events. Then she'd had to focus on *keeping* a roof over her head, putting away an emergency fund, staying out of debt and excelling at event planning—putting her own stamp on it. *Then* she'd had to focus on starting and running her own business. Moving to Knights Bridge. Buying a house.

Would Gabe regard buying *this* house, on his family's old campsite, as a fork in his eye?

If I ever come back to Knights Bridge to live, it'll be to the river. But I'll never come back.

He'd assured her *she* didn't have to hate Knights Bridge and he'd be fine if she came back here to live, but that was different from buying this place.

No question. He'd see her living on his grandfather's old campsite as a fork in his eye. Had Mark told him she'd bought the house? Was that why Gabe had decided to appear at the boot camp at the last minute?

She shook her head. *No.* If she could count on one thing never changing about Gabe Flanagan, it was his practical nature. The house and their shattered friendship hadn't been a factor in his decision to do the boot camp and sponsor the party.

Why was she getting herself worked up, anyway? Mark could have told him, *Oh, yeah, Felicity's a party planner now, why don't you hire her?* And Gabe could have said, *Done—let her know, will you?*

She gave up on work, shut down her laptop and drifted back outside, taking the deck stairs to the strip of lawn bordered by the woods on the steep riverbank. She took a deep breath, trying to stay in the moment and focus on the smells and sounds of the waning afternoon. She glanced at the open brick fireplace, still intact from when Gabe and Mark's grandfather had built it decades ago. Mark must have taken care for it to have survived construction of the house. She hadn't had a fire in it yet.

She brushed the fireplace's worn brick, remembering another hot summer day. She and Gabe had met at their favorite swimming hole on the river after their jobs, hers at her father's air-conditioned bank, his ripping apart a hot attic for an addition on a house near the village. They'd leaped into the river, laughing, enjoying the cool, clear water—by mutual agreement not talking about their impending departure for college. Afterward, they'd spread out a blanket from his car in front of the old fireplace. As daylight slipped away and the night turned cool, they'd built a fire.

Felicity could smell the wood smoke as if she were eighteen again, stretched out next to Gabe. Her heart raced, as it had that night—this time, though, because she knew what had come next, not because of her reaction to Gabe touching her bare thigh. He'd never done that before, and it'd been their undoing. The campsite was isolated, the night brightened only by the flames of the fire and the spray of stars above them.

Heat rose in her cheeks as that crazy night came back to her in all its clothes-tearing, laughing, exploring, reckless glory. *What* had she and Gabe been thinking?

Of course, they hadn't been thinking.

She'd worried they'd end up rolling down the riverbank given their exuberance. He'd been completely absorbed in the act at hand, and she'd followed him over the brink. There'd been a lot of fumbling, awkward touching and panting, a few nervous laughs, and then it was over, the virginity threshold never to be crossed again.

By dawn, they were back to being friends. Or at least Gabe was. She'd gone along with him and had pretended their night together hadn't been that big a deal.

"That wasn't…you know. Anything. Right, Felicity?"

"Right, Gabe."

She remembered his sexy half smile as he'd narrowed his eyes on her. "I didn't know I'd be your first."

She'd pretended not to hear him, and a few weeks later, they left their small, out-of-the-way hometown for college. She was positive no one else knew about their night together. When she'd returned home that morning, her parents assumed she'd camped out with girlfriends and lectured her about being sure she'd put out any campfires, stressing the importance of being responsible. Gabe had reported his parents hadn't even realized he hadn't come home. He'd shrugged off their obliviousness. "It's okay, Felicity. It's not like it's news they're flakes."

Live-for-the-moment, beloved and talented flakes. Mickey Flanagan could fix the fussiest imported car but on his own schedule. Lee had never been without a smile at the local assisted-living facility, where she'd worked as a licensed practical nurse. Dreamers, Felicity's father had called them, not without affection. Mickey had dropped out of college as a mechanical engineering major to travel. He'd never gone back. Born and raised in quiet Knights Bridge, he'd returned home after he'd satisfied his wanderlust, got a job as a mechanic and married a local girl. They'd had two sons together, both of whom had vowed to put action behind their dreams—which to them meant getting out of Knights Bridge.

Gabe had dropped out of college himself after his mother's death from an aggressive form of breast cancer. Mark had already been working as an architect in Boston. Their father had quit his job and gone on the road again, eventually returning to Knights Bridge and opening up his own shop specializing in vintage motorcycles and sports cars.

She and Gabe had never been destined to be anything but friends, and now not even that. He was a client. Nothing more, nothing less. That summer night with him was in the past. If they hadn't talked it over then, they sure weren't going to now. She wished they'd run into each other at the country store or at the mill on one of his visits and had gotten their reunion—however it would go—past them. Now they'd see each other at a high-profile event.

They'd be fine, Felicity thought, annoyed with herself for her angst. They'd be cordial with each other. Neutral.

Hey, Felicity, good to see you.

Yeah, you, too, Gabe.

She headed back up to the deck. The afternoon had turned hot and muggy. She usually didn't mind the heat since it rarely lasted long and she knew she'd be wishing for a hot day come January. Right now, though, the weather only seemed to emphasize her discomfort about seeing Gabe again. She doubted she'd be able to avoid him on Saturday.

"Neutral. He's not a positive or a negative in your life. He's a client. That's it." She groaned to herself. "Keep talking. Maybe you'll start believing it."

She'd see him—that was unavoidable—but maybe she wouldn't have to talk to him. He'd be schmoozing at the boot camp and then at the party, and the rest of his visit he'd be hanging out with family and buddies still in town. He wouldn't be staying long. He never did. He hadn't even before they'd parted badly.

Felicity wasn't afraid to see him. She just dreaded it.

Maybe it was best to get it over with and prove to herself he was a zero in her life. Be done with dreading to see him. She'd moved on a long time ago. She harbored no ill will or secret anything for him. No secret desire for revenge, no secret longing, no secret hope they'd renew their friendship—none of that.

She grabbed her handbag and went out to her car, a much-used Land Rover that she'd gotten off her brother in a great deal. "It's not sexy but it's a sweet machine," he'd told her.

She drove out the river road past the mill toward the village, turning onto another country road and following it until it ended at quiet, pretty Carriage Hill Road. She turned left, rolling down her window and taking in the slightly cooler air. The road eventually dead-ended at a Quabbin gate, one of more than forty gates that marked entrances to the reservoir and its surrounding protected watershed. She wouldn't go that far, but she knew the spot well. She and Gabe had obtained fishing licenses and gone out on the reservoir in his dad's rickety boat a couple of times, but neither of them had developed the fishing bug. She'd enjoyed being on the pristine water, envisioning life in the valley before the reservoir. She'd noticed signs of the lost valley towns. Old roads that now led into the reservoir, the occasional remnant of buildings long demolished. Gabe hadn't paid much attention. He'd focused on catching fish.

Felicity blinked back unexpected tears and cleared her throat. She had work to do before Saturday. "Best get to it," she said, and continued down the quiet road.

Felicity parked at the contemporary "barn" Olivia and Dylan McCaffrey had built on property he'd inherited from his father. It served as the base for Dylan's fledgling adventure travel business and entrepreneurial boot camps and was just up the road from the pristine antique house Olivia had turned into a destination inn—a coincidence that had led to their meeting on an icy March day over a year ago. They'd also built a house up a stone walk from the barn, finally moving in earlier in the summer. Mark Flanagan had designed both the house and barn to meld into the rolling rural New England landscape. Felicity didn't know if Gabe had ever seen them. Probably not.

Olivia greeted her at the front entrance. She was dressed in yoga pants and a long tank top, her dark hair pulled back. She was visibly pregnant, due in late autumn. "I had an urge for hot chocolate," she said, smiling as she held up a steaming mug. "I know. You'd think I'd have an urge for lemonade on a hot summer day. Come in, won't you?"

Felicity followed her into the barn. She'd checked out the space several times in the lead-up to Saturday's boot camp. The interior included a large, flexible open area with a sectional sofa and comfy chairs in front of a huge fieldstone fireplace, a kitchen, a study and, up spiral stairs, a loft with offices and storage space.

Olivia led Felicity to a long, dark wood table in front

of tall windows that looked out across wildflower-dotted fields to Carriage Hill itself. "Dylan's thrilled you were able to handle Gabe's add-on party on such short notice," Olivia said, sitting with her back to the view, still holding on to her hot chocolate. "I'm happy to help in any way we can."

Felicity sat across from her. "Thank you. I just want to be sure I have the logistics worked out. We're having lunch here, then another panel in the main room—I don't want to cause any distractions while setting up for the party."

"What if we have the party at the inn? The weather looks great for Saturday. Everyone will probably appreciate a walk and fresh air after a day of speakers."

"That's a great idea," Felicity said without hesitation.

"You can run it past Gabe and Dylan if you want, but they won't care if it's okay with me."

"I should take a look at the space, but I can't imagine any problems."

Felicity had arranged for one of the speakers—a diverse group—to stay in the area, but the rest, and all of the attendees, were commuting for the day. Dylan had deliberately kept the one-day event simple. Olivia was having work done at the Farm at Carriage Hill, but it only affected its handful of guest rooms. Felicity could help Gabe find lodging if need be, but he had family and friends in town. She doubted he'd have any trouble finding a place to stay. He hadn't asked for her help, and she assumed he had sleeping quarters handled.

"Maggie's catered a number of events at the inn,"

Olivia said. "She thinks it'll work out well, if that helps."

"It absolutely does. Maggie's a whiz."

Olivia smiled. "She's bringing dinner. Why don't you join us? Maggie always brings enough for days of leftovers."

Brandon Sloan, Maggie's husband, was in the White Mountains, leading the first group of Dylan's adventure travelers on a multi-day hike. He and Maggie had been together since high school and had two sons in elementary school. Brandon, the third of six siblings, had a day job as a carpenter with Sloan & Sons, his family's construction business. Gabe was friends with all the Sloans. Maybe he'd be staying with them.

Felicity frowned. Why was she obsessing about where Gabe stayed?

"I'd love to join you and Maggie for dinner," she said.

"Wonderful," Olivia said, obviously pleased. "Can I get you anything in the meantime? Water, iced tea— there's more hot chocolate if that appeals to you on a hot day."

"I think I'll walk down to Carriage Hill first."

"The back door's open. I'd go with you, but I've been a bit wobbly today. I'm sure it's the heat. Dylan will be back soon. Gabe picked him and Russ Colton up from the airport. I can't remember the last time he was in town. Mark and Jess's wedding, I think."

Felicity managed to get control of herself. She didn't swear out loud or even under her breath, but she was *not* prepared to see Gabe tonight—and she'd just accepted Olivia's invitation to dinner. "It'll be cooler on Saturday," she said, getting to her feet. "I'll scoot down to the inn."

"Maggie and I can answer any questions once you've had a look."

"Great. Thanks."

Olivia abandoned her hot chocolate and rose, visibly stiff. A hand on her lower back, she walked with Felicity through the main room and out the front entrance. Buster, her German shepherd mix, had materialized on the stone walk, lazing in the shade. He wagged his tail but otherwise didn't stir. "It was just Buster and me out here at first," Olivia said. "I liked that idea. Then Dylan came along..." She smiled, her hazel eyes warm with emotion. "It's not just Buster and me anymore."

"I'm happy for you, Olivia."

"Thank you." She patted her middle. "Pretty soon Buster will have to get used to a baby on our dead-end road."

She and Dylan also had kept his house on Coronado Island in San Diego. They might be starting new businesses and living relatively normal lives in Knights Bridge, but they were worth a considerable fortune. Felicity motioned vaguely down Carriage Hill Road. "Back in a few minutes."

"Have you seen Gabe lately?" Olivia asked as Felicity descended the steps to the stone walk. "You two used to hang out together."

"It's been a few years."

She debated saying more but instead continued past Buster. She heard Olivia gasp behind her and spun around. "Olivia—are you all right?"

Olivia swayed and reached out a hand, as if to balance herself, but there was nothing to grab hold of. Felicity launched herself up the steps, getting to Olivia just as she crumpled. She hooked an arm around her and eased her onto the landing. Felicity quickly checked for blood or amniotic fluid but didn't see any. Had the heat gotten to her? They'd only been outside a few minutes, but Felicity didn't know where Olivia had been that day or what she'd been doing.

She fumbled for her phone to call 911, but Olivia stirred and tried to sit up. "I'm okay," she mumbled.

"You fainted," Felicity said. "I'll call for an ambulance."

"What? Oh, damn. No. Really. I just..." She tried to sit up. "I didn't pass out. It was close, but I just got wobbly and couldn't... Don't call an ambulance. I'm okay, I promise."

"I can call your doctor."

"I'll call her. I just need a minute."

"And Dylan?"

"He's on his way. There's no need to worry him. Can you get me a glass of water? I think that's all I need. I'll be fine here." She smiled weakly, leaning against the doorjamb. "I have Buster."

The big dog had roused himself from his spot in the shade and was lumbering to her. Olivia patted him. She was clearly feeling better, but Felicity still had misgivings about not calling for help. "I'll fetch you some water, but if you feel at all faint, call 911." She folded her phone into Olivia's hand. "And if there's even the slightest question when I get back, I'm calling."

Felicity raced inside, leaving the door open. She filled a glass with water from the tap, moistened a dish towel and charged back out to Olivia with both.

Olivia was sitting up, Buster sprawled at her side. Her color looked better, and she didn't seem as unsteady. "Water or towel first?" Felicity asked her.

"Water." Olivia smiled as Felicity handed her the water. She took a few tentative sips. "I let myself get dehydrated."

"I can call your doctor. Really, I don't mind."

"I'll call in a minute." Olivia set the glass on the landing next to her and accepted the cool, wet towel from Felicity, placing it on the back of her neck. "That feels so good. You can go onto Carriage Hill. I'm fine."

Felicity shook her head. "It'll keep. I'll stay with you until Maggie gets here."

Olivia nodded and picked up her water glass again. The barn was air-conditioned, but she obviously needed to get her feet under her before she tried to stand up. She finished drinking her water. In a few more minutes, she started to get to her feet. Felicity eased next to her, but Olivia didn't need her assistance. They headed inside. Olivia sank onto the sectional and ran both hands through her hair, exhaling. "That was no fun," she said. "I have a bit of a headache, but all in all I feel fine."

"But you'll call your doctor while I'm getting you more water."

She smiled. "I will call my doctor now."

When Felicity returned with two fresh glasses of water—one for each of them—Olivia was more or less back to normal. She set her phone on a side table. "I spoke with my doctor's office about my spell." She stretched out her legs, settling in on the sectional. "All set. Plenty of fluids. Rest. Call if there's a problem."

"And Dylan? Are you sure you don't want to call him?"

"I'm sure," Olivia said without hesitation. "I'll tell him when he's back. I'm *fine*. Thank you for keeping me from splitting my head open on the steps."

Felicity sat on a chair across from her, Buster flopped on the floor between them. "You're welcome."

"Sorry if I scared you." She crossed her ankles and uncrossed them with a small moan. "Not a good position. I've *months* to go with this pregnancy, too." She patted her middle. "What do you think, boy or girl?"

"Healthy."

"There's probably a pool in town. Sex, height, weight, date of birth." She yawned, covering her mouth with the back of her hand. "Oh, my. I'm sleepy. I think I'll stay right here for now. I'll be fine if you want to scoot down to Carriage Hill now."

"It's okay. I have other work I can do until Maggie gets here."

"If you're sure—" Olivia stopped, drank more water and smiled. "Thank you, Felicity. I'd appreciate the company. Best to be on the safe side."

Felicity settled in at the table. Now it was just a question of who got there first, Maggie Sloan or Dylan, Russ and Gabe.

Four

Maggie Sloan arrived first, with dinner *and* brownies. "I thought you might want to try my brownies since they're on the menu now for Saturday," she said, setting a picnic basket on the counter in the barn's kitchen. She grinned at Felicity. "That's my excuse, anyway."

"As if you need an excuse to make brownies," Olivia said, now sitting at the table.

Felicity shut her laptop at the end of the table. "I've heard stories about your brownies, Maggie."

"They're one of my signature desserts. It's hard to mess up a brownie, but I do love my recipe." She lifted a foil-wrapped package from her basket. "I say we start with sharing a brownie. Plan?"

Olivia laughed, clearly fully recovered. "An excellent plan."

Maggie unwrapped the brownies and broke one into thirds, then distributed the pieces among three napkins. Felicity took one to Olivia before returning to her laptop seat with hers. Her generous chunk of brownie was moist, chocolaty and irresistible. She immediately thought of Gabe. Even if she'd made him brownies three years ago, they wouldn't have been this good.

"Incredible as always, Maggie," Olivia said, turning to Felicity. "People argue it's hard to have a bad brownie. Then they try Maggie's, and that's that."

"They'll work for Saturday?" Maggie asked, leaning against the kitchen counter.

"Definitely," Felicity said. "Thanks."

With Gabe on the way, she was tempted to skip dinner and just eat brownies, but she limited herself to the pre-dinner morsel and helped Maggie unload the rest of the food. There was plenty for the three of them. Olivia hadn't exaggerated.

"I made enough for Dylan and Gabe," Maggie said. "There's probably enough for Russ to have a bite, too, but I figure he'll want to get home to Kylie."

They set the table and enjoyed the simple fare of grilled chicken, summer squash and sliced tomatoes, but with Maggie's flair. Afterward they walked the short distance to Dylan and Olivia's new house. Felicity knew she was pushing it if she wanted to get out of there before the guys arrived. She'd skip checking the space at Olivia's inn. It'd be fine. She followed Maggie and Olivia inside through the side door and into the kitchen. It was dusk, the fields behind the house quiet on the still evening.

"You should get home to Tyler and Aidan," Olivia said, referring to Maggie's sons. "Felicity, you can head home, too. I'll be fine here on my own."

Maggie shook her head, clearly unimpressed. "I've had two babies, Olivia. I'm staying until Dylan gets here. The boys are with my mother. She's teaching them how to feed the goats. They're all excited. Brandon doesn't want to have anything to do with the goats, so they're taking advantage of him being away."

Maggie immediately filled up a glass of water at the sink and handed it to Olivia. "Drink up."

"The house is amazing," Felicity said, noticing the adjoining den also had a large stone fireplace.

Olivia smiled, water glass in hand. "Thank you. We love it. Mark was the perfect architect. He did a great job on your house, too. I envisioned a quiet country destination inn that I'd run while freelancing as a graphic designer, but then I wrote to Dylan, thinking he was his father, to clean up his eyesore of a yard or I'd do it myself…" She sipped some of her water. "I soon discovered his father had died before he had a chance to tell Dylan about this property and Knights Bridge."

Felicity knew the story, or at least the highlights. Duncan McCaffrey, a treasure hunter and adventurer, had gone on a search for his birth mother, never thinking he'd find her—or certainly that she'd still be alive. His search had led him to tiny Knights Bridge and Grace Webster, a nonagenarian retired English and Latin teacher who'd never married. She'd moved from one of the lost Swift River Valley towns in her late teens, while pregnant by an English pilot who'd gone home to the war. She'd given birth to a baby boy and he was adopted, unaware of her identity until he himself was in his seventies. Grace had just moved into assisted living when Duncan arrived in Knights Bridge. He'd bought her house, and a short time later, he died in a tragic fall on a Portugal treasure-hunting venture.

In the meantime, Olivia had purchased the center-chimney house, built in 1803, long before construction of the Quabbin Reservoir had turned Carriage Hill Road into a dead-end, stopping it from winding into the small towns of the now-flooded Swift River Valley. The house's previous owners had lovingly restored the property, including adding extensive herb and flower gardens. Olivia had set about converting the house into a destination inn, hosting parties, small weddings and other events. Her main obstacle was Grace's former house up the road. It had fallen into neglect, its unsightly yard, broken shutters and peeling paint not exactly conducive to Olivia's new business. She located its owner in San Diego and wrote him a letter. She'd confused Dylan with his father. When Dylan had received her handwritten note, he'd decided to head East and find out for himself what his father had been up to in little Knights Bridge and why he'd left him a dilapidated old house.

No one in Knights Bridge had realized that Grace had born a child. She'd met Duncan, her son, before his untimely death, and now she had Dylan—her grandson—in her life, and a great-grandchild on the way. Her English fighter pilot had died early in World War II, but no one doubted he'd have come back for the young woman he'd fallen in love with in New England the summer prior to the outbreak of the war, as her home and town were razed, the land scraped bare to make way for a reservoir.

Felicity liked Grace, who was preparing a lecture on Jane Austen for Sunday's tea.

She found herself not wanting to leave just yet and go home to her empty house and buzzing thoughts. "Was it difficult tearing down Grace's house?" she asked.

"In some ways," Olivia said. "Grace was for it, though. She'd lived in the same house since she arrived in Knights Bridge with her father and grandmother after they were forced out of the valley. When she turned ninety, she decided it was time to move to Rivendell. She loves it there. It's home now."

"Grace gained a grandson and Dylan gained a grandmother," Felicity said.

"And family in England," Olivia added, sinking onto a couch in the den with her glass of water. "Philip Rankin—Dylan's grandfather—was a widower, and his daughter and granddaughter welcomed us into the family."

Maggie pointed to the glass. "You're going to finish that, right, Olivia?"

Olivia smiled at her friend. "I'll keep it at hand. I've drank so much water I could float away." She turned to Felicity, who remained on her feet, half ready to bolt. "How do you like being back in Knights Bridge? Did you ever think you'd return here to live?"

"I never gave it much thought one way or the other. I'm good at planning events, but planning my life is a different story."

Maggie snorted in solidarity. "I can identify with that. I plan. Then I revise the plan when life intervenes, which it always does. I mean, an O'Dunn and a Sloan together? How could my life be anything but chaotic?"

"Also perfect," Olivia said.

"Mostly perfect. I have a tendency to take on too much in case you haven't noticed."

Both Olivia and Felicity laughed along with Maggie at her dead-on insight into herself. In addition to Brandon and their two young sons, his parents, feisty grandmother, four brothers and one sister, and her own three sisters and widowed mother, Maggie was also a caterer, innkeeper and budding entrepreneur of hand-made essential oils and goat's milk bath products. It was a full, busy life, for sure, but Felicity could see how it could get overwhelming. Any sense of "over-whelm" in her own life came not from the sort of abundance Maggie enjoyed but from her own bad habits.

"I hadn't really considered moving to Knights Bridge until Mark put the house up for sale," Felicity said. "Once I toured it, I knew. I've always loved that spot on the river."

Maggie tilted her head back. "Nothing to do with the Flanagans?"

She tried to look as if mention of the Flanagans didn't faze her. "I remember before Mark built the house. I assumed he and Jess would stay there, but they seem happy in the village. It makes sense they'd want to restore an old house."

"Gabe never wanted to live in Knights Bridge," Maggie said.

Olivia nodded. "That's why he let Mark buy out his interest in the riverfront property."

"Mark bought Gabe out?" The words were out before Felicity could contain them. "Never mind—"

"They pitched in together to buy the camp from their grandfather," Olivia said. "Didn't you know?"

Felicity shook her head. "I didn't know." She absorbed the news and shut down the dozen questions that erupted all at once. She forced a smile. "I guess it doesn't matter. I'm enjoying putting my own stamp on the place."

"You can plant all the flowers you want," Olivia

said lightly. "Jess says Mark didn't want so much as a petunia out there. He's more amenable to flowers in the village. I think he still sees the river house as a camp."

Maggie grinned. "I'd get a flower doormat, too. De-Flanagan the place altogether."

Felicity couldn't help but laugh, but she also decided a shift in subject was in order. Then a quick exit. "How did Dylan get Gabe to do the boot camp?"

Olivia shrugged. "I don't know the details. I imagine Mark was involved. Gabe has quite a reputation as a start-up entrepreneur. He'll have a lot to offer on Saturday."

"You two were always tight, Felicity," Maggie said, plopping onto a chair by the cold fireplace. "You didn't stay in touch?"

"We did for a while." Felicity left it at that and hoped it was a sufficient answer and didn't sound evasive. She didn't want to get into any details about her and Gabe's parting-of-the-ways. "I should get going. Thanks so much for dinner, and the company. Take care, Olivia, okay?"

"I will. Thank you again. I'm glad you were there when I went wobbly."

Felicity didn't argue, but she was convinced Olivia had actually fainted.

Maggie took another glass off an open shelf. "You'll have to join us for one of our girls' nights out, Felicity. We're overdue for one."

"I'd like that. The brownies are great, Maggie. They'll be perfect for the party."

"We'll have low-carb goodies, too," Maggie said. "It's awesome to have an event planner in town. I'm good with food, but party favors, guest lists, registrations, RSVPs, entertainment—my head starts to spin."

"We make a good team, then, because I'd poison everyone if I did the food."

"Accidentally, of course," Maggie said with a grin.

"Don't get Maggie started," Olivia said, tucking her feet under her on the couch. "She's got a list of people she'd merrily poison."

All in good fun, Felicity thought as she said goodnight and headed outside.

She took the stone walk back to her beat-up Land Rover. It was tucked in the back of the barn's discreet parking area. She understood that buying the house from Mark was naturally a source of curiosity in town, but she doubted anyone knew just how much work it had taken the past three years to get to the point where she could qualify for a mortgage. No doubt in her mind she'd have done it without Gabe's prodding, but she doubted he'd see it that way. He'd take credit.

Didn't matter. He didn't need to know her financial status.

And it was a reach, wasn't it, to think he might be interested? He'd had three years to show an interest in her, and he hadn't.

"Just as well."

She focused on the drive out to her house. It was a beautiful evening, the sort that used to draw her and Gabe out to the river to sit on a blanket and look up at the stars.

It was nearly dark when she arrived. She went inside, poured herself a glass of merlot and took it out to the deck. She was grateful she'd been there to help Olivia and that she'd only been a bit dehydrated. She didn't want to imagine what would have happened if she'd left two minutes earlier and Olivia had fainted without anyone around. If she'd hit her head... But she hadn't, and all was well.

Felicity listened to the river as she sipped her wine and forced herself to relax, calm her thoughts. "I love it here," she whispered. "Totally love it."

Gabe's arrival in Knights Bridge and his involvement with the boot camp party were temporary distractions. Get through Saturday, and her life would return to normal.

Felicity refilled her wineglass, lit a citronella candle and sat with her feet up on another chair, listening to the soothing sounds of the river as dusk gave way to night. She deliberately avoided thinking about work. Her days often didn't have hard start and stop times, and she always had eighty million things on her to-do list. All eighty million could wait until tomorrow.

Halfway through her wine, she heard a car out front. Hers wasn't a well-traveled road. She expected the car to continue on its way and loop back to the main river road, but instead she heard an idling engine and, in another moment, silence.

Company?

She set her wineglass on the table, jumped to her feet and trotted down the deck steps and out to the driveway. A gray BMW SUV was parked behind her car. A man was behind the wheel, but she couldn't make out his face. No one else was with him. She didn't recognize the car. Dylan McCaffrey, here to get reassurance about his pregnant wife's fainting spell?

Then the driver's door opened, and Gabe Flanagan got out, stretched and looked straight at her in the shadows. "Hey, Felicity. Long time."

"Almost three-and-a-half years."

He grinned. "I knew you'd remember."

She'd fallen into that one, hadn't she? Not off to a great start. What was he doing here?

He shut the driver's door, standing now in the light from the house. He was as strikingly good-looking and confident as ever. Visibly muscular and more obviously the successful start-up entrepreneur in his expensive, perfectly fitting clothes. Three years ago, he'd sit for hours at his laptop in a T-shirt and cargo shorts.

"We're all set for Saturday," Felicity said. "We're having the party at Olivia's inn. I need to take a quick look at it. Everything's well in hand, but we can talk tomorrow if you'd like."

"No problem. You'll do a great job."

It struck her as more than an offhand comment—as if what she did was so easy anyone could pull off a one-day boot camp of hard-driving, successful entrepreneurs and their aspiring audience. It was Dylan's first major event, too. But, sure. Anyone could do it.

Felicity gave herself a mental shake. Gabe didn't necessarily mean that at all. She knew better than to make assumptions. "Are you staying with Mark?" she asked. "Your dad? With Olivia and Dylan at their house? Did a room open up at Olivia's inn?"

"None of the above."

"Your grandfather at Rivendell? I don't think that's allowed."

Gabe walked to the back of the car, opened the hatch, took out a duffel bag and shut the hatch with a soft thud.

Why would he need his duffel bag?

He edged toward her. "Remember when you said you owed me for letting you sleep on my couch?" He hoisted his bag's strap on one shoulder, the light from the house creating shadows on his angular face, making his expression even more difficult to read. He didn't smile, but he didn't not smile, either. "I've come to collect."

"You want to sleep on my couch?"

"It's the best option," he said, pragmatic. "Mark says Jess has bad morning sickness. I'm not staying there. Olivia passed out this afternoon. Dylan found out when he got home. She didn't want to tell him, but he could tell something was up."

"Husband's instincts," Felicity said.

"New dad's instincts, too."

She tried to ignore the sensitivity in Gabe's tone. *Much* easier if he stayed the overbearing, mercenary jerk she'd convinced herself he was.

He wanted something from her. That was it. Had to be.

"Anyway," he said, "I'm not staying with them, either. I'd pitch a tent, but tents aren't my thing these days."

"What about one of the Sloan brothers? There are five of them. They all live in town."

"None of the Sloans were ever down-and-out enough to knock on my door and ask to sleep on my couch."

"I didn't ask. You offered. And I wasn't down-and-out. I needed space to think."

"What do you call no job, drowning in debt—"

"Reasons I needed to think. Obviously I should

have done my thinking in Paris. I had enough room on my credit card for one more good trip."

"Felicity math."

There was no animosity or note of criticism in his tone. He grinned at her, as if he knew she couldn't argue with him. Back then, she'd used time between jobs as an excuse to travel. Of course he remembered. This was miss-nothing, remember-everything, never-let-anyone-forget Gabe. He'd been that way in sixth grade. Now wasn't the time to argue whether she'd truly been down-and-out. By her standards, no, she hadn't been. By Gabe's standards? She probably still was in need of intervention. But she had reined in her credit-card spending.

He flicked vainly at a mosquito buzzing around his head. "I'm still not a fan of mosquitoes."

"If you think we can pick up where we left off three years ago—"

"I don't. I know we're not buddies anymore."

There was something in his eyes. She ignored it but felt its effect in the pit of her stomach. She flashed on being out here that night at eighteen. She hadn't noticed mosquitoes then. She hadn't noticed anything but him. *Gad.* His mosquito buzzed toward her and then disappeared into the darkness.

"We stopped being buddies when you told me I was in the wrong career."

"You were in the wrong career."

His tone was lighthearted, but she bristled. "Everything I learned as a financial analyst has helped me with event management."

"No doubt. I say the same thing about my failures."

"I wasn't a failure—"

"Didn't say you were but your jobs in finance didn't work out."

"Are we going to do this? I was in a tough spot when I knocked on your door. I could have used some support."

"I let you sleep on my couch and binge-watch *Judge Judy*."

"I do appreciate that."

"I also laid out the facts of your situation when you weren't ready to listen and hadn't asked my opinion."

"You told me I'd dug the hole I was in, and I needed to stop digging."

"Yep." No hint of remorse. "My goal at the time was to penetrate your one-track mind and get you to consider alternatives. As your friend, I felt I needed to say something. I did, and it pissed you off. You told me I needed to work on my people skills."

"Well?"

"Okay, you had a point. At least you knew I was being honest."

Honest? So that was it? She made no comment.

He glanced up at the starlit sky. He looked at her again, his eyes dark, taking on none of the light from the house or the stars. "I found your note at the bottom of my note. You told me you'd made me brownies as a thank-you."

She felt caught, trapped by her own behavior that day—by the memories of how she'd felt reading his note. "I did make brownies, but I ate them," she said, defiant.

He frowned. "All of them?"

"They weren't that good. I was mad. I forgot the baking powder or something."

"But you ate them, anyway?"

"A bad brownie is better than no brownie. It's one of life's rules."

He smiled then, taking her by surprise. "You're probably right about that."

Felicity felt the cool grass on her bare feet, let it pull her back to the present. She reined in the urge to launch herself into the emotions of the past and instead considered her current situation. There was no good option. Send him off to find other accommodations, and she risked the two of them becoming a source of gossip in town. Let him stay…same thing, but more manageable since no one had to know he was here. If not for the pregnant Frost sisters, she could at least try to persuade Gabe to bunk with the McCaffreys or his brother. She was backed into a corner. She *had* said she'd owed him three years ago, and Olivia and Jess needed rest.

"Inside," she said. "Before the mosquitoes start gnawing on us both."

"Ah, yes. Good to be back in Knights Bridge."

Five

Felicity switched on the lights in her living room, but it didn't change anything. Gabe had followed her inside and stood by the glass doors that opened onto the deck above the river. The man was as sexy and maddening as ever.

Sexier, maybe.

This wasn't a welcome thought as he turned from the view and set his duffel bag on the floor by her IKEA couch. It probably had cost her less than his pants. Less than his shoes. Maybe even less than his haircut.

She stopped herself. She didn't care if he had money. She never had.

He glanced around the living room. It had a wood-stove and glass doors that opened onto the main deck. Felicity hadn't left too much party-planning para-phernalia laying about, but she did have printouts of various badgers spread out on the coffee table. Gabe looked at them without comment.

"Different from the world of financial spreadsheets and such," she said.

"At least these woodchucks don't bite."

"They're badgers."

He raised his eyes to her and smiled. "I know. It was a joke."

"Ah. Right. You're still a New England country boy at heart. You know your badgers from your woodchucks. You just don't run into them often in your line of work."

"One hopes you don't run into them in your work, either. Badgers and woodchucks don't mix with parties."

"Morwenna Mills's badgers do. Have you met her yet? Her real name is Kylie Shaw."

"I haven't met her, no. I met her husband last night. He and Dylan flew from California together."

"Russ and I have discussed security for Saturday's boot camp," Felicity said, hating her awkwardness. "I'll go over the details of your party with him."

"It's not really my party." Gabe stifled a yawn and shuddered. "I'm still readjusting to East Coast time. I was in California for two months. Doesn't seem to matter it's three hours earlier there."

"Feel free to crash, but you don't need to sleep on the couch. I have a guest room. It's not fully set up for company yet, but it's got a bed."

"Thanks." His gaze settled on her, his eyes half closed. "It's good to see you, Felicity."

"You, too." She waved a hand vaguely. "I'll see to the guest room."

She was aware of Gabe watching her as she went down the hall to the linen closet. She dug out a stack of twin-size sheets and took them into the guest room, more or less where Gabe's grandfather would pitch his tent before the house was built. The windows looked out on the side yard, with a glimpse of the river down through the woods.

Gabe stood in the doorway. "I stayed here once while the house was being built and a few times after Mark moved in. He's good at what he does."

Felicity set the linens on the floor by the bed. "I didn't know until tonight you'd gone in together on this place. Maggie and Olivia knew, but they would—I've hardly seen Mark in the past few years, never mind you. I didn't buy the house because of the past."

"Mark and I were helping my grandfather."

"That was a decent thing to do." She lifted a box of party supplies off the bed and set it on the floor. "I weighed the pros and cons before I made an offer."

"Was I a pro or a con?"

She glanced back at him, slouched against the door-jamb. "Maybe I didn't consider you at all," she said lightly. "It's a little stuffy in here. Feel free to open the windows."

He stood straight. "I can make up the bed."

"I don't mind. You're my first company. It'll be good practice."

She didn't need to tell him that the guest room shared a bathroom with the house's third bedroom, which she used as her office—when she wasn't work-ing in the living room, out on the deck or in the town library. The master bedroom had its own bathroom. Mercifully, Felicity thought.

He stepped into the room and peered out a win-dow. "The trees are bigger now. Mark and I planted the apple tree out front when we were in high school. We promised each other we'd be out of here before it was big enough to climb."

"And now it is," Felicity said.

"The apples will be ripe soon. My mother talked about making pie with apples from that tree, once it was big enough. She didn't get that chance, but she liked coming out here when she was sick."

"I remember." Felicity could see it wasn't a subject he wanted to pursue. She pointed at the single blanket on her stack of linens. "There are more blankets in the closet. I've never lived anywhere but New England. I have lots of blankets."

"It's the humidity that gets to me compared to Southern California." He drew away from the window. "I'll take a walk. Don't let me keep you from anything."

"No problem."

"And, really, leave the bed to me—I still know how to make up a bed."

But he didn't, she realized. He had household help. She didn't. Every chore at her house had her name on it. "Enjoy your walk."

"I will, thanks."

He headed back down the hall. Felicity heard the front door open and shut. She made up the bed, fluffed the pillows and checked the towels and basic supplies in the bathroom. All set for a guest, if not for one accustomed to five-star accommodations. But he'd known what to expect. He'd been here before. He'd been a part owner of the place.

She went into the kitchen and pulled open her baking cupboard. She scanned the shelves and saw she had the ingredients for brownies. She could have taken some of Maggie's brownies home with her, but she'd been thinking of her waistline, not Gabe showing up in her driveway. She grabbed the ingredients she needed—flour, sugar, baking chocolate, vanilla—and set them on the counter, then collected eggs and butter from the refrigerator. She got out a bowl, measuring spoons and cups, turned on the oven to preheat and went to work.

She hadn't really made brownies that February morning. She didn't know why she'd lied, probably just an impulse after the shock of seeing him. What did the truth matter, anyway? She hadn't stuck around that morning, but she hadn't acted out of spite about the brownies. If she'd taken the time to make brownies, she could have cooled off, vacated the premises for the evening and come back for more pizza deliveries and *Judge Judy*. She'd have prolonged the inevitable, and so she'd skipped the brownies and left.

When she'd knocked on Gabe's door after losing her latest job as a financial analyst, she hadn't expected to stay for more than a day or two. She'd been broke, in debt, kicked out of her apartment, *desperate* not to go crawling to her parents for help. She'd turned to Gabe, then living in the smaller of two apartments in a house he owned on the Charles River in Watertown, just outside Boston. They'd known each other since nursery school. He'd taken her in, but he hadn't been that excited to see her. "*Again*, Felicity? Wasn't this job supposed to last three years?"

"It didn't."

"Did you quit or get fired?"

"I was outsourced."

"Fired, then."

He'd let her sleep on his couch and take as many hot showers as she'd wanted. It had been winter. The showers helped with her perpetually cold feet. After five days of putting up with her camped out in his living room, he'd read her the riot act. It couldn't have been more than an hour before he'd written his fateful note. Maybe he'd already had it written, because he'd started his speech while she'd been getting out of the shower.

"You need a career change," he'd told her. "You're a lousy financial analyst."

"How would you know? You quit college. I have an MBA."

"Your MBA isn't doing you any good, is it? You get jobs, but you don't keep them. Why is that?"

"Bad luck."

"Bad career choice. Do something else. You're hacking away in the wrong jungle."

She'd been incensed. How could he be so blunt? How could he not get how terrible she felt about herself?

She'd shouted through the bathroom door about his lousy people skills.

He hadn't responded, and she'd stared at her reflection in the mirror above the sink. She'd seen the truth of what he said in the dark circles under her eyes, the lines of fatigue at her mouth, the puffiness of her skin. Brown hair dripping, eyes somewhat bloodshot from too much television and last night's bottle of wine, full lips, high cheeks, a strong chin. In high school, Gabe had said she reminded him of Maureen O'Hara in *The Quiet Man*. Felicity had taken that to mean he'd wanted to spank her and told him as much, thinking it was funny—but he'd found it sexy, provocative.

She'd loved Gabe Flanagan then, as a teenager, before college and graduate school. Her first jobs after getting her degrees hadn't worked out, but she'd had high hopes when she'd landed a job at a large insurance firm in Boston's financial district. She hadn't known many people in Boston, and she'd been so busy keeping her nose above water, scrambling to learn the job, that she hadn't made many new friends. Certainly none who would take her in after she'd been fired.

There'd been Gabe, and she'd landed on his doorstep with her weekender bag in hand, explaining she needed a couple of days to regroup. She'd rented a house with two other women, but they had a friend willing to take her room, since she could no longer afford it. Gabe hadn't asked for details. He was successful and hard-driving and impatient, and he could read between the lines and didn't need her to spell out how broke she was.

She'd been making wrong choice after wrong choice. But it hadn't seemed that way. It'd seemed— she'd truly believed—she just needed the right fit, the right job. She just had to tough it out. Persevere. She wasn't a quitter, she'd told herself—and Gabe. But that had been part of the problem. She'd needed to quit. He'd pointed out he'd started businesses that failed. He'd made mistakes. "I learned from my failures. That's the trick, Felicity. Acknowledging your failures and learning from them."

In all the years she'd known him, she'd never let Gabe see her cry. Even when he'd broken her heart that summer after high school, she hadn't let him see her melt down. It wasn't as if it had been unexpected. That's what Gabe Flanagan did in high school. He broke girls' hearts. Everyone knew.

Still, they'd been there for each other through high school, college, their first jobs, various ups and downs. They'd go weeks without speaking, texting or emailing, and then she'd call him to tell him she'd just burned her mouth on a hot pepper or he'd send her a silly puppy video off the internet at 2:00 a.m.

She'd known their friendship had needed to change. They were proper adults. Gabe needed to be free to get on with his life. He'd sell his place and move into something grander, more expensive. He'd meet other up-and-coming, hard-driving entrepreneurs. People who got him. People he got. He'd come to rely on her, the hometown girl, to be there when he didn't have time or want to take time to socialize. She was easy, familiar and *there*.

She'd needed to figure out her life, but she resisted confronting how she'd managed to find herself out of *another* job. She'd had a five-year plan, but she'd kept having to restart the thing.

Back to Go, Gabe would tell her. *You can do it.*

By that day in his apartment, even he had lost patience.

And he'd lost faith in her.

After her shower, she'd put on clean clothes, including socks and shoes, dried her hair—Gabe had actually owned a decent hair dryer—and hung up her towel on a peg next to his threadbare towel. He had pegs, not towel racks. She didn't know why she'd noticed that or what it said about either of them. Probably nothing. When she'd emerged from the bathroom, she'd felt more in control of herself, but Gabe was gone.

That was when she'd found his note on the counter where he kept his recycling schedule, take-out menus, pens, stamps, paper clips, notepad and phone charger. There was a clear block with a photograph of the covered bridge in their hometown, a mile up the river from where he'd grown up with his brother and their unreliable but otherwise wonderful parents. They'd had dogs, cats, gerbils, hamsters and at least one cow. And chickens. Felicity was positive she remembered chickens.

After dashing off her response, she'd returned the Sharpie she'd borrowed to its mates. She wiped crumbs off the couch, folded the throws she'd used during her stay, fluffed the cushions, ran the vacuum and took her dirty dishes and various leftovers into the kitchen. She'd loaded the dishwasher, run the garbage disposal and taken out the trash, including her pizza boxes. She'd packed up her meager belongings, folded her blankets, put her sheets and towels in the wash—of course he had an in-unit washer and dryer—and gathered up her garbage. Twenty minutes later, she was on her way in the February cold.

By the end of the week, she had a job with a successful event planner in Boston. She'd meant it to be a temporary job—an ultra-temporary job, for that matter—to make ends meet and get herself on firmer financial footing. She wasn't going back to Gabe's couch, or moving in with her parents. But a few weeks turned into a few months, and then it was summer… and fall…and finally she'd realized she'd found a career she truly enjoyed and was good at. Serendipity, desperation, strategic thinking, accident—whatever it had been, she'd never looked back to emerging markets, municipal bonds and any of the rest of it.

She scraped the brownie batter into a pan and placed

it into the oven to bake. A peace offering, maybe. An acknowledgment that their fight three years ago was in the past and their drift apart had started before she'd stalked out of his apartment. For better or worse, they'd both changed since then, and there was no putting the Humpty Dumpty of their broken friendship back together again.

Gabe didn't return from his walk before she got the brownies out of the oven. She set them to cool on the counter and disappeared into her bedroom. She shut the door, something she seldom did when she was home alone. She checked her messages, tossed her phone onto her nightstand and grabbed a book she'd started the other night, reading to the faint, tempting smell of brownies.

Gabe figured he deserved every backhanded, aggrieved and otherwise vengeful comment and act on Felicity's part. He'd hurt her three years ago. He saw that now. He hadn't just pissed her off. They'd been friends—the best of friends—and he'd thrown a bucket of ice water on that friendship. So had she, but she wasn't looking at her role in their estrangement at the moment and might never get there. She was the injured party. That was how she saw it.

He hadn't been dishonest. Just the opposite. He'd been honest, maybe brutally so from her point of view. He hadn't taken into consideration her ego, her emotions, her hopes and her dreams. He'd flat-out let her have it without regard to anything except knowing he was right.

He had been right, too.

What did he want now?

He had no idea. Part of him wanted to pick up the pieces of their friendship—to get her back, counseling him, seeing through him, speaking her mind without any of the filters he so often encountered in other people. Hearing what was on *her* mind. Seeing through *her*, telling *her* what *he* thought. He'd never had that kind of open give-and-take with anyone else. For him, it defined a real friendship, and he missed it.

That didn't mean he could get it back, or that it was wise to try. Resurrecting their dead friendship, even if possible, wasn't necessarily good for either of them. The best he could do was to repair any damage caused by the way they'd ended things.

It would be easier if he hadn't noticed her curves and smile and the spark in her eyes.

And being here, he thought, taking in the familiar surroundings. It was night now, warm and quiet on the winding country road. He heard an owl hooting through the trees, somewhere down by the river. He wanted to stay in the moment, be here, now. He didn't want to hurl himself into the past, and yet he could feel memories tugging at him. Sneaking down to the river with Mark as young boys to throw rocks in the water. Riding his bike out here. Sitting by the fire with his grandfather. Fishing, camping, playing hide-and-seek.

The river—this land—had been the best part of his childhood. The smells, the trees, the river, the night sky were all unchanged. Felicity hadn't known he'd built the house with his brother. Would she have bought it if she'd known?

That was the least of his worries.

He turned around and walked back to the house, in no rush. He flicked away a few mosquitoes, but none landed. He remembered the night he'd made love to her, realized it was her first time. Damn, they'd been so young. Afterward she'd stood next to him in the dark. "If I ever build a house in Knights Bridge, I'd build it here. What about you, Gabe?"

"I'm never coming back here."

He'd meant it, too. He remembered her expression—a mix of understanding, acceptance and the slightest hint of disappointment, as if she hoped he might leave himself some wiggle room. But he hadn't. His future wasn't in Knights Bridge. He'd been sure of it.

He pulled himself out of his thoughts before he could examine them too deeply.

As he approached the house, he noticed the smell of brownies.

His imagination? A trick of his mind because he was lost in the past?

He shook his head, breathing deeply. No, it was brownies he smelled.

He went inside through the kitchen—Felicity had left the door unlocked—and found a pan of fresh brownies cooling on a rack on the counter.

He grinned. "About time, Felicity."

Three years ago, he'd read the note she'd left on his kitchen counter and had realized she was angry with him, but he'd figured she'd get over it—because they were friends and he was right. But when he'd opened his freezer and didn't find brownies, he'd known she wouldn't be back. Everything had changed. He'd known this because he knew Felicity.

Had she made brownies as a way of apologizing for overreacting that day?

No.

She was establishing control. She was in charge. This was her house, her town, her event on Saturday, and he could damn well toe the line.

She'd left him a note on the counter by the brownie pan.

Help yourself. Sleep well. I'm an early riser but
I'll be quiet.
Felicity

Gabe got a knife out of a drawer and cut a two-inch square, getting warm brownie on the blade. He wiped it with his finger and licked it. Felicity still made a hell of a brownie. He could pull together a decent stir-fry—or he used to. These days he seldom cooked.

He lifted out the brownie and ate it in two bites. It was one of the best he'd ever had, just the right balance between chewy and gooey. Perfect.

He smiled, feeling better, and took his duffel bag to the guest room. He set it on the floor and decided not to unpack. Keep his options open.

Sleeping well would be a trick with Felicity in the next room.

Gabe exhaled, hearing an owl somewhere in the woods. Tomorrow he'd see Mark and Jessica. There were other people he wanted to see while he was in town, and some he needed to see—but he didn't want to think about that.

He returned to the kitchen and checked the refrigerator. No beer, but he noticed an unopened bottle of a decent New Zealand sauvignon blanc. He decided not to open the wine and poured himself a glass of

milk, helped himself to another brownie and headed
out to the deck.

A citronella candle burned with a low flame in the
center of the table. He set his milk on the deck rail and
ate the brownie while he listened to the river down the
steep bank. On another night, perhaps, or for anyone
else, the sounds of the water would have been soothing, restorative after a long trip. For him, they were
unsettling, stirring up past longings and insecurities,
reminding him of the boy he'd been, managing an un-
stable if loving home. He'd always admired the Mac-
Gregors. They were solid, smart, stable, predictable.
He wasn't the only one who'd expected Felicity to be
the same. She'd expected it of herself. If she had been,
would they have become friends? Would he have slept
with her?

Not worth thinking about now.

He finished his brownie, drank his milk and got
back inside before the mosquitoes found him.

He heard the owl again.

He took *The Badgers of Middle Branch*, the first
book in the popular series, to the guest room with him.
Well, what the hell, right? He was in Knights Bridge.
Might as well read about badgers.

Six

Felicity awakened groggy and out of sorts and wandered into the kitchen in underpants and a T-shirt, saw the brownie pan and remembered Gabe was sleeping down the hall. It hadn't been a bad dream. She managed not to groan out loud as she about-faced and tiptoed back to her room. Her blanket and top sheet were in a tangle. Well, no wonder, with Gabe under the same roof.

She stood in the threshold and peered across the hall at the closed door to the guest room.

She'd done it, hadn't she? She'd let Gabe Flanagan stay.

Fully awake now, she took a quick shower, got dressed, pulled her hair back and put on a bit of makeup *and* sandals before returning to the kitchen. She put on a pot of coffee, toasted an English muffin, scrambled an egg and ate at the table. It was a warm, sunny morning, perfect for breakfast on the deck, but she didn't want to rattle around too much and wake up her houseguest. He hadn't been a late riser when she'd known him, but hadn't she heard he'd been in California? Had he mentioned it, or had Mark or even Kylie?

It didn't matter. She didn't need to dig into the details of Gabe's life.

It was another hour before he surfaced. She'd cleaned up her dishes and cut the brownies and wrapped them in foil and was running water into the empty pan when he padded barefoot into the kitchen. He had on jeans and a San Diego Padres T-shirt. "Morning," he said lazily.

Felicity shut off the water. "Good morning. Sleep well?"

"I dreamed about badgers."

"It happens." She pointed at his T-shirt. "I thought you were a die-hard Red Sox fan."

"I am. This was a gift from a Padres fan."

"I see. Provocative if you plan to wear it in Knights Bridge."

He grinned at her, and she went about putting on another pot of coffee. He offered to help, but she shook her head. She didn't need him buzzing around her. He was distracting enough as he pulled out a chair and sat at the table. The muscles in his arms, the fall of his shirt over his flat abdomen, the hug of his jeans on his thighs. Yeah, distracting enough.

"Who's the Padres fan?" she asked casually, trying to redirect her thoughts.

"Guy who bought my company. He's from San Diego, but he lives in LA now. I didn't dare put it on yesterday. I'm having work done on my condo. The painters probably would have let me live, but I don't know about Shannon. You remember her? Shannon Rivera. She's my assistant."

"I do remember her. She's stood with you through thick and thin."

"That kind of loyalty is a good quality," he said.

Felicity didn't detect any sarcasm or bitterness in his voice but still felt a pang at his words. At the time, he'd been starting a company—the one he'd just sold—and she'd intruded on his intense night-and-day schedule with her own problems. She'd met Shannon Rivera once, briefly—a super-organized, professional, personable and hard-working force behind Gabe and his high energy, multiplicity of ideas and impatience.

"Shannon didn't stay with the company after you sold it?" Felicity asked, flipping the switch to start the coffeemaker.

"She didn't want to. She'd have gotten a different job, but I still need an assistant while I figure out what's next."

"So the boot camp came up while you're at a loose end."

"You could say that."

Felicity leaned back against the counter by the sink. Sunlight streamed through the windows. "What would you like for breakfast?"

"You don't have to wait on me, Felicity."

"You're my guest."

"Your uninvited guest."

"Once I agreed to put you up in my guest room, you became invited." She thought that sounded diplomatic and pointed to the refrigerator. "I've got yogurt, eggs, cereal, English muffins, sunflower butter—"

"Sunflower butter?"

"My nephew's allergic to peanuts. He doesn't eat tree nuts, either, so it's safer for me to have sunflower butter. I keep anything with nuts segregated."

Gabe put his feet up on another chair and sat back,

making himself at home. "Little Max, right? Sorry to hear that. He's what—four or five now?"

"Five. He starts kindergarten this fall. He has a baby sister now. She just turned two."

"What's her name?"

"Elizabeth."

He narrowed his eyes on her. "Why so curt?"

"I'm not being curt."

At least, she hadn't realized she'd been curt. He'd shared her excitement when Max had been born. He'd missed Elizabeth's birth entirely. He hadn't been around when Max's allergy to peanuts had developed. Her choice, his choice. Nothing to do about it now. There was no unwinding the clock even if they'd wanted to.

"You haven't told me what you want for breakfast," she said.

"An English muffin and scrambled eggs, which I can make." He paused, eyeing her. "Max was a cute little guy. I imagine your niece is, too. Do they call her Elizabeth?"

"Lizzie."

"Must be nice being closer to them now that you live in Knights Bridge."

"It is." She sighed, dropping her hands to her sides. "Sorry. I appreciate your interest in my family. I'll make your breakfast. I don't mind. I know where things are, and you're my guest." She motioned toward the stove. "I'll get started."

"Thank you." He yawned again. "I'll set the table."

She got a frying pan out from a lower cupboard and set it on the stove. In a moment, she had butter melting, eggs cracked in bowl, a touch of water added, fresh chives snipped from the pot in the window—all under Gabe's watchful gaze as he got dishes from a cupboard.

"What are your plans for today?" she asked as she grabbed a whisk from a pottery container by the stove.

"I'm meeting Mark and Jess at the mill. What about you?"

"I'm working. I'll drive out to Carriage Hill at some point to take a closer look at Olivia's inn, but I don't foresee any problems. She and Dylan have so many irons in the fire—they seem to be having a great time. Olivia and Dylan are figuring out the details of the boot camp, adventure travel and the inn as they go along. They're not waiting for everything to be perfect."

"Smart approach."

"When it works. When it doesn't, people lecture you about being in debt and getting fired." She kept her tone light. "Sometimes it's hard to know if you're on the right path and just need to keep pushing forward, or if you're on the wrong path and need to—I don't know. Do something else."

Gabe kept his gaze on her. "No comment, since you're making my breakfast."

"Ah, yes, I can add all sorts of things to your eggs without your knowing—but I wouldn't, of course. I'm a good hostess. Anyway, Carriage Hill Road has certainly changed from when you and I would go blueberry picking out there."

He smiled. "Wild blueberries are the best."

Felicity didn't detect a hint of awkwardness in Gabe's tone. He got up and poured himself coffee, which he took black—still, she thought. He always had, from his first cup at thirteen. He returned to the table with it. She noticed his Padres shirt stretched nicely across his back. He was even more muscular and fit than when she'd last seen him. Well. Good for him. She wanted him to be healthy and in good shape, didn't she? They'd gone their separate ways, but it wasn't as if they'd been engaged or anything. He'd been a friend. Nothing more.

Nothing less, either.

She whisked the eggs, added the chives and dumped the mixture into the pan. She toasted the English muffin, buttered the two halves and put them on the plate just as the eggs were cooked.

"Looks great," he said when she set the plate in front of him. "Thanks."

"You're welcome."

He picked up his fork, but his eyes were on her. "Not being curt?"

"Nope. Sincere."

"The happy hostess, huh?"

"Least I can do." She went to the counter and poured herself a mug of coffee, then took it and sat across from him. "I saw you had a brownie before bed."

"I did. It was perfect. Thanks."

"I'm glad you enjoyed it. You can have the entire batch if you want—except for the one I plan to steal for lunch. I do all right with brownies, but Maggie's are the best. She'll make the brownies for your party."

"Sounds good." He dug into his eggs. "Do you like the idea of adding a party?"

"Sure," she said. "It's a fine idea."

He winked at her. "Now that was curt."

"Are you baiting me, Gabe Flanagan?"

"Not me. Totally innocent."

"*Innocent* isn't a word I associate with you." Felicity mimicked his wink at her. "Bet that's not a surprise."

He laughed. "Damn, I've missed you, Felicity. Thanks for breakfast. I'll take care of the dishes, get cleaned up and head out. Don't let me interfere with your plans. Anything you need from me for the boot camp party?"

"Not at the moment. I'll let you know. Helps that the weather forecast is perfect."

"Are you nervous?"

His question took her by surprise. "A little, I guess. I've been planning more events in town. So far, so good, but Dylan McCaffrey and Noah Kendrick are in a league of their own."

"You don't want to screw up."

"I never want to screw up." She set her mug on the table and considered whether she should continue. Why stop now? "But I have screwed up, and I survived. I got past it. I learned from the experience, my mistakes. I don't dwell on them. I moved on. If you expected to find me stuck in the past—"

"I didn't." Gabe reached for the pepper grinder. "You're welcome, by the way." He ground black pepper onto his eggs, skipping any salt. "You'd still be miserable, clawing your way to nowhere in the world of spreadsheets if I hadn't intervened."

He spoke without any hint of hurt, defensiveness, frustration or grievance. Just stating the facts. Felicity leaned back, accidentally brushing her foot against his under the table. At least she was wearing sandals, but, still, that split second of intimate contact didn't help with her focus. "Still honest to a fault with me, aren't you?"

"With everyone but less guarded with you."

"Not guarded at all. No filters as far as I can see." She gulped her coffee and jumped to her feet. "I should get busy. Find me if you need me for anything."

"Will do."

She headed into the living room with her coffee, stood at the glass doors and let out a long, cathartic breath as she gazed out at the trees in the morning sun. Gabriel Flanagan had her discombobulated. It was a word his mother had often used, and it fit how Felicity felt. She smiled sadly, thinking of Lee Flanagan. She'd sometimes envisioned building a house here, but it'd never happened. She'd died, but she and Mickey Flanagan never would have pulled off building a house. But they'd raised sons who had.

Felicity set her mug on the coffee table, but she launched herself back to the kitchen doorway. "When did you decide you wanted to stay here?"

Gabe looked up from his eggs. "Does it matter?"

"Yes."

"Why?"

"Because I think you're up to something," she said.

"Such as?"

"I don't know yet. Were you upset when you found out I'd bought this place?"

"Why would I be upset?"

"That's not an answer, but I'll tell you why. Because you think I bought it because of you. As a way to show you—I don't know. To shove your nose in my newfound solvency."

"To spite me, you mean. That would be a bad reason to buy a house."

"Yes, it would be, and it's not what I did. I bought this place because I love the house and love the location, and Mark gave me a good deal." She paused, calmed herself. "I'm not trying to be combative. You have some great memories here. I understand if you were taken aback I'd bought it. I'm sure Mark isn't aware of the details of our…history."

"Probably not. You're the owner of this property, Felicity. That's all that matters now."

"That's an evasive response—at best a polite way to tell me to mind my own business." She wished she'd stayed in the living room. She digested Gabe's words, his posture as he sat there eating his breakfast. She considered the timing of his presence in Knights Bridge. And she got it. "Lightbulb moment. You agreed to speak at the boot camp and came up with the idea of hosting the party after you learned I'd bought the house."

"The two aren't necessarily connected. I wouldn't jump to any conclusions."

"I'm dropping this," she said. "It's obviously not going to get me anywhere I want to go."

"I'm not here to cause you trouble, Felicity."

"Good."

She returned to the living room, collected her files and laptop and went out to the deck. She generally reserved mornings for computer work, but she didn't know if she'd be able to concentrate with Gabe wandering around her house. She didn't know why she felt so agitated, on edge—exposed. That was the word. *Exposed.* It was absurd. This was *Gabe.* They might not be the kind of friends they'd once been, but they weren't hostile to each other.

She breathed in the fresh morning air and sat at the table, the shade allowing her to leave the umbrella down while she worked. She opened the file on the boot camp party. Normally she liked more time to plan such an event, but she'd worked on enough similar parties that she wasn't worried about missing key elements. The boot camp itself wasn't an event with lots of bells and whistles. Dylan and Olivia wanted to keep it simple, allowing guests to enjoy their surroundings and network with each other without distractions— balloons, fireworks, games, speeches. Good food, good conversation, good surroundings. That, Dylan had told her, was enough. Her challenge, as always, was to keep her own role as the planner invisible, under the radar, allowing the festivities to feel natural and unplanned to hosts and guests.

She gave Olivia a quick call to make sure she was feeling okay.

"Back to normal, thanks," she said. "As normal as one can feel in the second trimester of a pregnancy, anyway. I always heard it's the easiest trimester. I don't know about that, but I'm fine. How are you?"

"Working away on my deck."

"Tough commute," Olivia said with a laugh.

After they disconnected, Felicity got to her work. She could hear Gabe in the kitchen—loading the dishwasher, running the water—and then his footsteps in the hall. Just as well she was reviewing RSVPs and the budget and nothing that required deep concentration.

Ten minutes later, her guest stepped out onto the

deck. "I'm off," he said, motioning in the general direction of his car. "I'll head over to Moss Hill to see Mark."

"Great, tell him hi for me."

"Feel free to join me."

"Thanks, but I have work to do—and I wouldn't want to intrude on your visit with your brother. Was the party actually his idea?"

"Felicity…"

"It was, wasn't it? Why? He has a great reputation in town. Was he trying to make sure you looked good?"

"It's my party," Gabe said. "Let's leave it there, okay?"

She shrugged and wished him a good morning. She watched him trot down the deck stairs. Just her luck he looked even better than he had three years ago. No matter, she told herself. In forty-eight hours, Gabe would be on his way out of Knights Bridge—back to his home in Boston, wherever it was, whatever it looked like.

She stood at the deck rail and looked down through the trees to the sunlit river. This was her home. This was what it looked like. She smiled. She loved it, especially when she didn't think about being here with Gabe.

When she returned to the table, she was relieved to see she had an unread email. One glance, though, and she had to read it again to make sure she wasn't mistaken:

Hi Felicity,
Allow me to introduce myself. My name is Nadia Ains-

worth. I work with Gabe Flanagan. I'm coordinating with you on plans for tomorrow's boot camp. I'm including my contact information, but I'd like to call you today. I only have your email address. Can you let me know your phone number and a good time? That'll get us started.
Thanks much!
Nadia

Felicity stared at the message. *Get us started?* It was a straightforward party. It wasn't Cinderella's ball. But if Gabe wanted this Nadia involved, so be it. The email signature didn't provide a job title, but she was in Malibu. A long way from Knights Bridge. Given Gabe's casual attitude about tomorrow, Felicity had no reason to doubt Nadia Ainsworth.

She typed her response:

Thanks, Nadia. My contact info is below. Everything's under control for tomorrow but I can chat at noon if you have any questions.
All the best,
Felicity MacGregor

"That ought to do it," Felicity said as she hit Send. Surely a busy executive assistant would seize the opportunity to check this one off her to-do list. Whatever her job description, Nadia Ainsworth had to have better things to do with her time than get involved with an event in a small town on the other side of the continent.

Five minutes later, Felicity saw she had a new message from Nadia:

Great! I'll give you a ring at noon.

Felicity didn't respond. She'd let Nadia assume she'd seen the message and be ready to chat at noon.

Gabe surveyed his brother's comfortable office at the Mill at Moss Hill. On his last visit to Knights Bridge, the mill had still been under renovation, opening day months away. Transforming the building from a nineteenth-century factory to twenty-first century contemporary offices, meeting space and apartments had been a feat of imagination, skill, financial and professional risk and not inconsiderable hope. Gabe was no architect, but he and Mark did share a capacity for risk and optimism.

He moved to the window and looked out at the river with its old dam and millpond. He and Mark had managed never to get too close to the dam in their boyhood adventures.

He and Felicity, either.

"Hey, Gabe," Mark said, coming through the open door from his assistant's office. "Sorry to keep you waiting."

"No problem. It's a workday for you. Good to see you."

"Yeah, you, too."

Gabe turned his back to the view and nodded to the spacious, gleaming office. "Damn, Mark, this place is great. Makes sense for an architect who specializes in old buildings to have his offices in an old building, but it feels brand-new."

"It's all about HVAC, water pressure and good windows."

"The fun stuff," Gabe said with a grin. "You kept a sense of the past without being nostalgic or hokey. How's the location working for you?"

"We're using it to our advantage."

"Gives clients confidence you can handle a major project wherever it is. Remember when we'd sneak out here and throw rocks in the millpond? This place was a wreck."

"I didn't see its potential then, that's for sure," Mark said, sitting at his spotless desk. "I went down to our old swimming hole before I sold the house. I found a few pieces of the rope we used to jump in the water."

A rope they'd liberated from the remains of the mill, as Gabe recalled. They'd tied it to a tree out by their grandfather's campsite and would swing out over the river and leap into the water. All in all, perhaps not the safest pastime, but he doubted their parents had ever realized what they were up to on those hot summer days.

"If it gets hot enough while I'm here, we can find another rope," Gabe said. "I'm staying with Felicity, by the way. Guest room in the back."

His brother tilted back in his chair. "That's a nice room. She's adding her own touches to the house. She's making it her own."

"Her touches involve lavender and balloons."

Mark laughed. "Of course they do. She's been talking about daffodils and hollyhocks, too."

Gabe grinned. Mark had gone for natural landscaping, without any non-wild flowers, even on the deck. "She's always liked the idea of a cottage garden."

"She'll find a way to meld one into the existing

landscaping, I'm sure. If she doesn't, I'll just have to endure," Mark said lightly. "It's her house now."

"She thinks I'm upset because she bought it."

"Why would you be upset? You sold your interest to me. If you'd wanted the house, you'd have said so."

"Yeah. I'm probably reading into things. It's a great house, Mark. You do good work."

Gabe wasn't even sure himself what he was getting at. He hadn't expected to feel ambivalent about the property going to someone else—out of Flanagan hands. Away from Knights Bridge, it'd seemed reasonable. He hadn't thought much about it.

Of course, that was before he'd found out Mark had sold the place to Felicity.

"Felicity seems happy there," his brother added.

"Yeah, she does. She always liked Knights Bridge just fine. She didn't have the issues you and I did, but she knew she needed to get out if she wanted to reach her potential as a financial analyst."

"I can identify. I never thought I'd be back here, but I couldn't be happier."

"That's great. Is Felicity happy as a party planner, as far as you know?"

"As far as I can tell. Hell, Gabe, ask her. You're staying there."

"I will." Time to exit that subject. "When do I get to see Jess? How is she doing as a mother-to-be?"

Mark shuddered and smiled at the same time. "Just don't call her that. You know Jess. She's adjusting."

"Ah. Got it."

"You don't have a clue and you know it." Mark pushed back his chair and got to his feet. "Come on. I'll give you the grand tour."

Gabe followed Mark out of the office, down a corridor with a display of the straw hats that had prompted the construction of the mill in the mid-nineteenth century. They checked out a function room with dramatic views of the dam and waterfall and then went downstairs to the ground-level inner workings of the building. "We use hydropower," Mark said. "Just like they did back when they made hats here."

"I should have paid closer attention to what you were up to out here," Gabe said as they headed out the back along the river.

"You were selling your company. You had enough on your mind without coming out here to watch the construction workers."

"They did a good job."

They walked along the edge of the quiet millpond to the separate building, connected by a breezeway, where the apartments were located. Gabe liked the industrial feel of the place, tempered by warm woods and tile along with the picturesque location and natural landscaping.

"We have a furnished apartment you can use while you're here," Mark said.

"Thanks. I'll let you know if I overstay my welcome with Felicity or decide to stay past Sunday."

"You're leaving then?"

"That's the plan."

"Kylie and Russ's apartment is on the second floor. They're doing cosmetic work on the house they bought up the road. Quite a whirlwind romance between those two."

"I met Kylie's badgers last night."

"You should stay for her book party next week,"

Mark said. "It's at the library. Felicity's planning it. It's Kylie's way of thanking people in town for giving her the creative space to work. She kept her identity as Morwenna Mills to herself until after she and Russ met in the spring."

"Secrets, secrets," Gabe said with a smile. "I can't imagine it caused too much of a stir."

"It's a good excuse for a party. That's what counts."

They exited to the front of the building. Gabe realized he was enjoying this time with his brother, getting the tour of the mill and a taste of what Mark did day to day. Yet in no way, shape or form did Gabe regret or even question his decision to get out of his hometown and stay out. Knights Bridge wasn't where he belonged. It never had been.

"Going to see Dad while you're here?" Mark asked.

"I imagine so."

"He has a new girlfriend. She owns an old BMW he's kept on the road."

Gabe grinned. "A match made in heaven."

"What about Gramps? Will you see him?"

Their paternal grandfather was now in assisted living in town. Gabe nodded. "I'll stop in before I leave on Sunday. I call them both once a week."

"Boston might as well be the moon as far as Dad's concerned, but you're never there, anyway. Any thoughts about where you'll go after you sell the condo?"

"Thoughts," Gabe said. "No decision yet."

"Good to have choices."

"Yeah, it is. Thanks for the tour. I'll see you later on."

Mark returned to his office, and Gabe climbed back

in his car and exhaled a sigh. He'd been all-in with his work since Felicity had left his apartment and stiffed him on the brownies that cold February morning. With remote employees and contractors, he could work anywhere, and he did. Or he had. Everything was different now, and despite warnings to have a plan for what to do after selling his company, he didn't. He'd figured that would sort itself out in time. Maybe that explained why he was here in his hometown.

He glanced at the renovated mill, remembering how Mark had talked about what could be done with it—neither of them ever imagining he'd be the one to make it happen. But they were both doers, achievers, guys who made things happen, unlike their dreamer father, who liked to sit around and think about making things happen. Still, he'd done all right, hadn't he? By Gabe's standards, absolutely. By his dad's standards for himself… he was a failure, living in a small New England town, working as a car mechanic.

Nothing Gabe wanted to think about now. He glanced at his phone and saw he had a text from Felicity.

I have a call at noon with your event manager.

Gabe stared at the text. Event manager? Since when did he have an event manager? And who the hell was it? Maybe it was Felicity talk for one of the hats Shannon wore as his assistant. "You don't want to be a control freak, Gabe," she'd told him. "I've been fired by control freaks. They bulldoze everyone in their way and they're inefficient. You want a life? Friends? A loyal staff? Delegate."

He'd delegated planning twice-a-year retreats to get his staff together to Shannon, but that was it. She'd have managed any contacts with the resorts. He texted her: Made it to KB. Let me know if you need anything for your call with Felicity MacGregor.

Glad you made it. What call?

Shannon didn't forget calls. Gabe typed his response: Did we hire an event manager to coordinate with Felicity?

No. No need. Do you want me to get in touch with her and sort this out?

He read Felicity's note again. No. TY. All okay there?

Eating too many doughnuts. Enjoy your hometown.

He texted Felicity: Just got your text. Who is your call with?

When she didn't answer immediately, he tossed his phone onto the seat next to him. He drove out to the house, but her Land Rover wasn't in the driveway. He wasn't going to hunt her down over a phone call. If she needed his help, she'd be in touch.

He backed out of the driveway, onto the narrow road and into the shade of a tall sugar maple he'd climbed as a boy. He didn't think Felicity had ever climbed it, but maybe she had.

"Damn," he said under his breath.

Being back here wasn't easy, but it was good—and it was necessary.

He'd head to Carriage Hill Road, check out the setup for tomorrow and say hi to Dylan and Olivia. So far, his reentry into his hometown and Felicity's life was going just fine, despite the bursts of nostalgic memories. To be expected, and reasonably under control.

Seven

Felicity entered Smith's, a house converted into a restaurant—the only restaurant—in Knights Bridge village, on a side street off the town green. After a brief conversation on the phone, she and Nadia Ainsworth had agreed to meet for lunch. Smith's wasn't crowded on the warm summer afternoon, and Felicity recognized the smattering of people there, except for a woman alone at a booth. The woman—in her early forties, with long, auburn-dyed hair—rose and waved. Felicity waved back and joined her. "Nadia?" she asked. "I'm Felicity Mac-Gregor."

"I thought so. Thanks for coming."

Nadia was dressed professionally in slim black pants, a white blouse and a lightweight camel-colored jacket. A bit formal for Knights Bridge, maybe, but Felicity tended to go in the opposite direction and sometimes felt she should be less casual. She sat across from Nadia, who already had a glass of iced tea in front of her.

"What a great place," Nadia said, returning to her seat. "I've heard the turkey clubs are to die for and the pies are not to be resisted—although I'm not sure pie is ever to be resisted. You got here quickly. I thought you lived farther from the village. I hope you didn't run any red lights."

"There are no lights," Felicity said with a smile. "I'm out on the river. It's not that far. How can I help you?"

"Please, order something to drink first. I took the liberty of ordering us each a turkey club. I have a feeling we could have split one. I've been watching plates get delivered to various tables. They do believe in big portions out here in the country. I guess a gigantic sandwich makes sense if you plan to run ten miles or chop a cord of wood or something this afternoon." She smiled, her tone cheerful and casual without any overt condescension. "I like to walk."

"You're from California?"

"Mmm. Malibu. I'm out here on family business. Did you tell Gabe I was calling you?"

That struck Felicity as an odd question. Wouldn't he know? The waiter arrived, and she ordered iced tea.

Nadia lifted her glass of iced tea. "This entire boot camp event is very last minute, as you know. Sorry if we're cutting any corners."

"Happy to help if I can."

"I hear your hesitancy," Nadia said. "I don't blame you. This party's a big deal, and you don't know me from a fence post, as they say. That's why I suggested we meet in person."

"When did you get in?"

"I arrived in Boston late yesterday and drove out here this morning. Gabe's here, too, isn't he? I spoke to his assistant. Shannon Rivera. She's incredible, but she's very protective—you'd think she was with the

Secret Service sometimes. We've both worked with Gabe since the early days. But you've known him forever, haven't you?"

"We both grew up here."

"This is my first time in Knights Bridge. It's adorable."

Felicity smiled. "It has its charms."

Her iced tea and the two club sandwiches arrived, made with Smith's signature roast turkey. Nadia's eyes widened. "I see I was right about the portion, but I bet I eat every bite. At least I didn't order fries, and I did skip breakfast this morning." She picked up a triangle of her sandwich. "I'd like to start by going over the boot camp guest list and schedule with you. You can email me the guest list if that's easier for you."

Felicity tried a bite of her sandwich, giving herself time to respond. An experienced event planner would know she couldn't provide access to the guest list without first clearing it with her client. "I'm not sure of your role here," she said finally.

Nadia shrugged. "Friend more than anything else, I guess. I specialize in customer development, but I helped plan retreats for Gabe when he had his company. I'm familiar with his preferences."

It was an admission, more-or-less, that she wasn't particularly experienced. She'd likely worked with the event planners on staff at the various retreat venues. "I can't send you the guest list," Felicity said. "If there's anything you think Gabe needs, just let me know, and I'll see what I can do."

"What's the final head count for tomorrow?" Nadia asked. "Can you tell me that much?"

"Around fifty."

"Is that inclusive of workshop leaders and staff?"

Felicity nodded. She pried loose another triangle of her sandwich. If this meeting was heading south, she wanted to get some food in her.

"Gabe's a great public speaker, but he doesn't like it," Nadia said. "He doesn't have a phobia or anything, although a lot of people do. I might be one of them. Given the choice between speaking in front of fifty people or getting a root canal, I'd pick the root canal."

Felicity took a break from her turkey club and drank some of her iced tea. Nadia was nibbling at her lunch. She wasn't the sort of liaison Felicity usually dealt with. She often coordinated with venue and client staff, but she wasn't even sure Nadia actually worked for Gabe. She seemed anxious and uptight, brimming with nervous energy.

She gave a self-conscious laugh. "As I said, my main job isn't event planning, in case you couldn't tell. You have to stay nimble and versatile these days. I'm sorry Gabe's involvement in Dylan McCaffrey's boot camp came at the eleventh hour."

"It's all in hand," Felicity said.

"That's great. No surprise, now that I've met you. The retreats we did were planned months in advance. That was very manageable, although it would get intense the closer we got to the actual date. The last one was in Aspen. Ever been?"

"Once, when I was between jobs."

"Take those vacations when you can, I guess. I'd probably have been afraid to spend the money." Nadia sank against the cushioned back of the bench. "I'll miss the retreats. I imagine everyone who worked for Gabe will. He's an important client, and he's a dream to work with. We're all waiting to see what he does next, I'm sure."

"Did you come out here to meet with him?" Felicity asked.

"I'm settling my grandmother's estate. She died over the winter. She lived in Groton. That's not that far from here. I figured I might as well stop in town and meet you, take a look at this barn where the boot camp's being held. It's on Carriage Hill Road. I think I'll be able to find my way there. I plugged the address into my rental car's GPS."

"The road dead-ends. You'll know if you've gone too far."

"Nothing subtle about a dead end."

Felicity laughed, finding herself less suspicious of Nadia's involvement. Maybe she was overstepping, but that was Gabe's problem—and possibly a result of miscommunications. "We have a few dead ends around here," she said.

"It must be nice to be able to work in your hometown. I lived within walking distance when I was a kid. Then my parents up and moved my two younger brothers and me to California. My dad had a new job in LA. We all hated leaving Grandma behind."

"Was she ever tempted to move to California with you?"

Nadia shook her head, her affection for her grandmother evident. "She said she didn't want to get settled in California and have my dad get a job in Chicago or somewhere else. I visited as often as I could. She was eighty-seven when she died. The last time I saw her, she told me she'd had a good run. I think she knew we wouldn't see each other again. Anyway." Nadia sat up straight, obviously making an effort to stay cheerful. "Did you always want to move back to Knights Bridge?"

"Yes and yes-and-no." Felicity debated how forthcoming to be with a woman she'd only just met. "I'm glad I made the decision to move back, though. My parents love having me here, so I can feed the cats while they travel."

Nadia laughed. "Life could be worse."

"Look, there's nothing to worry about with the boot camp. You can leave it to me and focus on your personal reasons for being on the East Coast." Felicity got her wallet out of her handbag and left enough cash to cover lunch. "My treat. I hope everything goes well with your grandmother's estate. Sorry I have to run, but it's been nice to meet you."

"What, you're skipping pie?"

"I recommend the peach pie this time of year. They get peaches from Elly O'Dunn's farm. Take your time so you have enough room after the club to enjoy every morsel." Felicity slid out of the booth and got to her feet. "I'll let Gabe know we chatted."

Felicity left Nadia in the booth, looking a bit stunned—but better to be abrupt to the point of rude than to get in too deep with this situation. Whatever was going on, it clearly had to do with Nadia and Gabe and nothing to do with her, the party, the boot camp or his presence in her guest room. Whether he or his assistant had anything to do with Nadia coming to Knights Bridge or she was acting entirely on her own initiative, she was on a find-out-about-Gabe-and-Felicity-MacGregor mission. She hadn't even been that subtle.

Felicity jumped back in her Land Rover and checked her phone, saw the text from Gabe about her noon call, now in the past along with lunch. She debated what to do next, but, really, there was no debate. She grabbed her phone and texted Gabe: Where are you?

Carriage Hill barn.

Felicity didn't hesitate before she typed her response: On my way. We need to talk.

I'll be here.

Felicity didn't charge off to find Gabe. She needed to get her bearings first. It wasn't just Nadia Ainsworth and whatever was going on with her—and between her and Gabe—but being around him, his energy and drive. She didn't want to get sucked in and lose herself, or at least her focus. She had a high-profile event coming up in her hometown. She was *working*. She had a job to do.

She looked up the street to Smith's, with its hanging baskets and pots of summer flowers on its front porch. A turkey club and peach pie could defuse a determined troublemaker, if that was what Nadia was. Let her take some time to calm down. Maybe their chat had helped her stop herself from spooling up further, whatever her true agenda for being in Knights Bridge.

Go back and join her for pie, after all?

Felicity shook her head. As tempting as Smith's peach pie was, she wasn't going back there. She spotted Christopher Sloan walking toward the popular restaurant from Main Street. He was the youngest of the five Sloan brothers, a firefighter in town. Heather, the only sister and the youngest of all six siblings, was in London for a year with her husband, a Diplomatic Security Service agent. Felicity remembered Brody Hancock from high school. He'd had a run-in with the Sloan boys back then. All in the past now. She'd never known what the fight was about. She hadn't been part of that crowd. She'd always stood a bit apart, the banker's daughter with good grades and a natural aversion to trouble.

Mark and Gabe had always been tight with the Sloans. Really, why couldn't Gabe have stayed with one of them? Christopher was on his own and lived in the village. Surely he had space.

Of course, a Sloan hadn't bought the old Flanagan place.

Gabe would be gone in a few days, and if his stay helped him get over any emotions about the property being out of Flanagan hands, that wasn't a bad thing.

Felicity noticed her Rover was getting warm. She turned on the engine and rolled down the windows just as Evelyn Sloan walked up the street from her house. She was in her eighties, using a cane these days but otherwise in good shape. She was the widowed grandmother of the six Sloan siblings, still living on her own. She paused at Felicity's old Land Rover. "I thought that was you. How are you, Felicity?"

"Doing well, Mrs. Sloan, thanks."

"You can call me Evelyn. I don't mind. I understand your parents are traveling a lot these days. Good for them. Go while you can."

Felicity smiled. "They're enjoying retirement."

"They've earned it." She leaned in closer, as if she

had a secret to share. "I heard Gabe Flanagan is staying at your house on the river. Are you two back together?"

"We've always just been friends." And for a while, not even that.

Evelyn frowned. "Just friends? Okay." She straightened, adjusting her cane. "Have a nice afternoon. I don't care for this hot weather, but it does feel nice on my old bones today. Back in the day I'd be tempted to take a dip in the river myself. Gabe stopped at the farm for a rope. I understand he plans to go out to your swimming hole on the river. You kids used to have a blast out there. It's a lovely spot. Still, it's never a good idea to swim alone."

The "farm" wasn't a working farm these days, its old barn instead the offices for Sloan & Sons, a respected, busy construction company in town owned and run by Evelyn's son and his wife and grandchildren. Gabe had worked for them through high school and until he dropped out of college.

Felicity started to say something about swimming holes, but Evelyn was already on her way up the street. "A rope," she said, rolling up her window. "Leave it to Gabe."

Eight

On Wednesday, Gabe sat on the stone steps outside the spacious, airy, contemporary "barn" where he'd be speaking tomorrow. It was an impressive place, but he was more impressed with how happy, content and comfortable in her own skin Olivia Frost—now McCaffrey—was. She sat on the steps next to him. He hadn't seen her since Mark and Jess's wedding almost a year ago. Olivia had left Knights Bridge for Boston and a career in graphic design, but she'd always wanted to return home. From what Gabe had heard from Mark, she'd had a few knocks and kicks along the way, but she was here now, married, expecting a baby, enjoying her and Dylan's new home and business ventures. Olivia and Jess's parents owned a small sawmill on the other side of town that specialized in custom woodwork. Need a twelve-by-twelve late-eighteenth-century window replaced, the Frosts could do it. Mark often used or recommended them. Jess still worked with her parents. Gabe hadn't stepped foot at the Frosts' sawmill since he'd gone swimming in its small, frigid millpond as a kid, never expecting Jess would marry his big brother.

Olivia stirred next to him. "I should get back to Carriage Hill. That's what I call my inn down the road."

"I drove past it to have a look. I like the chives on the sign."

She smiled. "You might be the first person to recognize they're chives."

"Felicity snipped a few chives into my eggs at breakfast. She has a pot in the kitchen window."

"What a great idea—I love chives." Olivia stood, placing a hand on her lower back with a wince, then smiling down at him. "Don't worry. I'm not going to pass out. I did that yesterday."

"Not funny, Olivia."

She waved a hand, clearly unrepentant. "Now you sound like Dylan. I didn't *really* faint. I just sort of fainted. I suppose it's easier to make light of it when you're the one who got wobbly and know you're fine and were never in any danger."

"I suppose it is," Gabe said.

"Dylan wasn't thrilled I delayed telling him, but I have to be— I can't explain it. I guess I just want to maintain my independence. I'm pregnant and I've had a few minor incidents, but I'm not an invalid. You know?"

He smiled. "Never been pregnant."

Olivia rolled her eyes, laughing. "Mark would say the same thing. I can tell you two are brothers. I had Felicity and Maggie here, but I'd have been fine without them. I keep my phone handy." She held up a water bottle. "And now I keep water handy, too."

"Glad you're figuring out what works for you."

"Thank you. Me, too." She patted him on the shoulder. "I'll see you later. Let us know if you need anything."

Gabe watched her head down the stone walk to the driveway and then onto Carriage Hill Road, turning left toward her early-nineteenth-century inn. She looked steady on her feet. She and Dylan had invited him to join them for lunch at their new house, but he wasn't hungry. He'd had a big breakfast—chives and all.

He went back inside and helped himself to iced tea from a pitcher in the refrigerator in the barn's kitchen. He looked out across the fields to Carriage Hill itself. A century ago, the region's plentiful lakes, ponds, rivers and streams had drawn engineers and politicians from Boston in search of drinking water for the growing metropolitan area to the east. The massive Quabbin Reservoir had been the result, requiring the building of Winsor Dam and Goodnough Dike, the emptying and razing of four small towns and the relocation of their population, and then the flooding of the picturesque Swift River Valley—all long before Gabe had been born.

It'd been a long time since he and Mark had set off into the protected woods with nothing but a jackknife and a compass. He'd been good with the knife. Mark had been good with the compass. No surprise, maybe, given where they'd ended up in life.

"As if you're a hundred years old," Gabe said aloud, turning from the view.

Usually when he got this restless and reflective it meant he was about to do something new—start a company, sell a company, go on a trip. Take action. But he *was* doing something new. He was getting ready to speak at an entrepreneurial boot camp for the first time, and he was sleeping under Felicity's roof for the first time. That both were in Knights Bridge was part of the problem, maybe. Visits to his hometown had a tendency to stir him up. Even just breezing in and out would drag him into his past. He wasn't trying to forget his childhood so much as, simply put, accept that he'd moved on. He wasn't *that* Gabe anymore. He didn't have to worry he'd be like his father, dreaming without taking any steps to accomplish anything beyond getting through the day, and then brooding on the inevitable disappointments that resulted from his inaction.

He needed to be wary of giving in to impulse when he was in this mood. He didn't want to do something stupid and then leave town, get back to normal and ask himself what the hell he'd been thinking. Easier to resist the urge in the first place than to have to clean up a mess afterward.

He took his iced tea out front and sat on the shaded stone steps, taking in the quiet and the welcome breeze. Dylan and Olivia's setup out here on their dead-end road was great for what they had in mind—the occasional boot camp, adventure travel, meetings, parties, weddings, girlfriend weekends and such—but most important, it was the perfect spot for starting a family. They were unquestionably happy here, and with each other.

Gabe was pleased to be in on the inaugural boot camp. He figured he had time on the family part.

"Loads of time," he said under his breath, before he could get carried away.

He heard a vehicle on the road and then the driveway, until it finally came to a stop in the parking area off to the side of the barn. He recognized Felicity's old Land Rover from when her brother had driven it. It was dented and rusted in spots, but it looked to be in good shape. Even if she could afford one, Gabe doubted Felicity would ever go for a BMW or Mercedes-Benz. She was into function these days, and the Land Rover was well-suited to trekking on the area's back roads in any weather as well as to hauling her party supplies.

He got to his feet slowly as Felicity came up the stone walk. "Hello, again," she said. "Enjoying the shade and breeze, I see."

"Feels good." He studied her as she approached the steps. She had a tight look about her. "What's up?"

She waited until she was standing in front of him before she replied. "Who is Nadia Ainsworth?"

Not what Gabe was expecting. "Nadia? Did she contact you?"

"We just had lunch together."

"Where?"

"Smith's. Where else? I don't know her. I wasn't about to invite her to my house, and I gather she's not the type for a picnic on the town common."

Gabe took a couple of steps deeper into the shade, not quite onto the grass. Nadia. Hell. How had she managed to follow him to Knights Bridge? Why? He'd seen Nadia last week in Los Angeles. She'd mentioned she needed to close out her grandmother's estate in New England, but she hadn't indicated she had plans to head East anytime soon. She was a top-notch customer service specialist, but her life was complicated these days. Her husband, David Ainsworth, had bought

Gabe's company and then walked out on Nadia a few weeks later.

That was a few months ago. David had assured Gabe the two events weren't connected, but Gabe hadn't asked. What went on between the Ainsworths was none of his business—and he wasn't going to let Nadia drag him into it. She'd tried in Los Angeles, and she hadn't been particularly subtle about it. Now she'd lured Felicity to lunch. He had every reason to be annoyed with Nadia's games, but Felicity had enough on her mind with the upcoming boot camp. He'd deal with Nadia.

He tamped down his irritation. "What did Nadia want with you?" he asked.

Felicity tilted her head to one side, eyeing him, then stood straight and sighed. "Steam's coming out of your ears, Gabe. Did this Nadia step out of the lines by contacting me? Did I step out of the lines by meeting with her?"

Of course she'd seen through him. "It's the humidity," he said, not bothering to try to sound as if he was serious. "I'm not used to it. I was in California too long."

"The humidity. Good one."

He ignored her light sarcasm. "Where is Nadia now?"

"Enjoying Smith's peach pie, I think. She had a turkey club but didn't seem inclined to resist pie. Does she work for you or did she make that up?"

"No one except Shannon works for me since I sold the company." He took a moment to soak in the breeze, listen to the birds. Didn't help particularly. Steam probably *was* coming out his ears. "I'll speak with Nadia.

She must be confused about her role. I'll straighten things out. I'm sorry she troubled you."

"It wasn't any trouble, really. I needed lunch, and I love Smith's turkey clubs. I love their pie, too, but I've been into the brownies. Anyway, it worked out. I got the impression Nadia was fishing for information more than anything else. There was only so much I could tell her." Felicity put one foot on a step and leaned forward, as if giving her thigh a stretch. She straightened, eyeing Gabe again. "You don't have a good expression. Nadia isn't some deranged stalker who's going to boil your pet rabbit, is she?"

"Don't worry about her."

"Is she going to boil *my* pet rabbit?"

"Felicity, you don't have a rabbit. I don't have a rabbit. It'll be fine."

"Is she an ex-girlfriend?"

"No, but I'll take care of the situation. She's not your problem. She's excellent at her work, and she's smart. She understands the necessity of getting immediate feedback from customers and using that information to revise products and plans. She knows how important it is to pivot quickly in the business we were in."

"Doesn't sound like an event planner," Felicity said.

"She coordinated with resorts on a couple of small corporate get-togethers." He changed the subject. "Do you have anything you need to do here? If you need a hand, I can carry a box inside—"

"No boxes." She stood in a patch of bright sun and squinted at him. "I'll check on a few things here at the barn and then walk down to Olivia's inn. That's where we're having your party."

"Perfect. Thanks." He motioned toward the parking area, where he'd left his car. "I'll go see if I can find Nadia."

"Good luck."

Madly curious. That was Felicity, always digging, probing, a natural for ferreting out people's secrets. Interested in people, she'd say. Gabe had no intention of further discussing Nadia with Felicity, no matter how curious she was. He didn't need to explain. What he needed to do was to find Nadia, settle her down and draw some clear boundaries she couldn't miss.

Felicity started up the steps, paused and glanced back at him with a knowing sigh.

He bit. "What?"

"You and Nadia. You weren't straight with her, were you?"

"Straight with her how? She's a terrific customer development specialist. She knows that."

"She has some kind of personal interest in you."

"Not that kind, Felicity. Trust me."

"Maybe, but I know you, Gabe. You're the guy who says he'll call even if it's bad news and then doesn't, and when people get upset, rationalizes his behavior by saying not calling is easier on the other person. Your way of letting people down gently whether in a personal or a business relationship. Let them figure it out on their own instead of telling them straight what the score is."

"Didn't we part company because I was *too* straight with you?"

"That's different. We've known each other since nursery school."

"I can't remember back that far," he said lightly.

"It's possible that not keeping a promise to call allows the other person the chance to realize what's going on and come to terms with the situation in private."

"Spares them, huh?"

"It could." He had no idea what he was saying but was arguing to argue. He and Felicity used to have back-and-forths like this all the time. "Someone who's going to freak out and be emotional might rather have a chance to regroup before a conversation happens."

"Told you," she said with a note of victory. "You're that guy."

He grinned at her. "You're as big a know-it-all as ever."

"Me?" She snorted. "That's a good one. My advice— not that you asked—is to be straight with Nadia. Don't leave her guessing or twisting in the wind. It's too easy to read things between the lines that aren't there, and if they are there—then get them out in the open."

"A lot of assumptions in that advice."

"What's between you two is none of my business. I don't want it to be. I'm not sticking my nose into your life. If Nadia's a problem, she's your problem."

"I'm sorry she contacted you. I'll handle the situation."

"Good." Felicity continued up the barn steps. "See you later."

Gabe waited until the door shut behind her. Then he cursed under his breath and stalked along the stone walk to his car. He noticed Felicity had parked her Land Rover crookedly. She'd been agitated but not upset. Nadia had stuck her nose in Felicity's business, but she hadn't made any threats. The woman was a mess but not that kind of mess. Her grandmother had died, her husband had dumped her and Gabe had sold the company she'd helped build, leaving her with an uncertain future if in no way financially destitute.

It was added salt in her wounds that her ex-husband had been one of the buyers.

When she was on her game as a customer development specialist, Nadia was the best, but she hadn't been on her game in a while. That wasn't Gabe's problem to solve, but she was in Knights Bridge. He needed to straighten her out. Bad enough that Felicity had been stuck dealing with her. He didn't want Nadia pestering Dylan and Olivia.

As he started up Carriage Hill Road, he glanced back up toward the barn. Quite a spot it was. His brother had done a fine job in designing the house and barn, making them seem part of the rolling New England landscape. Gabe was suddenly sorry he hadn't been out here sooner. Maybe his delay had prompted Mark to hire Felicity on his younger brother's behalf.

Gabe smiled. "No. If Mark was pissed, he'd just threaten to throw me in the river."

The party had made sense, and he appreciated Mark's help.

Now he just had to make sure Nadia Ainsworth wasn't going to cause problems.

The village of Knights Bridge with its oval-shaped green had changed little in decades—probably not since well before Gabe was born. The oldest house, located on South Main Street, had been built in the late eighteenth century, the newest—across the common on Main—before World War II. The library had gone up in the 1870s, and the Swift River Valley Country

Store had opened in 1910, or close to it. Gabe didn't remember every date in his hometown's history. A few businesses had come and gone—a yoga studio had opened in what once had been a hardware store—but the houses, shops and offices had never been destroyed by fire, bulldozer or well-intentioned village renewal.

Gabe eased into a parking space on Main Street, in front of the small bank Felicity's father had shepherded through several decades. He turned off the engine and sat for a moment, pulling himself together. He was off balance, and he hated it. It wasn't just Knights Bridge or Nadia sneaking into town and manipulating Felicity into lunch. It was Felicity herself. He'd thought he was in control of his "reentry."

"Yeah, right," he muttered. "Should have known better."

He got out of his car, shut and locked the door and looked across the street to the common, dotted with shade trees, benches and monuments. He'd already spotted Nadia sitting alone on a bench. He had no idea if she'd noticed him or even would have recognized his car.

He crossed the street. She glanced up, smiled and waved.

He waved back. So far, so good. She hadn't leaped up and run screaming to him. She'd done that in February in a Beverly Hills restaurant. He'd contacted each of his workers personally to let them know he had a buyer for the company. With Nadia, he made it a face-to-face meeting. David, her about-to-be-ex-husband, had asked him to give her the news that he was the buyer. Gabe had managed to get her to calm down before someone called the cops. She hadn't said so in as many words, but she must have known the sale would be the death knell to her marriage.

He crossed soft, sunlit grass to her spot in the shade. "Hey, Nadia," he said casually. "Nice day to sit in the shade."

"I'd have sat in the grass but there are ants." She pointed at a small mound by the bench. "See them? They're little bitty black ants. I've been watching them do their ant thing." She raised her chin to him, squinted. "It's something to do in a small town."

"How long do you plan to stay?"

"As long as I want."

"It was just a friendly question, Nadia."

She made a face, as if chastising herself. "Sorry. I was going to drive out to Carriage Hill Road, but I decided to take a walk after lunch. I faded pretty quickly." She tucked her legs up and wrapped her arms around her shins. "It's lovely here, but it's humid today. I don't like it. I overheard kids talking about swimming holes. Gah. It was like listening to Tom Sawyer."

"There are some great swimming holes in the area," Gabe said.

She smiled up at him. "No wonder you left. I bet you couldn't wait to get out of here."

"Nadia…" Gabe realized he had no game plan. "Nadia, you can't be here, pretending you work for me—claiming that I asked you to get involved in the entrepreneurial boot camp. Pretending to be something you aren't isn't going to help anything."

"Is that what your friend Felicity told you? Did she accuse me of harassing her?"

"No. And it's not what I'm saying, either. Look, why don't we go for a walk—"

Nadia leaped to her feet. "I should have known I'd be misconstrued. I was just trying to do a good deed. I know how you are about this place. Your hometown. And I know you can be impulsive. I was worried about this boot camp and this last-minute party."

"How did you find out about them?"

"David mentioned them. We had—" She brushed hair off her face. "We had some matters to discuss, and he told me. From what little contact we had, it's obvious Felicity is perfectly capable of handling everything. She's a pro. She has good experience. There's no reason for concern."

"Nadia, I appreciate that you want to help, but you don't work for me anymore."

"I know, Gabe. I'm a *friend.* And I never did work *for* you. I wasn't your employee. I was a contract worker. The same as this Felicity MacGregor, except we didn't go to nursery school together." Nadia crossed her arms on her chest, looking more annoyed and aggrieved than embarrassed or apologetic. "Don't worry. I'm not going to send you a bill for checking her out."

It wasn't a bill that concerned him, and she knew it. Gabe decided not to argue with her. "Where did you park? I can walk you to your car."

"I'm parked by the library." She waved vaguely across the common toward South Main. "I might walk around a bit more—I'll just be sure to stay in the shade. Maybe I'll take a look inside the library. I bet it has a great reading room. Did you spend a lot of time there growing up?"

"I wasn't much of a student."

She grinned at him. "Had your eyes on the girls instead, didn't you?"

He smiled, feeling some of his irritation ease. "The library does have a great reading room. I'll walk over there with you."

"Great, thanks."

They took a paved walkway into the sunshine. Gabe noticed perspiration beading on Nadia' upper lip. "You're not dressed for the heat," he said. "Especially since you're not used to it."

"No kidding." She flipped her hair behind her shoulders and shuddered. "I'll skip the walk and go straight into the library. I hope it's cooler in there. Isn't this humidity killing you?"

"It's like riding a bike. You never really forget. It won't last, though."

"Here and then gone. My grandmother used to say that. Damn, Gabe. I'm going to need an inhaler." She smiled sideways at him. "Not really. I shouldn't joke about that. My little brother had asthma as a child. He outgrew it, but I remember how awful and scary it was when he had an attack."

"Is he helping settle your grandmother's affairs?"

She shook her head. "I'm the executor."

They came to South Main and crossed to the library, built by the same small-town industrialist and benefactor who'd built the Mill at Moss Hill. His former house, a sprawling Victorian on a side street off South Main, was up for sale—or had been. Mark had mentioned it in a phone call a while back. It could have sold by now.

Gabe stopped at the steps into the library. "Enjoy your visit. You'll want to be on your way before it gets dark. There aren't a lot of streetlights out here. You're not used to driving without streetlights."

"That's for sure. At least it doesn't get dark early this time of year."

He didn't argue with her. He started to ask if she had a place to stay tonight but decided that would only risk opening up a fresh can of worms. He couldn't say for sure what she was thinking. Theirs had always been a friendly but strictly professional relationship. He'd seen her in person perhaps a dozen times since she'd started working with him. She'd always been reliable, professional and very good at what she did. He'd tried to hire her as a senior manager two years ago, but she'd turned him down—because of the husband who'd left her a few months ago. David had wanted her to continue freelancing. Easier, better for him. He'd had the bigger job. He'd been on the move, looking for a company to buy.

Clearly, Nadia was struggling to let go of the life she'd had.

"Enjoy the rest of your stay in New England," Gabe said.

"I will, thanks," she said. "If there's anything I can do for tomorrow—"

"There isn't." Too abrupt. He took the edge off his response with a smile. "Thanks for the offer. Take care, okay? Good luck settling your grandmother's affairs. I know it's not easy to say goodbye to a loved one."

"It's not, and on top of David—" She blew out a breath, then smiled awkwardly. "I'd go back to him in a heartbeat, you know. It's sick, but I have a feeling Smith's peach pie will help. I have no regrets. I'm glad to see your hometown. It's a cute place. I think it's growing on me."

"It's the peach pie. Take care, Nadia."

"You, too."

She hesitated, as if she expected him to kiss her on the cheek or take her hand—make some kind of friendly physical gesture. He didn't, and she turned abruptly and ran up the library steps as if she suddenly realized she was late for something.

Gabe felt uneasy about their conversation, but there wasn't much more he could do. He headed back across South Main. As he crossed the common, he received a text from his brother: Join us for dinner tonight? Six o'clock, here at the house.

Gabe didn't hesitate before he responded: Perfect.

Jess promises not to barf.

He grinned at Mark's text. No barf at dinner would be a very good thing, but how could Jess promise? He typed what he thought was a diplomatic response: I have no say on barf.

Ha, neither do I. She's feeling better.

That's what counts.

Olivia and Dylan will be at dinner, too. Bring Felicity.

How to respond to that? Gabe decided to keep it simple and neutral: I'll let her know.

When he reached his car, he looked across the common toward the library. Nadia was already descending the steps. She hadn't lasted in the library for a whole ten minutes. Too noisy? Never intended to spend time there?

Gabe shook off his questions. Not his problem. Nadia was a free agent. She hadn't broken any laws. She didn't work for him. She could do what she wanted to do. He hoped she'd leave Knights Bridge without bothering anyone else, but it was her call to make.

He got in his car and turned on the engine, taking a moment to collect himself. He felt the temperature drop as the air-conditioning kicked in. Didn't matter that his father was a great mechanic, he'd always driven beaters, and he hated air-conditioning. It hadn't been a matter of principle. He just didn't like it.

Neither had his mother, Gabe remembered. "Makes me cold," she'd say. "The air doesn't feel real."

Gabe laughed, thinking of her with affection, missing her but without the intense pain that had lingered since her death. She'd died with so many unfulfilled dreams. She'd always believed there'd be more time. But she hadn't been bitter. She'd made the best of the time she'd had, determined not to squander a minute. In her last weeks, she'd loved just to sit on the porch and listen to the birds. "I'm happy here," she'd tell Gabe. "I always have been happy here."

Her way of saying, maybe, that he shouldn't be too hard on his father.

Maybe, but Gabe wasn't going there.

Talk of peach pie had made him hungry, and he was certain that however many brownies Felicity had eaten that morning, she couldn't possibly have eaten them all and still had room for one of Smith's turkey clubs. A brownie, a walk down to the river...and maybe a dip in their swimming hole.

Nine

Felicity was relieved Olivia looked as well as she did. After getting a better sense of the space for the post–boot camp party tomorrow, they wandered in the well-established flower and herb gardens behind Olivia's antique house—the one that had helped bring her and Dylan together. The gentle buzz of bumblebees hovering in catmint and lavender highlighted the quiet and stillness of the warm afternoon out here on the edge of the Quabbin wilderness. Even the birds seemed to be off for naps.

"Thank you for yesterday," Olivia said, not for the first time.

"No problem."

She pointed at a clear-glass pitcher on the table on the stone terrace. "I now keep water at hand at all times. Sorry if I scared you. I'm glad you were there, though."

Felicity ran a palm over the tops of the lavender. "I'm glad I was, too."

Olivia patted her middle, swelling under her deep-blue T-shirt. "I have a ways to go, but I'm more than halfway there. It'll be cool weather when the baby comes. My mother is knitting a sweater and booties. I'd forgotten she knew how to knit."

"Did you learn to knit?"

"I did, but it never took. I always liked the colors and patterns better than the knitting-and-purling. What about you?"

"My mother got into quilting for a while. I learned to knit on my own in college. Maybe I should find a knitting project this winter for quiet, cold nights out on the river." Felicity smiled. "I wouldn't count on me finishing booties before the baby outgrew them."

"My mother's waiting a few more weeks before she starts anything for Jess—she doesn't want to jinx her." Olivia paused, bending slightly to pinch faded yellow daisy blossoms. "Mom's much better, but having two pregnant daughters has roiled the anxiety waters. She says she'll be fine. She's looking forward to being a grandmother."

Felicity remembered when Olivia and Jess were in a car accident in high school. Trapped but not badly injured, they'd gone missing for several hours. Their mother had developed an anxiety disorder that had worsened over the years, until she could barely leave town. She'd finally sought therapy and now was off on trips with her husband, planning new ones. Everyone in town was thrilled for both of them.

"What about your dad?" Felicity asked.

"Can't wait to be a grandfather. He and Dylan are making plans to paint the nursery."

Felicity wasn't surprised Dylan would want to paint his baby's nursery himself, with his father-in-law's help. His own father wasn't around any longer, but she had a feeling he was with Dylan in spirit. As dramatic as the turns in their lives since meeting early last year, he and Olivia were grounded, tackling their new ventures a step at a time and—most important and very obvious—clearly as madly in love with each other as ever. Felicity breathed in the fragrance of the summer garden. She'd never been madly in love. Well, sort of with Gabe, but that had been teenage hormones. Maybe she wasn't wired to fall head over heels in love.

Not exactly what she wanted to be thinking while listening to bumblebees and enjoying a pleasant walk with a friend, but to be expected with Gabe in town, camped out across the hall from her. Why couldn't she have found him *less* physically appealing these days? But no. That hadn't happened. Not even close.

She and Olivia continued on a mulched path toward the stone terrace by the kitchen door. An addition to the house was in the works and would serve as a suite for a live-in innkeeper yet to be hired. Olivia's original, modest plans for her antique house had expanded without getting out of hand, at least as she'd explained to Felicity. With the promise of favorable weather, guests at Gabe's post–boot camp party could meander out to the terrace and gardens. The logistics were simpler with the party being held here instead of at the barn, although Felicity could have managed at the barn. She'd managed far more complex events. She liked the contrast between the barn's newness— even the grass looked new—and the Farm at Carriage Hill's centuries-old house with its wide pine board flooring, multiple fireplaces off its center chimney and beautiful landscaping.

"Anything else you need ahead of tomorrow?" Olivia asked.

"All set, thanks."

"You look so calm, cool and collected."

Felicity laughed. "Do I? I feel more like the old saying about the duck who looks calm on the surface but is paddling like crazy under the water."

"I can identify, except I doubt anyone's ever said I look calm."

They stepped onto the terrace, passing Buster sprawled in the shade, and went through a tidy mudroom to the big, country kitchen, located in one of the "newer" parts of the house. Felicity noticed sprigs of fresh basil on the butcher-block island. "Did I catch you in the middle of making something?" she asked Olivia.

"I had optimistic plans to make pesto. Now the thought of pesto…" She grimaced, waving a hand in dismissal. "I'll throw some on some mozzarella and tomatoes with a little salt, pepper and olive oil. I have way more than I need. You like basil, don't you? Take some with you."

"I'd love to. I have a few chives in my kitchen window."

"Gabe mentioned you'd snipped a few chives into his eggs this morning. I imagine he's not your average houseguest. It's decent of you to put him up for the weekend. Dylan invited him to speak at the last minute, but it's not as if Knights Bridge is overflowing with hotels and inns."

"He's an easy guest," Felicity said.

"Mark and Gabriel Flanagan aren't what I'd call easy, but they're great. Anyway, I love chives. Hence, they're my logo for this place."

Maggie Sloan burst into the kitchen through the

front door, a brown paper bag on each hip and her two young sons, Aidan and Tyler, charging in behind her. "Not staying," she said, hefting the bags onto the counter by the sink. "I'm dropping the boys off to swim in a friend's pool. Why did my parents never worry when my sisters and I took off to the brook? Freezing-cold water, slippery rocks, slugs, leeches, spiders, ticks. Never occurred to them we'd be anything but fine."

"And you *were* fine," Olivia pointed out.

Maggie grinned. "Yes, we were. Even after Dad died and Mum started buying goats, we never were seriously hurt. The occasional cuts and bruises, but that's to be expected. Which," she added emphatically, "I will remind myself if Aidan and Tyler come back with Band-Aids on their knees. Cuts and scrapes I can handle. I don't want broken bones, concussions—" She sighed. "I'll stop now."

Felicity helped Maggie unload the bags, an array of fresh vegetables they would use at tomorrow's party. In her short time back in Knights Bridge, she'd discovered Maggie was far more organized in her work as a superb caterer than she was in her home life, but she seemed to thrive in the chaos.

Aidan and Tyler ran through the mudroom out to the terrace. Door banging, dog barking, boys yelling happily for no apparent reason.

"I'll make them wash off the dog slobber before they get in the pool. I didn't swim in a pool until I was in my teens at least," Maggie said. She shut a cupboard and turned to Felicity. "Tomorrow's going to be great. You're not nervous, are you?"

"Just enough to keep me on my toes."

"I'll be here early if you need to find me."

But she didn't wait for an answer, instead heading out through the mudroom with such energy one of the empty bags blew off the counter. Olivia started to reach for it, but Felicity grabbed it, folded it and tucked it next to the refrigerator with a few other bags. "Are you going back up to the barn?" she asked.

"Not yet. Dylan's meeting me here," Olivia said.

Felicity glanced out the window above the sink and noticed Maggie and her sons heading through the side yard to her van. "I could use a dip in a cold brook right now myself."

"Not me," Olivia said with a smile. "I'd have to dash to the bathroom."

They laughed, and Felicity took a moment to double-check Maggie's groceries. Of course, everything was there, in order. As much as Felicity enjoyed the company of both women now, she hadn't stayed in touch with Maggie or Olivia when they'd all been living and working in Boston. They'd run into each other on occasion when she visited Knights Bridge. Felicity remembered craving anonymity when she'd moved to the city, relishing a chance to do things without the intimacy of life in her small hometown.

She did like to think no one in Knights Bridge had a clue she'd slept with Gabe Flanagan the summer before college. It was their secret, and no matter what she did with the rest of her life, he would always and forever be her first lover.

She put that thought out of her mind and walked back up to the barn, past the sign for The Farm at Carriage Hill with its signature clump of blossoming chives, designed by Olivia herself. Her career change from full-time Boston graphic designer to innkeeper hadn't been as radical as Felicity's from financial analyst to event planner, but it hadn't been without its drama, either. It had led, after all, to Dylan, his long-lost grandmother, marriage, a new home, new businesses—and, now, a baby on the way.

There was Buster, too, of course. The big dog had appeared on Olivia's doorstep in the weeks before she'd written to Dylan in San Diego. She often joked he'd adopted her rather than the other way around.

Olivia also had dealt with the emotional and career fallout of a vampire friend who'd sucked her dry and stolen her job—something like that, anyway. Felicity had picked up bits and pieces of the story since her move to Knights Bridge but gathered the friend was now an ex-friend and no longer a factor in Olivia's life. She was generous and trusting by nature, and the betrayal had obviously been difficult for her.

Felicity wondered if there was more behind Nadia Ainsworth's trip to Knights Bridge and invitation to lunch than a desire to help Gabe and curiosity about her, the boot camp and his hometown itself. Whatever the case, Felicity would mention her when she spoke to Russ Colton about security tomorrow before the boot camp got rolling.

And Gabe?

Perfectly capable of watching his own back.

As she reached her Land Rover, she mentally went through everything that needed to be done before tomorrow's party. Satisfied she had finished here, she got in her Rover and drove back out Carriage Hill Road and onto her quiet river road.

Gabe had left her a note on the kitchen counter.

Meet me at our old swimming hole. It's hot. Time to cool off.

She let out a long, controlled breath.

Their swimming hole.

They'd tied a rope to a branch and nailed ladder rungs to the tree trunk to allow them to swing out from the steep bank and drop into the water without killing themselves. The rope had disappeared, and most of the rungs had been dismantled or rotted years ago.

But Gabe had been out to the Sloans' for a rope...

And it *was* hot. Felicity decided she could use a break before she tackled her final checklist for tomorrow's party.

Why not take a refreshing dip in the river?

Felicity changed into a swimsuit, added shorts and a T-shirt over it and slipped into flip-flops. Before she could change her mind, she set off on a path down through the trees toward the river. Gabe's car, she'd noticed, wasn't in the driveway. Either he hadn't arrived yet or he'd parked farther down the road and taken a shortcut to the swimming hole. That meant she could either walk back on her own or ride back with him in her wet swimsuit.

She followed the path through trees, grass and ferns. She almost talked herself into turning back twice before she reached the quiet, deep spot where she, Mark, Gabe and other kids had leaped into the river.

Mostly she and Gabe.

She spotted him by an oak tree that clung to the steep riverbank, and for a moment, he might have been the teenager she remembered, playful, dreaming of all he'd do in life, making plans so he wouldn't end up "stuck" in Knights Bridge. He was more muscular now, all man with no hint of boy as he tied the fresh, new rope to a branch of the oak that reached out above the water.

He tugged on the rope. "It should hold." He grinned at her. "Want to go first?"

"No way."

"Why not? What could go wrong?"

"The rope could come loose, and I could end up dropping onto the rocks instead of into the water."

He peered down the bank and shook his head. "There aren't any rocks you need to worry about. You might hit shallow water, but it's unlikely you'd get hurt. You'd compensate and fling yourself out to deeper water."

She shook her head. "You first."

"We could take the rope down to the edge of the river, but it wouldn't be as much fun as swinging from up here." He frowned at her. "You're swimming in your shorts?"

"I have a suit on underneath."

"Ah." He hooked the rope onto a chunk of one of the old rungs they'd nailed into the tree years ago. "I didn't pack swimming trunks. Shorts will have to do."

Felicity made no comment. He pulled off his shirt and tossed it into the grass at the base of the tree trunk. She averted her eyes from his bare chest, the taut, developed muscles a reminder they weren't kids anymore. They could relive the past with a quick dip in the river, but they hadn't gone back in time.

He kicked off his sandals and grabbed the rope. He'd tied a knot at the lower end to provide footing. He gave the rope a tug, seemed unsurprised when it held and hopped up, swinging out over the steep bank and silvery water. He shouted *woo-hoo* and plunged into the deep pool.

He shot up instantly, swearing. "Holy hell, the water's colder than I remember."

Felicity laughed, catching the rope as it swung back toward her. "You're used to heated pools."

"Damn right." He gave his head a toss, flicking river water off his hair, and swam to a boulder a few yards below her. He hopped up onto it and sat, stretching out his legs on the sun-warmed rock. "Feels good on a hot day, though." He pointed up at her. "Your turn."

She peeled off her shorts and T-shirt and tossed them onto the ground next to his shirt. She adjusted her swimsuit, hoping it wouldn't hike up or tug loose and expose more than she wanted to as she was swinging on the rope—something she never used to consider.

She tugged on the rope, making sure it was still secure after Gabe had used it. It held firm.

"Use your muscle memory," he said from below her on his boulder. "You've done this before."

Many times, she thought. She shut her eyes, concentrating on the still, hot air, the faint coolness rising up from the water below her, the sounds of the river coursing downstream, the chattering of a red squirrel in the trees. She could feel the roughness and newness of the rope. She remembered hanging on too long as a teenager and getting rope burn. Gabe hadn't sympathized. "Let go sooner next time. Lesson learned, Felicity."

She wouldn't screw up or chicken out now, with him watching her.

She opened her eyes, pulled herself up onto the

rope, one foot on the knot as she swung out over the water and dropped before she naturally swung back, pendulum-like, to the bank. She tucked up her knees and cannonballed into the river, plunging underwater. She'd had fair warning it was cold, and it was. At the same time it felt good, and she resisted shooting to the surface. She swam a few yards underwater, toward Gabe's rock, and then came up, taking in the warm, humid air.

Gabe swam next to her. The water probably wasn't over their heads here, but she didn't want to touch the bottom and disturb mud and debris and risk stubbing a toe on a rock. "The water feels fine now," he said. "Either that or I have hypothermia and can't tell the difference."

"Too soon for hypothermia."

"Easy for you to say. You're a forever New Englander."

She smiled. "Don't you forget it."

They swam to the boulder and climbed onto it together, sitting next to each other, dripping as they watched the river. Felicity pointed to mallards clustered by rocks on the opposite shore. "I wonder if they're related to the ducks from last time I was out here," he said.

"When was that?"

"Summer after my sophomore year at UMass."

"I remember."

"We went to a Red Sox game that summer. We sat in the bleachers."

"That was the next summer."

He leaned back on his elbows and stuck his feet in the water. "Was it?"

She nodded. "We drove together. I worked at my dad's office that summer."

"Oh, right. I picked you up after work. You were wearing eyeshades like Bob Cratchit."

"I was not," she said, grinning at him. "We drove straight to Fenway. You drove, actually. I don't know why you didn't get a speeding ticket. Pure luck."

"I didn't go that fast."

"You were mad at Mark *and* we were running late."

"What was I mad at Mark about?"

"Something to do with your father."

He splashed water with one foot. "Right. Take your pick. Mark steered clear of his charming dysfunctions sooner than I did."

"You both have done well. Your mom and dad did something right."

"They did a lot right," Gabe said. "I just didn't see it when I was racing to Boston to see the Red Sox beat the Yankees."

"They lost to the Yankees by three runs."

He kicked water on her. "Wet blanket."

"You're the one who told me to look life square in the eye."

"Your career choices and your debt," he said. "Not my rose-colored glasses memory of a Red Sox game."

"You remember they lost," she said, not making it a question.

"Tied going into the eighth and the Yankees stole second base with two outs and ended up getting the lead. Red Sox got two men on base in the bottom of the ninth but didn't score." He sat up straight. "We should take another dip before we get too warm."

"Good idea. I don't want to have to get used to the water all over again."

"It's not as cold as the brook," he said.

"That's not saying much."

He stood on the flat boulder, backed up as far as he could and cannonballed into the water. He swam out of the way and flipped onto his back. "You're next."

Felicity stood up, the rock slippery where she and Gabe had dripped. Since he'd gone ahead of her, it was wet where he'd stood to get his running start into the water. A breeze floated across the river as if from nowhere, sprouting goose bumps on her arms and legs. She was grateful she wasn't wearing a revealing swimsuit.

"I'll count to three," he said.

"Make it five."

"Whatever happened to reckless, fear-nothing Felicity MacGregor?"

She glared at him. "All right. Make it three."

"I'll split the difference and make it four."

"Nobody does anything to the count of four."

He groaned and started counting. On three, she leaped into the river in a sloppy cannonball. The water felt good now, just cold enough on the hot day. She popped up, and Gabe was there. He caught her around the waist. "I'm standing on a rock."

She knew the rock at the river bottom, allowing him to stand up in water that otherwise would have been over his head.

"You know what to do," he said with a grin.

Felicity did, indeed. She threw her arms around his shoulders. "Okay. Go ahead. Fling me."

He hoisted her up, and she put her feet flat on his

thighs. Then he tossed her into the water back first, as they'd done countless times as teenagers. She went under, swam into deeper water, away from the riverbank but not so far she'd get swept into the current. She flipped onto her back and looked up at the sky, pretending she was fifteen again, with no worries beyond her summer reading list and saving enough money from her part-time job.

She swam back to him. "I wish I could flip you but you're too big these days."

"All grown up," he said with a grin.

Yes. Definitely. She cleared her throat. "I should get back. I have a few things to do before dinner."

"One more jump from the rope?"

"I've got all summer."

"Yes," he said. "You do."

"All right. I'll stay while you jump once more. Someone needs to be here in case you split your head open."

"You're all heart, Felicity."

She climbed out of the water onto the bank and, grabbing a skinny poplar sapling by the trunk, hoisted herself up to the steep path. She had to crab-walk midway, holding on to embedded rocks and tree roots. She finally launched herself to the oak tree where they left their clothes.

Gabe was right behind her. She hadn't realized it. He hopped up and grinned at her. "You still have a nice butt."

"Gabe."

"What?"

"Never mind."

He leaned out and grabbed the rope. Ideally, he'd

have stayed on the bank on her turn and caught the rope as it swung back, but he'd been in the water. As kids, they'd tied the rope farther out on the branch, allowing for a landing in deeper water, but one of them would have had to crawl out along the branch to reach the rope. This worked fine.

"I'll catch the rope when it swings back," she said.

"Why don't we go together?"

"What? It won't hold—"

"It'll hold just fine."

And he hooked an arm around her middle, lifted her and leaped for the rope, using the momentum to swing them out over the river. He let go of the rope, and down they went in a tangle of limbs. She clung to him as they hit the water, went under, disentangled and surfaced.

She spit out water and brushed wet hair out of her eyes with one hand. He treaded water next to her, grinning. "That was fun," he said.

"It was *insane*."

"You used to like insane."

"Within reason. This wasn't within reason. We both could have split our heads open."

"But we didn't."

She sighed. "No, we didn't." She treaded water next to him. "Now I have to climb up the bank again. I should make you carry me."

"Now that would be dangerous."

"Are you suggesting I'm too heavy?"

"No. Not suggesting anything of the sort."

She saw it in his eyes then. Lust. Plain and simple. She recognized that look for what it was and flipped on her stomach and swam away from him, toward the riverbank. She lifted herself onto a small boulder next to the path. "You first, Mr. Flanagan."

He swam toward her, his strokes strong and smooth— which only added to her sense of physical awareness. "Your turn to watch my butt?"

"I didn't say that."

He grinned. "I did."

"I was thinking I don't need you watching my butt."

"Since when are you self-conscious?"

"Gabe, we're flirting with danger here. You're bored."

He flicked a drop of water off her chin. "What if I kissed you right now?"

"Where would that get you?"

"Gee, I wonder." He ran his hands through his hair, squeezing out some of the water. "I'll go first. Enjoy the view."

He wasn't the least bit self-conscious, she realized. He took the path quickly, using momentum to carry him up the steep bank. He only needed to grab one tree root. When he got to the top, he reached down, took her hand and all but hoisted her up next to him. "Should I have gone slower?" he asked. "Given you more time?"

"I had plenty of time."

"And?"

"I think you should kiss me and get it out of your system. Then we can go back to my place and check for ticks. Nothing to do with your kiss, of course. Just summer."

"The thought of ticks could ruin the moment, but that was your point." He smiled. "And the operative word is *could.*"

Felicity found herself leaning against the oak, feeling grass, dirt and small rocks under her bare feet, aware of the outline of her body—breasts, hips—under her wet swimsuit. It might not be a sleek bikini but she wasn't hidden under jeans and a sweatshirt, either. "Okay," she said. "Go for it. Kiss me."

"Is that supposed to deter me?"

"Does it?"

"No." He cupped the back of her neck with one hand and lowered his mouth to hers. "Not even close," he said, touching his lips to hers. She thought he would back off immediately, but he didn't. He let it be a real kiss, as if he'd been thinking about it for a while. Then he stood straight and sighed. "That was good. You're a little out of practice. You should let guys kiss you more often."

"If I could throw you in the river, I would."

"Should I expect a sneak attack?"

"It wouldn't be a sneak attack if you expected it, would it? No. You should expect never to kiss me again."

"But you liked it?"

"Consider us even for three years ago. A bed, brownies, a kiss. We're good." She brushed off something small and brown crawling on his shoulder. "That, my dear Gabe, was a tick. Let's go."

"It was a spider but we'll go."

"My brother once got a tick on an unfortunate part of his anatomy—"

"Let's go, Felicity."

"Are you going back to my place?"

"Yes, I am."

"Great." She grinned at him. "I have a hand mirror for de-ticking."

"Trust me, sweetheart, if I find a tick on my privates, you'll be the last to know."

"Not me. I find one, I'm screaming. You don't have to rescue me, but you'll know."

He adjusted her swimsuit strap, pulling it back onto her shoulder. "This was fun," he said. "It was like being kids again. Thanks for joining me."

"A trip down memory lane."

Again that look in his eyes. "Yeah. Something like that."

They came to their senses by the time they returned to her house, Felicity by way of the path, Gabe in his car, giving them a few minutes to cool down. She slipped her shorts and T-shirt on over her swimsuit. He put his shirt back on. That helped with her distractibility. Once inside, they retreated to their rooms to change into dry clothes.

Their teenage souls had crept into the present and dragged them back to the past.

Without any warning, Felicity felt the touch of Gabe's lips on hers as if he was kissing her now. She bit down on her lower lip, hoping to dispel the feeling. It didn't work.

She'd wanted more to their kiss.

"To be expected," she whispered to herself.

Seriously, she thought. She'd put all her resources into her work and her move to Knights Bridge—buying this place, moving in, getting settled. She'd neglected any semblance of a romantic life.

"Sex," she said under her breath. "You haven't had sex in…forever."

Gabe had been her first lover. Her best friend. All that history was bound to bubble up now that he was camped out across the hall. That he was comfortable with himself—comfortable in his own skin—only made her more aware of how much he'd once meant to her.

She picked up her swimsuit and laid it across the edge of the tub to dry. Just as well it was cold and damp. She'd let it snap her out of her haze of arousal or whatever it was. She wanted to slip into boxer shorts and a T-shirt and crawl onto the sofa and read a book she'd picked up on color schemes. She didn't know if it'd help her in her work, but it couldn't hurt—and it was perfect for reading with Gabriel Flanagan in the house. Interesting but not taxing, and easily reread if her mind wandered.

And it would. No point reasoning with herself, overthinking, rationalizing or otherwise driving herself nuts. Let it be. Two adults with a past jumping into a river on a hot day could get in over their heads in more ways than one, but they'd caught themselves before they'd ended up in the grass.

"Imagine the ticks," she said with a laugh, sitting at her desk with her laptop.

"We're invited to dinner at Mark and Jess's place," Gabe said, matter-of-fact, as he walked into the room.

"We?"

"Uh-huh. Mark says Jess is up to it. Check for those ticks and be ready at six."

Ten

Gabe had only seen photos of Mark and Jess's house off South Main Street, a few doors down from Maggie and Brandon Sloan's "gingerbread house," another of Knights Bridge's older homes. Gabe would have been at a loss with all the fixing up. He'd worked for Sloan & Sons through high school and college, and even for a while after he'd dropped out, but he'd never been taken with construction. It was a job to Brandon, but Mark lived and breathed this stuff. He gave Gabe the grand tour, including the attic and cellar.

"We're taking our time," Mark said as they descended the stairs back to the entry. "We painted and did the floors and a few other updates when we moved in, but the house is in good shape. We can take our time."

Gabe noticed the bright white walls and polished hardwood floor, peeking out from cheerful throw rugs. "Now that my schedule's eased up, you can put me to work if you have an unfinished project."

"Jess wants to plant spring bulbs in flowerpots."

"Sure you don't have a wall for me to knock down instead?"

Mark grinned. "Where did this sudden urge to grab a crowbar come from? I thought you were planning your next trip."

"I am, but I can help out here." He shrugged. "Maybe it's the prospect of being an uncle."

"Uncle Gabe has a nice ring to it, does it? Come on. Let's see what's happening with dinner."

They joined Jess, the McCaffreys and Felicity in the kitchen and helped set up dinner outside on the patio, at a long table with a sweeping umbrella. It was simple fare: grilled chicken, fresh local corn on the cob, salad and peach pie.

Jess, not yet visibly pregnant, sat next to her older sister, both looking healthy and happy. They had no trouble eating dinner that Gabe could see. As Mark brought out the pie, Felicity eyed him and then Gabe. "What are you doing?" Gabe asked her.

"Noticing the similarities between you and Mark. I don't think I ever paid attention. Jess and Olivia are obviously sisters and you two are obviously brothers."

"Mark's taller and leaner," Gabe said.

"He's more precise in his mannerisms and thinking, too. You can see how he became an architect. You're more abrupt and action-oriented. A natural start-up entrepreneur."

"Ah, so that's it."

She smiled. "Let's just say I'm glad Mark's the one who designed my house. But you two have so much in common, too. Coloring, your smiles, your eyes. Brothers."

Gabe had expected a few digs at him, given their parting three years ago, but maybe their dip in the river had helped. He'd initiated staying with her in part be-

cause he wanted closure on their relationship. They'd
never cleared the air. They'd moved on with their lives.
The lingering feelings from their falling-out weren't
impeding them, but it still felt like unfinished business. Now that she was living in Knights Bridge—on
his grandfather's old campsite—it was time to smooth
any ripples in the waters between them.

Olivia and Jess pulled everyone into a conversation on the various merits of peach pie, peach cobbler,
peach shortcake and just a fresh, perfect peach. There
was no shortage of good-natured opinions. It was the
sort of pleasant discussion on a lazy summer evening
Gabe hadn't been a part of in ages. He thought he
might get restless or bored, but he didn't. He smiled
to himself. He had a strong opinion about peaches.

The Frost sisters struck Gabe as content with their
lives, not just because they were settled into good mar-
riages, expecting their first babies, but because they
were grabbing hold of their own hopes and dreams.

After dinner, Gabe joined Dylan and Felicity in
cleaning up the dishes. With the inaugural boot camp
in the morning, it was an early night for everyone. No
one seemed nervous, including Felicity. Gabe had done
the driving, and she sat next to him, her window rolled
down as she gazed out the window. "It's a beautiful
evening," he said.

She nodded without looking at him. "It is."

"Boot camp on your mind?"

"Not right now, no. I'm enjoying the scenery."

It could be true. Gabe said nothing.

Back at her house, instead of going straight inside,
he decided to build a fire in the fireplace his grandfather had built at the edge of the woods, above the

river. "Would you mind?" he asked as Felicity came around to the front of his car.

"Not at all. There's wood in the garage. Help yourself."

"Great, thanks."

"I haven't used the fireplace since I moved in. I keep thinking I will, but I haven't gotten around to it. Maybe when my niece and nephew spend the night. I'm happy Mark kept the fireplace when he built the house." Felicity bit her lip. "You and Mark, I mean."

"Demolishing it wasn't an option either of us considered. If a fire turns out to be more work than I expect it will, I'll skip it." He narrowed his eyes on her, debating whether to say something—invite her to join him, something—but he merely pointed at the fireplace. "I'll see how it goes."

"I'll grab some kindling and matches," she said. "I keep some by the woodstove."

She was off before he could thank her. He went into the garage and collected an armload of wood from a half cord neatly stacked along a wall, probably left over from winter when Mark and Jess had moved out. He carried the wood to the old brick fireplace and set it on the cracked cement that passed for a hearth.

Felicity returned with an armload of kindling, a box of matches and a faded patchwork quilt. "I thought you might want to sit out here for a bit," she said, spreading the quilt on the grass.

Gabe arranged some of the kindling in the fireplace. "Join me?" he asked casually.

"Sure," she said, the slightest hesitation in her tone. "Why not?"

They had a fire going in minutes. Felicity sat on the

quilt and stretched out her legs. She'd kicked off her sandals and was barefoot, still in the maxi dress she'd worn to dinner. Gabe had on khakis and a polo shirt, and he slipped off his shoes before he sat next to her on the quilt. His left leg was so close to her right leg that she swore she could feel the warmth of his skin.

It was past dusk but not yet fully dark, the flames glowing against the silhouettes of trees and the glimpses of the river. "Talk to me about your life, Felicity," Gabe said cheerfully as he leaned back on his elbows and stared at the fire. "Tell me what you've been up to the past three years. Working, going out on your own, buying a house, moving back here. I'd like to hear all of it—whatever you've a mind to tell me, anyway."

She started tentatively, maybe harboring a touch of resentment that he didn't know the details of her life. Maybe with more than a touch. But if that were the case, she got past it, and he thought it was because she wanted to tell him—and because he wanted to listen. Being a man of action, he had to remind himself not to pepper her with questions, judgments and opinions, and to just let her talk. Three years ago, he hadn't reminded himself of any such thing. He'd barreled in with what was on his mind without considering what might be on her mind, or even asking. Never mind he'd meant well. It hadn't been the best approach— obviously so, given her reaction.

Now, in the fading light, with the crackle of the fire, she told him about getting that first job in event management and how it had changed her life. Once back on her feet financially, she'd worked to exchange the hectic life of a Boston-based event planner for the one she had now, on her own in Knights Bridge. She'd done big conferences and corporate board meetings and all the rest and would continue to do so from time to time, but she liked planning small-town events best.

"Some people think I've given up on my ambitions," she said, tucking her feet under her. "I haven't. This is what I want to do, where I want to be."

"No guy out here?"

"Where did that question come from? Never mind. Don't answer. I can say for certain I didn't come back to Knights Bridge because of a man—one I left in Boston or one here."

"What about one of the Sloan brothers? I could see you and Adam Sloan together. Quiet guy. Stonemason. You two wouldn't clash."

She smiled. "Ha. Adam's a great guy. All the Sloans are."

"Brandon and Justin are married, and Eric's engaged to a paramedic. Mark isn't sure the paramedic is going to last if Eric doesn't get his act together and set a wedding date. I don't see you and Eric together, though. He's the eldest of six. He likes order. You'd rebel. It wouldn't be pretty."

"Think so, huh?"

He grinned at her. "Uh-huh. What about Christopher? He's a firefighter—he's a bit younger but not by much."

"He's getting over Ruby O'Dunn."

"Ah. Ruby. I understand Hollywood called to her."

"She's happy out there but homesick. Maggie wants to get out to California before Ruby comes home."

Gabe got up and tossed another log on the fire. "I'm staying out of it."

"This from a man who just suggested I should go out with one of the Sloan brothers."

"You're different," he said without missing a beat. "We have a history."

"So that's your excuse."

He heard amusement in her tone and turned to her, the light from the fire catching her smile. He sat back down, one knee up as he eased close to her. "I have never tried to run your life."

"Are you kidding? Gabriel Flanagan, you can't be serious. You told me I was a lousy financial analyst and I needed to change careers."

He shrugged. "I stated the obvious. You already knew. You got mad at me for telling you what you didn't want to admit to yourself."

"You commented on my debt," she said.

"You were sleeping on my couch."

"That makes it okay?"

"Not my point. If you'd been solvent, you wouldn't have needed my couch. Your financial situation was the elephant in the room. And I made it clear it was up to you to figure out what to do with your life. It wasn't my decision."

He was being straight with her, as he'd been then— if not diplomatic. He'd been mystified at how she could have taken offense to his comments. Everything he'd said that day at his apartment had seemed straightforward and obvious to him.

"Felicity…" He hesitated. "In my world, it's a gift to figure out you're on the wrong course. Then you can figure out how to make the corrections you need to get on the right course."

"I can see that. I guess sometimes we all need a

bucket of cold water dumped on our heads to figure out we're on the wrong course."

"I was your bucket of cold water?"

She grinned. "You added ice just to make sure I got the message."

"I missed that."

"Mmm. You thought you were just being a friend."

He said nothing, and they watched the fire die to red coals. The night had turned dark. He saw bright stars above them. He'd never been good with stars. The protected reservoir and small size of its surrounding towns curtailed ambient light and often brought stargazers to the area.

"You could get into stars now that you live out here," he said absently.

"What? Yes—yes I could." She turned to him. "Thanks for asking me to tell my story, and for listening."

"Would you have become an event manager if I'd kept my mouth shut?"

"I don't know. I probably would have slept on your couch and watched television for a few more days."

"And made brownies?"

"That stuck in your craw, didn't it?"

"That was the idea, wasn't it? My mouth was watering, and there were no brownies to be found."

"Should have made some yourself."

"Not the point."

"Have you ever made brownies?"

He shook his head. "Never. Easier to buy them."

Her eyes glowed in the firelight, her cheeks pink with the warm night—or something else. Gabe didn't want to think about that right now. How attracted to her he was, how much he wanted to kiss her. "It's your turn, then," she said abruptly, as if reading his mind. "Tell me about your life the past three years. I'd like to know what you've been up to."

"Making money. Working. Traveling. That's it." He slapped at a mosquito that landed on his knee. "Missed. Looks as if the mosquitoes have found us."

Felicity gave him a skeptical look. "All right. We'll talk about you another time."

"You have a big day tomorrow. Why don't you go on in? I'll put out the fire and bring in the matches and the quilt."

"You're the one speaking."

"It's a panel. I'll speak for maybe ten minutes. You'll be on all day. Anyway, I'm on California time. Go on." He blew her a kiss. "See you in the morning."

She got to her feet, stepping on the hem of her dress, adjusting it quickly. "I sometimes wonder how many times you sat out here as a kid."

"A lot," he said. "And later, with you."

"I remember." She blew him a kiss back. "Good night, Gabe. See you tomorrow."

He watched her head back to the house and waited until she mounted the deck steps and disappeared inside before he turned back to the fire.

So many memories…

Gabe pulled the quilt closer to the fire. Mosquitoes really weren't a problem tonight, but it didn't matter. He'd be out here for a while, mosquitoes or no mosquitoes.

He watched the flames flickering against the night sky, but his mind was in the past.

He was seventeen again, aching to get out of Knights Bridge, knowing it meant leaving behind all he knew—the people, yes, but he'd see his family and friends and stay in touch with them. It was the day-to-day life of his small hometown that he'd be giving up forever. Pieces of it, anyway. Hiking and fishing in Quabbin, swimming in the river, ice-skating on the ponds and the rink on the town common, watching the holiday parades. He'd wanted a different life from the one he had, but what that life looked like had been unformed, based more on hope and dreams than firm goals and plans.

Too much like his father.

Gabe remembered figuring that out, deciding to get serious about specifics, dates, actions, deadlines. He wasn't going to drift through life, always dreaming. He'd also known he'd do just that if he stayed in his small, out-of-the-way hometown.

He'd come out here to the river on a cool late-summer night before his freshman year in college. He got a fire going in the fireplace. Felicity stopped by, sat on his blanket with him, chatting about her plans. She already had everything set for her departure for college in upstate New York. He'd been procrastinating, which he'd done with college applications, too. He hadn't applied to a single college early, in part because he'd known college—whatever one he ended up attending—would be a stepping-stone, not an end in and of itself, and he hadn't had any patience with steps. He'd wanted to get where he was going even if he didn't know exactly where that was.

He'd been driven, no question. Still was.

He'd known whatever he ended up doing, it wasn't

going to involve remaining in Knights Bridge. That was for the Sloans, the Frosts, the O'Dunns, if not all of them, most of them. It wasn't for him. Mark had already left town, and Gabe wasn't going to get sucked into staying.

He still could smell the fire that night. He'd gone swimming in the river and he'd been enjoying the heat of the flames on his bare feet. Even now, years later, he could feel the contrast of the chilly night air and cold grass as he'd considered his future. His parents hadn't provided any wise counsel—any counsel at all. "It's your life, Gabe," they'd tell him. "Do your thing."

He'd seen their laissez-faire approach as disinterest, an abdication of their parental role, even selfish. Why take the time and trouble to engage with him on his plans for his future when they could just indulge whatever they were up to at the moment?

Gabe bit back a wave of emotion. What he wouldn't give now to have his mother go on with him about her latest craft project. She'd always had something in the works that was bound to make her "good money." She loved starting new projects but she'd inevitably lose interest and rarely completed one. They were all, at best, a wash financially and, at worst, a money pit. But he'd never known anyone more cheerful or filled with life.

She'd never talked to him about the cancer that would take her life. "I want you to remember the good times, Gabe," she'd told him. "My smile, my laugh, my love for you and your brother. If I don't beat this—this beast…" She'd paused, getting a faraway look. "Never mind. I will beat it."

But the fight wasn't in her. It was playacting, as if she was reciting certain prescribed lines—as if it'd be wrong to accept she was at the sunset of her life. She hadn't wanted her sons to think she was giving in, somehow hastening her departure from them.

She'd loved this camp, too. Money had always been tight for his parents, and they'd come out here, pitch a tent and enjoy themselves, never mind they lived a few miles up the river. For them, their times there were a break from their day-to-day routines, a low-cost vacation. They'd cook over the open fire, swim in the river and not go anywhere near town.

Now Felicity MacGregor owned it. What would his mother say about that?

She'd be fine with it, Gabe knew. His mother had liked Felicity. "She's focused and direct," she'd say, eyeing him in her knowing way. "You could do worse, you know."

Gabe had never seen Felicity as particularly focused. Direct?

He smiled. Yeah, she could be direct. No one gave it to him straight the way she did.

No question he could do worse—and he had. At the same time, he'd resisted any romantic impulses toward her.

Mostly resisted, anyway.

Felicity had joined him that night in front of the fire, out of the blue. Her impending departure had been on her mind. "We'll stay friends," she'd told him, her words perhaps a cover for the uncertainty bubbling inside her. "We'll always be friends, won't we, Gabe?"

"Always, Felicity. Always."

"Good. I don't know what I'd do without you. I wish we were going to the same college, but we'll only be a couple of hours apart, and we'll see each other when we come home."

"Yeah, that'll be great. It'll all work out."

He'd watched the flames flicker in her wide, luminous eyes, and for the first time, he'd thought about what it would be like to make love to her there in front of the fire—what their lives would be like if they were more than friends. Gabe Flanagan, son of a fun-loving pair of flakes, and Felicity MacGregor, daughter of a small-town banker and an accountant.

He'd glanced at Felicity, who had been clearly annoyed with his sudden silence. He'd been so preoccupied with the sheer absurdity of the idea of making love to her. But then they had gotten carried away.

Everything had changed that night.

But nothing could happen between them.

Nothing.

That was what he needed to remember. No more kisses at the swimming hole. No more deluding himself that he could have it both ways—Felicity in his life, Knights Bridge out of his life. She lived here, and he needed to back off and let her go about her business. He'd made a success of himself and he'd gotten out of town, but in many ways he was that kid again, with his hand on fire and his plans for the future up in the air.

Gabe put out the fire and went inside, but he knew he wouldn't fall asleep anytime soon. Lying on his back in his boxers, on top of the sheets, no blanket, he listened to the portable fan oscillate, appreciated the intervals when it hit his overheated skin. He and Mark had opted against air-conditioning, although it was easily added. They'd never had air-conditioning when they were growing up. It was expensive, and rarely needed, especially so close to the cooling waters of the river. But he could have used AC now.

This place…

He didn't belong here, in the town of his chaotic boyhood. Did Felicity? She didn't strike him as living in the past, but what if she was? What if she was stuck—couldn't move on with a personal life?

Not his concern. Not his business.

Not his responsibility, either. Their tight friendship had ended several years ago. If it had deterred her from finding a guy, getting married, having kids—whatever—she'd had plenty of time to move on. He had.

He winced in the darkness of the small room. *Had* he moved on?

It wasn't like him to think about such things, never mind overthink them.

He shut his eyes, instead thinking about kissing Felicity. It was hot and humid tonight, but if they'd gone to bed together…

He gritted his teeth. "Forget it, pal. Just forget it."

But as he felt himself drifting off to sleep, he couldn't put the thought aside. He was a teenager again, making love to his pretty, eager best friend. He hadn't done much thinking then, that was for damn sure. Then again, neither had she.

He remembered how she'd cried out when he'd thrust into her.

"You're a virgin."

"What did you think I was?"

And *was* had been a key word. That was all they'd

said. Need, hormones, longing, desire—they'd been lost. He knew she'd orgasmed. He'd felt it, heard her soft moans of release. They hadn't come to their senses quickly, not like today at the swimming hole. They'd made love again, exploring, experimenting. They'd made sure they were protected.

He could still feel himself inside her. Feel her warm skin, her breath, her lips. He could hear her cries, her laughter. She'd relaxed her natural guard and enjoyed some real wild abandon that night. For those hours, he'd been a part of her inner world, sharing an intimacy—a union—that he'd felt more than could explain.

Felicity had awakened first, slipped out of their sleeping bag, gotten dressed and greeted him as if nothing had happened. For a moment he'd wondered if she'd thought she'd dreamed their lovemaking. Then she'd said, "You're my best friend, Gabe," and he'd known. It was the summer after their high school graduation. They had their lives ahead of them. They couldn't risk falling for each other. She'd needed him as a friend not as a lover—definitely not as an ex-lover.

She'd decided that was what he'd needed, too, and they'd headed to Smith's for breakfast and gone over their plans for college.

Now, more than a decade later, he wondered where they would be tonight if he'd taken her by the hand that summer night and told her he wanted to marry her.

He almost choked at the thought. It never would have happened. They'd have broken up within months. Weeks, even. Felicity had been right to put on the brakes between them that morning. He'd needed to get away from Knights Bridge and figure out who he was, and he'd have messed up her life in the process.

On some level, maybe they'd both known that. Staying friends had kept them in each other's lives, at least through college and their first jobs.

They'd never talked about that night.

His doing.

But what was the point of talking now? They'd both moved on.

Gabe got up and switched off the oscillating function on the fan. He needed the air to blow directly on him all the time.

Only way he'd get any sleep.

Eleven

Felicity took a shower, got dressed for the day and tiptoed into the kitchen at six, certain she was up before Gabe, but he greeted her by the coffeemaker. "I see we're both up with the crows," he said.

"I thought you'd sleep in a bit longer. You had a later night than I did."

"Did I?" He flipped on the coffeemaker switch. "Thought you might have stayed up late, with the boot camp today."

"There are often last-minute changes to accommodate, but so far, so good for today."

"That's great to hear. My party and Nadia Ainsworth aren't causing you trouble, then."

Felicity got mugs down from the cupboard. "Well, we'll see. What about you? Any butterflies?"

"Nope."

She smiled. "Why am I not surprised?"

"Because you know me. What about you?"

"A few, I guess. I've managed big, high-profile events, so it's not that."

"It's because this one's in Knights Bridge and involves friends and neighbors." He opened up the bread box and pulled out whole-grain English muffins. "Am I right?"

"In a nutshell, yes. People remember great content but they *really* remember late coffee, bad food, cold rooms, long lines, impenetrable programs, bathrooms without proper supplies—you get the idea."

"A lot of moving parts with an event like this."

"Yes."

"Do you celebrate afterward?"

His question caught her off guard. "Celebrate?"

"You know. Kick back with a six-pack or a bottle of champagne."

"I have a Jane Austen tea tomorrow at Rivendell. I can't—"

"I was thinking you'd share the six-pack and bottle of champagne." He popped two halves of the English muffin in the toaster. "It's good to celebrate a job well done."

"Did you celebrate selling your company?"

"I took off to New Zealand for a vacation."

"By yourself?" She held up a hand. "Don't answer— I didn't mean—"

"Yes," he said. "By myself. Alone. Just me, myself and I for a week seeing the sights and decompressing."

"It must have been intense, selling the company. Look, I'm going to wait and grab coffee and a bite to eat at the barn."

"Not going to drive over there with me?"

Felicity shook her head. "I need to get there early."

"Okay." He grabbed the carafe and poured coffee. "Do you have a to-go mug? I can send you off with coffee."

"In the cabinet," she said, pointing. "Top shelf. I

still have it from when I went into an office. I hardly use it now."

He filled the mug, splashed in half-and-half from a bottle he already had on the counter. "I figure you must still take your coffee with half-and-half since it's in the fridge. I'll drink it if I jumped the gun."

"You didn't."

He screwed on the top and handed her the to-go mug. "Need help carrying anything out to your Rover?"

"No, all set, thanks." She held up the mug. "And thanks for the coffee."

"Anytime."

"Help yourself to whatever you want here. I'll see you later at the barn."

He nodded. "Looking forward to it."

"Good," she said absently, heading outside.

As she got in her old Land Rover, she saw she had a text message: Good luck tomorrow!

Nadia Ainsworth. It'd come late last night, but Felicity hadn't noticed it until now. Answer? Don't answer?

She deleted it without answering. Something was off about Nadia. Best not to encourage any level of friendship or intimacy. She was Gabe's problem.

Felicity took a few sips of coffee and backed out of her driveway, past Gabe's BMW. She dismissed a few knots in her stomach. It'd been a while since she'd felt such pressure to make an event perfect. She always had perfection as a goal but seldom felt a small glitch here or there would sink an event—or her. Today *wasn't* different on that score. She knew it, even if her stomach didn't.

By the time she reached Carriage Hill Road, she was focused on what she had to do for the day. Maggie Sloan's good cheer and utterly relaxed attitude when she greeted Felicity in the kitchen didn't hurt. "Do you ever get pre-event jitters?" Felicity asked as she downed the last of Gabe's coffee.

Maggie, red hair pulled back, apron on over a simple knee-length dress, shook her head. "Not since the food-poisoning incident in Boston."

"Food-poisoning? No way."

"Not buying it, are you?" Maggie grinned. "You're right. There was no food-poisoning. It's what I tell myself before an event. If I don't poison anyone, anything else can be managed."

Not a bad way to manage any jitters, Felicity thought, and it fit Maggie's personality.

Her older sister, Phoebe, came into the kitchen, her fiancé, Noah Kendrick, a few steps behind her. They'd arrived last night from Noah's winery on California's Central Coast and had stayed at Phoebe's former home in the village, a cottage around the corner from the library. She'd been the library director for several years and had always expected to stay on until she retired.

Felicity had known Phoebe forever, but it was her first time meeting Noah, a lean, quiet man, a tech genius and a billionaire. "I'm not much on public speaking," he said, as if he, too, had a few butterflies.

"I imagine the attendees today will be interested in anything you have to say, even if you stumble here and there," Maggie said.

"Just don't make any jokes," Dylan said, joining them. "You're the worst."

Noah grinned. "Now you tell me. All these years and you've never hinted I'm not funny."

"I hinted. You just didn't take the hint."

The two longtime friends laughed, and Phoebe shook her head, smiling at her sister and Felicity. "I'm imagining bad jokes at board meetings."

"Many bad jokes," Dylan said. He sipped coffee from a mug he'd brought with him.

Noah winced, good-humored. "You're not kidding."

"Best to stick to relevant anecdotes—like how you found me sleeping in my car and asked me to join you at NAK because you needed my instincts about people to offset your cluelessness."

"Utter cluelessness," Noah added. "Except about Phoebe here."

Felicity left them to their friendly banter and went into the main room to check on the setup for the day. Maggie joined her, but everything for the coffee and muffins that would get the day started was laid out. Whatever she might say, Maggie was an experienced professional. She wanted everything to be perfect today, too.

Satisfied things were in order, Felicity slipped out the kitchen door and to a pebbled path behind the barn. She followed it along the field and an old stone wall down to Olivia's inn. She slipped through a gap in the stone wall and took her time walking up a mulched path among the lavender and mint.

Russ Colton waved to her from the terrace, as if he'd been waiting impatiently for her to get there. "I heard you were on your way." He pointed at a padded envelope on the wood table. "That arrived for you."

"Here?"

"Yes. Here. It's not something you're expecting?"

Felicity shook her head. "No, it's not. How did it get here? Did someone drop it off?"

"It was on the steps at the front door when I got here. I haven't asked if anyone saw who delivered it. I wanted to talk to you first. If it's nothing, great." He fastened his gaze on her, a reminder that he was an experienced security consultant. "Who's Nadia?"

Felicity peered at the handwritten label:

For Felicity MacGregor.
From Nadia.

"Gad, Russ," she said. "I'm sorry. I should have told you."

"Told me what? Is she helping you today? What's going on, Felicity? This woman's name isn't on any of my lists. Am I overreacting? I'd rather overreact than underreact."

"Her name is Nadia Ainsworth. She used to work with Gabe Flanagan. She was in town yesterday. We met for lunch."

Russ's eyes narrowed. "Your body language suggests she's a problem. Is she?"

"I don't know if she is or she isn't. Is it okay if I open the package?"

He nodded, standing to one side as Felicity picked up the padded envelope. It was soft, as if it held fabric. She pried it open and, under Russ's watchful eye, withdrew a folded tea towel depicting Knights Bridge's one-and-only covered bridge.

"There's a note," Russ said.

It was tucked in a red ribbon tied around the towel. She lifted it out and opened the small, folded white card. The note was handwritten in deep red ink, perhaps to match the towel and ribbon.

> *Dear Felicity,*
> *Have a wonderful time today! I'm sure every-*
> *thing will go well. A pleasure meeting you yes-*
> *terday. Look me up if you're ever in Malibu.*
> *We'll do lunch again.*
> *Best wishes,*
> *Nadia*

Felicity handed the note to Russ. He read it quickly and tucked it back into the ribbon. "Seems innocuous," he said, some of his tension visibly easing. He paused, studying her. "Not to you?"

"I really don't know."

"What's your gut say?"

"That she's got a hidden agenda, but that's only my gut take on her. I only met her briefly yesterday. Gabe's the one to ask about her."

"Where is she now?"

"I have no idea. She mentioned she's settling her grandmother's estate somewhere in the area."

"I'll ask Gabe. You focus on the boot camp and let me handle this, okay?"

"Sounds good to me," Felicity said.

And that was that. Russ stuffed the towel and note back into the envelope, not taking any particular care, and held on to it. "In other news, how are the badgers coming along for Kylie's launch party?"

Felicity knew Russ wasn't looking for an actual answer—he just wanted to change the subject and lighten the mood. "Coming along great." She motioned toward the kitchen. "I should get to work."

"Take care today," Russ said. "Give me a shout if you need me. Don't hesitate."

She smiled. "Overreact rather than underreact."

"You got it," he said, almost smiling back at her.

Russ stayed out on the terrace while Felicity went through the mudroom into the old house's spacious country kitchen. It was quiet now, but that wouldn't last. She pushed a hand through her hair, realizing she hadn't pulled it back yet. She dug a clip from her bag and headed through the dining room and living room in the original part of the house. Mark Flanagan hadn't been involved in the house's first major contemporary renovation, several years before Olivia had bought the property, but he'd designed the addition that was in progress.

She ducked into a powder room off the main hall and, using Olivia and Maggie's goat's milk liquid soap, washed her hands and dabbed water on the back of her neck to cool off from her walk and the tension of finding Nadia's package. She felt awkward more than upset or angry. She'd let Russ and Gabe deal with her, should any problems arise.

Maybe the covered-bridge towel had been a genuine, well-intentioned gift.

Best, Felicity decided, drying her hands, to let it be and not read anything into it. She hoped Nadia had dropped the package off on her way out of town.

A glance in the mirror told Felicity that her tension was showing in her face. She practiced a few cheerful smiles and did thirty seconds of deep breathing, then clipped her hair back, freshened up her makeup and returned to the kitchen.

Her phone rang. She expected it was Maggie but recognized Nadia's number on the screen. She almost let the call go to voice mail but decided to answer. "Hello, this is—"

"Felicity MacGregor. Hi, there. It's Nadia Ainsworth. I wanted to call before you got too busy. Did you get my package?"

"I did—I just opened it. Lovely. Thank you."

"I know what it's like to be in your position with so much going on. Dylan McCaffrey, Noah Kendrick and Gabriel Flanagan all speaking today. That's pressure. And that's just for starters. It's a diverse group of men and women for a relatively small event. These boot camps are going to be special, I think."

"I think so, too," Felicity said. "Can I call you back later? I really can't talk right now."

"Of course. I understand." Nadia didn't sound the least bit put out. "You need to focus. You don't want to screw up this event. Believe me, I know."

"Where are you now?"

"I'm in my car."

"Heading to your grandmother's—"

"Why don't you call me when the party's over? There's no urgency. I got a real kick out of the covered bridge towel, I have to admit. I bought it at the country store in your sweet little village center. It's so quaint. Okay, talk to you later."

Felicity exhaled in relief when she realized Nadia had disconnected. Next time she'd let the call go to voice mail. Whatever Nadia's true intentions, her behavior was verging on intrusive and inappropriate.

The call didn't strike Felicity as a genuine effort to reach out in solidarity and appreciation. Nadia had no reason to reach out. They'd only met yesterday. They didn't know each other.

"This isn't about me," Felicity said under her breath. "This is about Nadia and Gabe."

She heard voices and went back outside. Russ was chatting with Gabe on the terrace. She felt Gabe's gaze settle on her and knew Russ had already told him about Nadia's present. He'd changed into a sleek, medium-gray suit since she'd left him in her kitchen. He looked like the successful entrepreneur he was.

Gabe followed her into the kitchen. "Are we in your way?"

Felicity shook her head. "No, not at all."

"Russ showed me Nadia's gift."

"A covered-bridge towel. Makes a good gift." Felicity debated whether to tell them about Nadia's call. It didn't add to what they already knew, but they'd want to know. No question. "She just called, actually. Wishing us well today. She didn't say where she was."

Russ stood still next to the table. "You asked?"

"Yes."

"I'm sorry about this," Gabe said. "I don't know what her game is, or if she even has one. She texted me to tell me she's flying back to California today. I came down here to let you and Russ know."

"What about her grandmother's estate?" Felicity asked.

"Something came up at home, and she has an offer on her grandmother's house." Gabe patted Buster, who'd stirred from his spot in the shade. "She must have dropped off the package on her way to the airport. If she calls again, find me. I don't care if I'm speaking."

Russ shook his head. "Find *me*, Felicity. I'll handle Nadia. Gabe, you're here to share your wisdom with aspiring entrepreneurs. I'm here to make sure someone like Nadia doesn't cause trouble."

Gabe stood straight, Buster flopping back into the shade. "Fair enough. Thanks." He paused, nothing about him suggesting he'd relaxed. He turned to Felicity. "Don't let Nadia get inside your head."

"No problem."

"Right." He gave her the faintest of smiles. "Not saying you can't handle yourself. I'm doing my best not to let Nadia get inside my head, too."

"I think she's already there, don't you?"

"That's part of her game right now," Russ said. "She's messing with you to keep herself from thinking about her own life."

"I think she wants something from Gabe," Felicity added.

He picked a stray dog hair off his expensive suit coat, but there was nothing casual about him. "She hasn't said anything to me."

"Sometimes people don't say so outright."

"I'm not good at mind-reading," he said.

"I'll head up to the barn," Russ said. "See you two later."

He was off, down through the garden and the gap in the stone wall to the path up to the barn. Felicity watched him, trying to ignore a twinge of irritation with Gabe—his take-charge attitude, his crack about mind-reading, his impossible-to-miss physical presence. The rush of pure physical awareness got to her more than the rest of it. It wasn't helpful, this rekindled attraction to him. She wasn't eighteen anymore.

She hit the pass code on her phone and handed it to him. "That's Nadia's number, right?"

Gabe glanced at the screen. "Yes."

"Then it wasn't someone pretending to be her. She's never done anything scary, has she? Threatened to hurt you, someone else—in theory, even. For example, the girl you slept with in high school who's now a successful event manager in your hometown."

"No. Nothing like that."

"Good. I didn't think so. If she's on her way to the airport, she isn't going to crash today's boot camp. She's just…" Felicity paused, wondering how frank she should be. "She wants your attention. Why, I don't know. Does she think you have any influence with her ex-husband? Could she want you to intervene on her behalf?"

He tapped her temple. "Can't read minds, remember?"

"I'm talking about interpreting cues, Gabe."

"Cues such as when you were camped out on my couch eating cold pizza and pad thai and I was supposed to know you didn't want advice? Never mind. We have work to do right now. I don't know what Nadia is thinking or why she left you a towel."

"Do you suspect she's lied to you about her reasons for coming out here?"

"Probably, but she did lose her grandmother a few months ago." He sighed, looking less tense. "I'm sorry she zeroed in on you."

"It's okay, Gabe. I've dealt with worse." Felicity took her phone and slipped it in her tote bag. "You can have the towel. Put it in your condo powder room or something. It can remind you of Knights Bridge. You and Mark used to fish off that bridge, didn't you?"

"First time was with Gramps. I must have been four or five."

"And you remember?"

"Yeah. Mark and I got after him for throwing his cigarette in the river." Gabe grinned suddenly, winking at her. "The Flanagans are an incorrigible lot. That's what my mother used to say."

"I remember," Felicity said with a smile.

"Gramps did quit smoking."

"Good for him. Gabe…" She considered her words. "You just sold a company for a lot of money. You're not an unattractive guy. Do you think Nadia has set her sights on you now that she's divorced? She's— what, ten or twelve years older than you? That's not unheard of."

"Nadia was married the entire time she did work for me, and I hardly ever saw her. We were never together, and we're never going to be together. Whatever her reasons for pestering you, that's not one of them."

"Got it. Right. None of my business, anyway."

Gabe studied her. "Are you sure Nadia didn't say anything else?"

"I'm sure. I just hope she gets on her flight—for her sake, too. Don't worry, okay? I'm fine. Russ is on the case. We all have work to do today."

"I speak for an hour. You work behind the scenes for hours and hours. Doesn't seem fair." Gabe grinned at her. "I've got it a lot rougher."

She laughed, genuinely amused at his teasing. She waited, watching as he made his way through the garden and out to the pebbled path. No question the man was good-looking, sexy and damn near irresistible—but resist she would.

She returned to the kitchen and acknowledged a surge of relief when she found Maggie Sloan bustling around, preparing for her part of today's inaugural entrepreneurial boot camp.

On with the day's work.

Once he arrived at the barn, Gabe conferred with Russ on Nadia as the two of them grabbed a quick cup of coffee before attendees started arriving. "We don't know where she is now," Russ said. "We don't know what flight she's on. It'll take her a couple of hours to get to the airport, and she'll need to arrive early to get through security. I would guess she's on her way to Boston, but I don't like to guess."

"Do you want me to call her?" Gabe asked.

Russ shook his head. "Don't stir the pot. Do you have a photo of her in case she turns up here?"

"I don't. She's always been a pro, Russ. She's going through a hard transition right now, but she's never made any threats, overt or implied, and she's never disrupted an event."

"How well do you know her?"

"She's freelanced for me for several years from her home in Malibu. We've met face-to-face no more than a dozen times."

"And her husband bought your company and filed for divorce," Russ added. "I don't like that she's contacting Felicity the way she is. Is she obsessed with you?"

"Felicity basically just asked me the same question,"

Gabe said. "I don't think so. We've never had a relationship if that's what you're asking. It's never entered my mind, and as far as I know it's never entered hers."

"Professional contact only?"

"Totally. I'd tell you if it were otherwise. Nadia believes I have influence over David, her ex-husband, but I don't. I had no idea their marriage was on the rocks. I'm not sure she did, either. He seemed to dump her out of the blue. He's one of those narcissistic asses who can turn on the charm when it suits him, but I don't have anything to do with him."

Russ nodded thoughtfully. "Sounds as if Nadia's had a lot come at her at once. What about you and Felicity?"

Gabe drank some of his coffee. Yeah, he thought, what about him and Felicity? It was a damn good question. "We grew up together," he said finally. "We stayed friends after we both left Knights Bridge. We drifted apart. This is the first time I've seen her in a few years."

"Any big falling-out or just less and less contact?"

"There was a falling-out," Gabe said, downing the last of his coffee. He set the mug on the counter, where one of Felicity's helpers, already on duty, swept it away. "She got mad at me for giving her unsolicited advice."

"Ah." Russ pointed his mug at Gabe. "But you hired her to plan the party today."

"Sort of. It was through Mark."

Russ grinned. "I have a meddling big brother, too. He's out in Hollywood pouring drinks and writing screenplays. Hates to fly or he'd come out here for a visit. Does Nadia know about your past with Felicity?"

"I didn't tell her. My assistant knows, but she's not one for spreading gossip, just listening to it. A lot of people in Knights Bridge know we grew up together and were friends."

"Easy to find out that sort of history in a small town," Russ said. "I wouldn't be surprised if people here know more about what happened between you and Felicity than you two do yourselves."

"And you're only half kidding."

"Not kidding at all."

Gabe laughed, relaxing for the first time since he'd heard about Nadia's package on the doorstep. "You're getting to know your new town."

"Bit by bit." Russ turned serious again. "If Nadia is looking for reasons to be jealous, a history between you and Felicity could do it."

"Nadia has a lot going for her. She doesn't need to be jealous of anyone."

"It's not necessarily about that kind of need, Gabe. Maybe she just wants to see your life screwed up since hers is so screwed up. Maybe she doesn't want to see you reunite with old friends in your hometown because she feels alienated and alone." He set his mug on the counter. "I could go on, but I'm only speculating. Don't worry about anything today, okay? That's what I'm here for."

Gabe nodded. "Thanks," he said. "It's got to be hard to get worked up about a present of a towel with a covered bridge on it."

"You'd be surprised," Russ said. "If you hear from Nadia, let me know."

"Will do," Gabe said, irritated that Nadia had inserted herself into today's event.

"And don't contact Nadia yourself," Russ added as Gabe started toward the main room.

"No chance of that."

When he entered the main room, Gabe noticed several people arriving for the day. Felicity was at the front entrance to greet them. He glanced back toward the kitchen, but Russ had slipped away to do his thing. Gabe had an urge to disappear, too. He didn't like the limelight. He liked his work, and he wanted to help people—but he wasn't a big networker. From self-made billionaire Noah Kendrick's uncomfortable expression as he arrived, Gabe figured at least he was in good company.

He resisted an impulse to call Nadia and tell her to back off, but he'd do as Russ, the security pro, recommended and avoid contact. He didn't want to think about her. That, he was certain, was at least one thing she wanted. Sending notes and towels to Felicity was Nadia's way of exerting control. She might not be aware of what she was doing, but that didn't matter.

He made eye contact with Felicity and smiled at her. She smiled, looking relaxed and confident. He figured now wasn't the time to point out he was right about her not following her parents and brother into finance. She loved her work as an event manager. He could see it.

Or maybe her smile was meant for him—she was relaxed because her old friend Gabe was in town?

He grinned.

Not a chance.

Twelve

By six o'clock, the boot camp had wound down, and most of the attendees and speakers were on their way home. Felicity looked forward to handling future larger, more complex events out on Carriage Hill Road, but it felt great to have the inaugural boot camp behind her. She kicked off her shoes and sat out on the terrace at Olivia's house with a glass of iced tea and a small plate of Maggie's delectable hors d'oeuvres, left-over from the party. The cleaning crew had swooped in right on time and was doing their thing. Felicity would take a moment to catch her breath, then wrap up for the day. Olivia, Dylan, Noah, Phoebe, Maggie, Gabe and Russ were up at the barn, no doubt relaxing in their own way. Felicity had a feeling they would stay on for the evening to celebrate what had been a successful inaugural event.

She would go home, take a shower, have a glass of wine on the deck and head to bed early with a book.

And Gabe?

She drank some of her tea and listened to the bees in the mint. Gabe could do his Gabe thing. She didn't need to be a part of his evening plans.

Her phone vibrated on the table with a text message. She glanced at the screen: How'd it go today?

Nadia.

Felicity groaned and didn't touch her phone. She had no intention of responding. She didn't want to encourage further contact, but she didn't want to deal with Nadia right now, either, regardless of her intentions. Nadia was a professional with at least some experience with event planning. She wouldn't expect an instant response.

But another text came in: Why don't we share a bottle of wine to celebrate?

Not at the airport or boarding a flight to California, apparently.

Felicity snatched up her phone, but it had been a busy day, and she didn't trust herself not to start typing a tart response. She put the phone back on the table and picked up her tea glass with both hands, hoping that would help her not to tell Nadia to leave her the hell alone.

If not for her iced tea and moment to relax, Felicity doubted she'd have noticed the texts immediately, anyway. She refused to let them ruin her quiet few minutes before she finished up for the day. She only had a few loose ends to tie up.

She popped a stuffed mushroom into her mouth from her small plate of leftover goodies. Having a caterer of Maggie's caliber in town had made everything so much easier today, but she was clearly stretched thin with her husband out of town, two small boys, the inn, the goat's milk products and her complicated family. Maggie thrived on having a lot of irons in the fire, but everyone had limits.

As if Felicity's thoughts had conjured them, Maggie's two young sons scrambled over the stone wall, bypassing the gap, and ran up a mulched path through the garden, apparently in the middle of a game that involved a chase. From what Felicity could hear, it involved running from a pretend monster.

Then Nadia Ainsworth leaped over the stone wall, laughing as she chased them up the path. "You can run but you can't hide!"

The boys squealed in delight, Nadia, obviously, the monster after them.

At that moment, Russ Colton materialized seemingly out of nowhere and eased between Nadia and the two boys. "Can I help you?" he asked her.

"Oh, sorry." She clutched her chest, breathing hard. "My name's Nadia Ainsworth. I ran into Tyler and Aidan in the field, and we got a game going. They told me they're meeting their mom here. Maggie. The caterer for today's entrepreneurial boot camp. I have two brothers myself. It's okay. Really. Gabe Flanagan and I are friends." She pointed toward the terrace. "Felicity knows me."

"Let's go have a seat," Russ said.

"And you are—"

"Russ Colton."

"Oh, right. You're married to Morwenna Mills. I saw a bit about her at the local library. She has a new book coming out." Nadia spoke cheerfully, getting her breathing under control. "I'd love to sit down for a minute. I'm not used to this humidity. I'm dripping."

Russ had her go ahead of him, and they joined Felicity at the table. The boys had run inside in search of goodies. Nadia plopped onto a chair and wiped her brow with the back of her wrist. She smiled at Felicity. "I thought you might have your feet up. Good day?"

Felicity nodded. "Everything went well, thanks."

"I decided to hike up Carriage Hill. It's on state land. I got *maybe* a third of the way to the top before the heat and humidity turned me back. I'm not used to New England summers anymore. Gabe said we could easily be in sweaters tomorrow. I guess I'm a real Californian nowadays despite my Massachusetts roots." She screwed up her face, eyeing Russ. "Gosh, you look so serious. I hope I didn't cause any problems."

"Maggie had her eye on the boys," he said. "They play in the field on a regular basis. She saw you—"

"Oh, no. I frightened her. She doesn't know me, and here I was chasing her sons. No wonder you beelined for me." She didn't sound that chagrined or apologetic about her behavior. "The boys needed a monster for their game. I obliged. I should have asked Maggie's permission first. Yikes. I can see how that must have looked from afar. Sorry. As you can see, I'm harmless."

"We understood you were flying to California today."

"Mmm. Los Angeles. That was the plan, but I changed my mind." Nadia shifted to Felicity. "Did you get my texts?"

"Just now," Felicity said.

"Great. I wasn't sure if they went through. The cell coverage out here is spotty at best. It looks as if most of the people at the boot camp have gone home, or wherever. Good time to catch your breath. I'm sure you made the day easy for everyone involved. That's the role of a good event manager, isn't it?" She didn't wait for an answer and glanced around the garden, in its full mid-summer glory. "What a perfect setting for a party. I got a decent look at the McCaffreys' barn, too. Amazing. What a great setup."

Felicity didn't detect an undercurrent of hostility in Nadia's tone or demeanor, but Russ remained quiet and watchful. There was no question he didn't like her sudden appearance, particularly with two young boys who didn't know her. A lecture about strangers was no doubt in their immediate future.

"Could I talk you into something to drink?" Nadia asked. "I'm afraid I wasn't prepared for the conditions and let myself get dehydrated."

"Iced tea okay?" Felicity asked, rising. "I'll get it."

"Oh, no, you don't need to go to the trouble. I'll get it—"

"It's no trouble," Russ said. "Relax, Nadia. Catch your breath."

"Okay, no problem. Unsweetened tea would be great, thanks."

She stayed put while Felicity went inside. Maggie arrived through the front door and was setting up the boys at the table with drinks. "Is that woman still here?" she whispered. Felicity nodded, and Maggie made a face. "She doesn't know where the line is, does she? But you should have seen Russ go into action. My goodness. We had no idea she was here on a hike. She must have parked at the Quabbin gate and taken the back way to Carriage Hill."

"That makes sense. I didn't see her until she came over the stone wall."

"The boys are fine. All that counts."

"Does Gabe know?"

"Oh, yes. He's on his way."

When Felicity returned to the terrace, Gabe had joined Russ and Nadia at the table. Nadia thanked Felicity for the iced tea. She'd already helped herself to a mini cream puff on Felicity's plate. "Delicious," she said, looking less sweaty. "I could eat a hundred of them right now, but the tea is the best. Just what I need. I didn't even bring a bottle of water with me."

Felicity stayed on her feet. Nadia seemed oblivious to Gabe's glowering look.

"Where's your car?" he asked her.

She swallowed the last of her cream puff and gulped her tea, then set the glass on the table. "I parked at a yellow gate down the road. I wanted to see the reservoir up close, but I took a wrong turn and ended up on the trail up Carriage Hill."

Gabe gave no indication how he felt about her story. "Why aren't you on your flight?"

"Last minute change of plans." She shrugged. "Nothing nefarious. What, do you guys think I'm some kind of stalker? Wow. I'm glad I wasn't met by the cops."

"The boys' uncle is a police officer," Gabe said.

"Ah, yes. Eric Sloan. I met him at lunch at that little restaurant in town. I resisted pie today." She sat up straight and licked her lips, looking somewhat more self-conscious. "Apologies, okay? I didn't mean to flip any paranoia switches. I would check the boys for ticks, though. I guess that's par for the course around here in warm weather."

"The ticks are bad this year," Russ said. "It's a good idea for you to check yourself."

"I will, believe me. I have a cousin who had Lyme

disease. It was awful, but he made a full recovery." Nadia grabbed a tiny brownie and pushed back her chair. "Thanks so much for the tea and goodies. I'll run along now."

Russ stood. "I'll drop you down to your car."

"It's not far. I'm cooled off and rehydrated. There's no need to trouble yourself—" She stopped, obviously finally tuning into the moods around her. "Okay, let's do this your way. I would appreciate a ride. Thank you."

"My car's out front," Russ said, nodding toward the yard. "Let's go."

Nadia glanced at Gabe, as if expecting him to offer to take her since they knew each other. He gave her a steady, not-quite steely look. "Have a good flight back home."

"Thanks. I'll probably go tomorrow, but I might yet make it out tonight." She turned to Felicity. "Congratulations on today. It's been great meeting you."

"You, too," Felicity said politely.

Nadia started to say something else but smiled without comment. Russ motioned for her to go ahead of him off the terrace and then got in close to her, leading her to the side yard and around to the front of the house.

Felicity sat down and frowned up at Gabe. "Do you think she's just clueless?"

"No."

"You're irritated," she said.

"You could say that."

"Boiling mad? That more accurate?"

He sighed. "Felicity."

"Russ will see her off. I would definitely describe

him as boiling mad, but all's well that ends well. I wouldn't mess with Maggie, though. She has access to kitchen equipment and she knows how to use it, and her boys are Sloans. Dumb move on Nadia's part."

"Her behavior was inappropriate. I'm sorry."

"You're not answerable for her, Gabe." Felicity decided to drop the subject of Nadia Ainsworth and her antics. "I overheard a lot of positive comments about what you had to say today. Everything seemed to go smoothly. We can both take a bow."

He leveled his deep, warm blue eyes on her. He was focused and serious—the high-flying, risk-taking, successful young entrepreneur taking her in. "The day went well," he said. "You did a great job. The party went off without a hitch despite the short notice. I don't know about taking a bow, but I'm glad my part's done."

"Did you throw up before you spoke?"

"Felicity…" He sighed. "I did not throw up."

"After?"

"No, not after, either."

"Were you queasy? Did you get dry heaves? I've seen that happen plenty of times in my work."

"Felicity."

"I'm helping you to see the bright side." She decided not to mention Nadia's texts. Having her swoop in as a pretend monster after two small boys was enough for Gabe to digest. "I have a few things to check on, but most of the loose ends involve my laptop. I can take care of them at home. Enjoy your evening. I'll see you later on."

"You could stay," he said.

"I'd fall asleep on the floor next to Buster."

She grabbed the tea glasses and the goody plate,

aware of Gabe watching her. Was he looking for a sign Nadia had upset her? It didn't matter, she told herself. She smiled at him, said goodbye and headed back to the kitchen. Maggie had her sons helping her load up her van. They'd be on their way in a few minutes. The clean-up crew was experienced and competent. Felicity didn't need to stay until they finished.

She left through the front door and started up the road to the barn, where she'd parked.

Gabe fell in next to her. She smiled at him. "Afraid Nadia will break loose from Russ and come find me?"

He flinched. "I don't know what she'll do next."

"Okay, no joking around. Got it. Russ would agree. Have you met Kylie yet?"

"Not yet. I look forward to it. She and Russ had other plans or they'd have joined us for dinner last night."

"I'd never have put them together, but they work," Felicity said. "He sort of reminds me of Sherlock Badger. Stoic, tough. Better-looking, though."

"A week ago I'd have no idea what you were talking about." He studied her a moment, less tense and annoyed. He surprised her with a smile. "Didn't your piano teacher call you incorrigible?"

"I was eleven. Aren't all eleven-year-olds incorrigible?"

"I wouldn't know."

"I wouldn't, either, but I'm going with it."

He leaned close to her. "It's been good seeing you, Felicity."

"You, too. Are you staying another night?"

"That's the plan. I don't know what time I'll be back. Are you sure you won't join—"

"I need to do a few things," she said, interrupting him.

"All right. If you see a fire outside, that'll be me."

He opened her Land Rover door for her and shut it once she climbed in behind the wheel. He stepped back, waiting as she backed out, turned around and headed down the driveway to the road. She probably should have made one last check at the barn, but she knew everything was fine.

As she started up Carriage Hill Road, she glanced back at Gabe and noticed a protective air about him, as if he was worried he'd missed something—*knew* he'd missed something but couldn't put his finger on exactly what it was. She suspected it was the residual effect of Nadia's intrusive behavior. Gabe felt guilty, even if he knew he wasn't responsible for this woman's conduct. Felicity felt a little of that same guilt herself. When she arrived at her house and got out of her Rover, she welcomed the coolness of the river and the quiet rustle of a breeze in the trees. Just as well she'd have some time to herself tonight.

She almost knocked over a bottle of wine on her doorstep. A note was tied to it with a red ribbon, just like the one on the covered-bridge towel. Felicity recognized Nadia's handwriting:

> *Door's locked or I'd have left it in the fridge to chill. Congrats on a great day!*
> *Xo*
> *Nadia*

Felicity shivered, unsettled. She quickly checked Nadia's earlier text messages. She must have left the wine before she'd sent them. Keep it as a surprise, maybe? She'd expected Felicity to accept her invitation to get together, at which point she would have suggested meeting back here.

Kind of pushy but not really creepy and dangerous.

Felicity picked up the wine. It was a decent New Zealand sauvignon blanc. It'd been in the shade, so it wasn't hot. Nadia had some boundary issues going on, but the situation hardly warranted smashing a perfectly good bottle of wine on the rocks. Felicity took the wine inside, keeping it with her as she checked the house in case her wannabe new best friend had given Russ the slip, doubled back to town and was hiding under a bed.

But she didn't find anything—she hadn't seriously expected to—and put the wine in the refrigerator. She'd let it chill while she took a shower.

In the bathroom, stripped to her skin, she received another text: Russ followed me out to the highway. He's quite the stud. Did you get the wine?

Felicity debated. Pretend to be in the shower already, or answer?

"Get it over with," she muttered, and typed her response: I did. Thanks!

Lovely.
Safe travels.
I hope our paths cross again soon.

Felicity didn't respond.

She got into the shower, welcoming the lukewarm water. If nothing else, today had reminded her that Gabriel Flanagan wasn't the teenager she'd known in high school—or even the man he'd been three years ago. He'd worked hard for the life he had now. He'd turned his dreams into reality. He'd had the drive, the commitment and the focus to be the kind of entrepreneur the attendees at today's boot camp had wanted to hear from. Felicity had her own business, but she didn't have any ambition to turn it into anything but what it was. That had been part of the point in moving to Knights Bridge, hadn't it? She'd wanted to work for herself, on a variety of projects, and still have time for a life.

She shut her eyes and let the warm water soothe her fatigue and tension. She'd done her job today. Gabe had done his job. Their paths in life had diverged from their days hanging out together out here on the river.

When she emerged from the shower, she slipped into yoga pants, a T-shirt and sandals. She decided that drinking Nadia's bottle of wine might not be a good idea given her mood. She'd give it to friends who didn't know Nadia or Gabe and could just enjoy it.

Instead she opened a bottle of inexpensive pinot grigio, poured herself a glass and took it outside to the deck, where she sat alone and listened to the river course downstream.

Thirteen

⮜⮜⮜⮛⮞⮞⮞

Gabe returned to Felicity's house after dark, expecting to find her tucked in bed. Instead he spotted her sitting cross-legged on her quilt in front of the fireplace, watching the fire die down. He walked over to her and stirred the coals. She didn't say anything. He added a log to the fire and sat next to her. "Sleepy?" he asked.

"Mmm. I was just about to go in. I keep dozing off. The fire's nice." The flames were already picking up. "How was dinner?"

"Low-key. Everyone was tired. Olivia went to bed early. We met at her and Dylan's house."

"Quite the place, isn't it?"

"That brother of mine is good at his work, but they had a vision of what they wanted."

"Just like this place," Felicity said, uncurling her legs. She was barefoot, dressed in yoga pants and a baggy hoodie. "You and Mark had a vision of what you wanted."

Gabe pulled off his shoes and set them in the grass, away from her and the fire. "You could say that. Russ made sure Nadia got to the airport."

"She'll get home to Malibu and get on with whatever is next for her, especially with an offer on her grandmother's house. My guess is she got out here and started flailing with all that's gone on in her life lately."

"Doesn't excuse her behavior."

"We don't have to talk about her. The post–boot camp reviews are coming in. You were definitely a hit today. People wanted to hear what you had to say. You didn't mince words." She smiled. "Big surprise there, huh?"

"I'm straightforward to a fault," he said.

"It's what people wanted today. Needed, maybe. You've been in the trenches as a start-up entrepreneur."

"I have scars, you mean."

She smiled. "You love your scars."

Her eyes were half closed, shining in the glow of the revived fire. Gabe noticed the empty wineglass on the blanket next to her. "How much wine have you had?"

"One-and-a-half glasses. Not enough to wander off into the woods and get eaten by a bobcat."

"Wouldn't want that. Did you drink alone?"

"Unless my woodland friends opened a bottle up in the pine trees. There's an abundance of squirrels and chipmunks out here. And I heard an owl."

"I heard one last night," Gabe said. "I thought you'd go out with friends. You could have joined us. We all assumed you were tired and had other plans."

"Both true. It's fine, Gabe."

"You do have friends here?"

"I do. I'm still settling into new routines, but, yes, I have friends."

"I like Russ. He and Kylie are new to town. You all seem to have hit it off. Are they friends or just clients?"

"The friendship came first. It's probably easier to be

friends when you're planning a fun party than doing other client-based services. Knights Bridge has been keeping me busy lately, but I don't work exclusively here or even in the area."

"You're doing well on your own," he said.

"Thank you, yes, so far, so good. Buying a house was a big step for me, but I'm saving now for a trip. It killed me to give up traveling when I was broke—well, once I acknowledged I was broke. Technically I was broke and traveling. If I had room on my credit card for airfare and a decent hotel, off I went."

"But never to Wyoming," Gabe said quietly.

He thought he heard her breath catch. "No," she said. "I did poke you in the eye with that, didn't I? Sorry. I was taken aback about the party, I guess."

"Mark and I could have handled that better. He didn't know what he was stepping into."

"It all worked out," Felicity said.

"Are you happy?"

She stared straight ahead at the fire. "If I say yes, what will that mean to you?"

"That you're happy."

She glanced at him. "That simple, huh?" She faced the fire again. "Well, I'm happy right now, at this moment. That doesn't mean I don't have wants."

A couple of ways he could take that, but Gabe decided to be careful, a little judicious for a change. "But you're where you want to be, doing what you want to do."

"I could do without a mosquito finding me—" She stopped herself, sighing. "I'm being flippant. Sorry. Yes, Gabe, I enjoy my work, and I love living out here on the river."

"I always had a feeling you'd appreciate this place. I made a few suggestions to Mark about what kind of house would work here, the light, the views of the river. He was more into the technical aspects of the design and construction."

"He made sure the house wouldn't fall into the river," Felicity said.

Gabe laughed. "Something like that. I considered buying him out while we were building. I had it in my head I could loan or rent the house to family and friends, stay here when I was in town, but it wasn't practical at the time. I never saw myself spending much time in Knights Bridge, and I'd just had a start-up go bust and was throwing myself into the next one."

"The one that just sold for a gazillion?"

"Not a gazillion but yes, that one. Instead Mark bought me out." Gabe steadied his gaze on the flames. "I had you in mind when I made my recommendations about this place. I'd ask myself, *What would Felicity want in a house?*"

He turned to her in time to see red spread up her neck and into her face. It had nothing to do with the heat of the fire. He'd hit the wrong notes in his comments. She swooped to her feet, grabbed her wineglass and glared down at him. "Ruin the place for me, why don't you? Damn, Gabe. Now I get to sit out on the deck and wonder if you figured out it would have a nice view of the river."

Hell.

"This is my house now," she said. "*Mine.* There are no Flanagan ghosts here."

He said nothing as she spun around and stormed across the yard to the house. He heard her pound up the steps to the deck, tear open the French door and bang it shut. Since the windows were open he heard her bedroom door slam shut.

Gabe rubbed the back of his neck. He could feel the sweat. He'd screwed up. Being in front of young, eager would-be entrepreneurs had stirred up every hope, dream, insecurity, regret and frustration he'd had when he'd started out. Being around people he knew and respected, who were making a difference here in his hometown, living full lives, happy—he'd thought about his tarp-covered furniture at his sterile condo in Boston, a metaphor for his life.

He'd assumed Felicity would get where he was coming from, but how could she? He hadn't explained himself, had he?

"Idiot."

He hadn't tried to bring her into the conversation, or to take into account or ask what she might be thinking.

He could do better.

He walked barefoot across the cool grass and up to the deck, hesitating before he went inside. He continued down the hall to her room. Her door was shut. "Felicity…" He took a breath. "I made assumptions. It didn't occur to me you have a genuine attachment to this place. I should have asked."

She ripped open the door. "For about thirty seconds I let myself believe—I don't know what I let myself believe. You're not here because of me, and that's fine. It really is. You want or need or whatever to relive your past before you go back to Boston and your life."

"Now who's making assumptions?" He'd tried to insert a bantering note to his voice, but from her combative stance, he knew he'd failed. He held up a hand.

"Don't slam the door in my face, okay? You're not wrong, Felicity, but maybe this isn't about right and wrong." He searched for the right words but knew he'd never find them, not tonight. "Being here isn't what I thought it'd be."

"I have no idea what that means."

He smiled. "Me, either."

Her squared, stiff shoulders relaxed visibly, if only slightly. "All right. Truce."

"Let's put another log on the fire and talk," he said. "We can pour wine."

"All right." She sounded wary but not hostile or angry. "It's been a while since I was into the pinot grigio. It's not that good. I have a much better bottle of sauvignon blanc. It should be chilled by now." She gave him the slightest of irreverent smiles. "My new best friend Nadia left it for me. I wasn't going to tell you, but—well, what the hell. She'd appreciate the two of us splitting her wine while we talk about burning my house down."

"No one's going to burn your house down, Felicity, and Russ is making sure Nadia's boarding her flight."

"Shall I open the sauvignon blanc?"

"I don't want to drink Nadia's wine."

"It wasn't a test, but we can split the last of the pinot grigio."

"I don't really need wine," he said. "I just want to talk."

"Uh-oh. Then I might need wine." Felicity paused, her smile fading, their eyes connected. She sucked in an audible breath. "Oh. You're serious." She motioned behind her. "I'll grab the bug spray and be right out."

It wasn't the most romantic of gestures, but Gabe merely nodded. "I'll go put that log on the fire."

They dabbed on insect repellant and sat on the quilt side by side, legs stretched out in front of the fire. They skipped opening Nadia's bottle of wine. Wrong timing as far as Gabe was concerned, and Felicity agreed.

"You first," she said. "You gave me the three-second recap of your life since I vacated your couch. I'd like to know more."

He told her more but not everything—because everything would be tedious for both of them. She could fill in what he meant by working hard. "I had a good team," he said. "I did my best to respect them and treat them well. Everyone benefited when I sold the company."

"Including Nadia?"

"Yes, but I had no idea David would end their marriage. I don't believe David's buying the company had anything to do with the friction between him and Nadia, but it was bad timing for her. That's been the only issue since the sale."

"You're selling your condo," Felicity said. "Do you think you'll stay in Boston?"

"I've flirted with the idea, but I don't know where I'd go. I'm a die-hard Red Sox fan. Reason enough to stay right there. Then there's Shannon. She's irreplaceable, and she's rock-solid Boston. I'd hate to start from scratch with a new assistant unless the move was worth that aggravation."

"Has Shannon ever been to Knights Bridge?"

"Once, out of curiosity. She and her husband and kids stopped by on their way to the Berkshires one weekend. I think she was surprised to find flush toilets out here."

Felicity laughed, no hint of her earlier irritation. "What's next for you then?"

"I'm in the process of figuring that out. That's part of why I'm here. Dylan and I are talking. He invited me to participate in the boot camp." He shrugged. "It'll all work out."

"Now that's the Gabriel Flanagan I know. Don't get bogged down in the details. Just set a goal and get rolling. I'm glad you're doing well, Gabe. I have faith in you figuring out what's next."

"Thanks. That means a lot to me."

She rolled onto her knees and then stood up and grabbed a chunk of birch wood, its peeling bark lighting up the moment she placed it on the fire. "I should have saved that one for getting a fire started," she said, returning to her spot on the quilt.

He took the opportunity to switch the conversation back to her. "You seem to enjoy party planning, event management—whatever you want to call it."

"I do, very much. I only do the occasional wedding—it's its own specialty, really—but I might yet. I never say never. I learned so much working for a small, high-end event manager in Boston. She focused on corporate events. I traveled a fair amount, but most of my job was details." She smiled with a small shudder. "Lots and lots of details."

"What prompted you to go out on your own?"

"Several factors were involved. I wanted to buy a house and couldn't realistically afford Boston prices, and I wanted more control over my own schedule and what projects I worked on—and I knew I could do it.

I could make enough money as a solo entrepreneur to have the life I want."

"Here in Knights Bridge," Gabe said, as if he couldn't imagine such a thing.

"I love it here. I love the river, I love my gardens—I want to plant a vegetable garden. I want to put up a clothesline and hang my own laundry to dry. Boston's my city and I love it there, but Knights Bridge is home."

"Do your parents approve?"

"I haven't asked them, but they seem to."

"What about growth? Do you want to hire staff, expand—"

"Not right now. I hire contractors as needed."

"Today was a good day for you," Gabe said. "You impressed everyone there."

"Well, thank you. I hope so. Wine by the fire was my way of celebrating a job well done. What about you? I get that you're never satisfied, but do you take time to celebrate?"

"Celebrate what?"

She rolled her eyes. "Do you *ever* look back with a sense of pride or do you always feel unfulfilled—that there's one more hill to climb, hurdle to clear, million to make before you can celebrate?"

"I can do both," Gabe said, amused. "Celebrate and clear the next hurdle."

"Not at the same time. It's a good way to fall on your face."

He laughed. "I guess you have a point. I'm not dissatisfied or unfulfilled, Felicity. I just have a lot of ideas and like to stay busy."

"Do you want to take time to have a relationship, start a family—make a home for yourself?"

"Sure."

"When that becomes a goal, world, watch out."

"I do tend to laser-focus on any goal I set."

"Like telling me I don't belong in finance."

"I was right."

She smacked him playfully on the knee. "It's not about being right. It never was." She sighed, leaning back on her elbows, watching him. "But you *were* right. Sometimes I wish I had stayed and had it out with you—that I'd fought harder to maintain our friendship."

"Fight harder? You didn't fight at all, Felicity. Neither did I."

"Maybe our parting of ways was meant to be. I don't know that I'd have taken that first event management job with you breathing down my neck. I might have tried again as a financial analyst just to prove to you I could do it."

"Not a good motivation," Gabe said.

She shook her head. "No, definitely not. I also didn't want to admit failure to you. I didn't want you to criticize my new career as a backward step. I thought you'd want it both ways. I face my failure as a financial analyst *and* come out on the other end in a stable, high-paying job."

"You thought I'd look down on you for taking a job in event management?" He could hear the surprise in his voice. "Felicity, that's not who I am."

"I know that. I projected a lot onto you then. Turns out I like the work, and I'm good at it. I paid down my debt, reined in my spending and bought a house. Not bad, huh?"

He smiled. "Not bad at all."

She looked up at the starlit night sky. "I've never seen stars as bright as out here."

"It's a great night for stargazing."

An owl hooted in the woods. Gabe could hear the flow of the river. He noticed shadows in the darkness and the bright flames, slowly dying down. He shifted away from the fire's heat. It was by no means a cool night, but he liked having a fire, its atmosphere—its connection with his past. He absorbed the moment, being out here, now, with Felicity, talking with her about their lives—work, family, friends, plans. This was the Felicity MacGregor he'd known forever but also a new Felicity, more at ease in her own skin, less impulsive, not as hard on herself. He'd told her about his life, but there didn't seem much to tell. He worked. He traveled. He had friends all over the world. He had family in his small hometown that he didn't see often enough. He didn't have a community, not like Felicity did, now that she'd moved back to Knights Bridge.

She couldn't stop yawning next to him on the blanket. The mosquitoes weren't bad tonight, if only because of the bug repellant. The last flame flickered and started to go out, as if cueing them to head inside, call it a night. "I'm no good at sleeping in even after a late night," Felicity said, stirring next to him. "Do you want to stay out here for a while longer?"

Gabe considered how to respond. They were friends again. If she had any desire for something more, she had it tamped down deep. More likely it was nonexistent, despite their kiss yesterday. Nerves, probably. The moment. The past catching up with them. He could think of a dozen ways she'd dismiss what had happened, but he'd be lying to himself if he tried to pretend he didn't want something more. It wasn't nonexistent for him, and it wasn't even tamped down that deep. He just wasn't going to act on it. Not tonight, anyway.

Finally he nodded. "I'll wait for the fire to die down." He leaned toward her, kissed her on the forehead. "It's been good talking to you, Felicity. Really good."

"What time do you leave tomorrow?"

"Sometime in the morning. I don't have to rush back."

"Will you go straight to Boston?"

"For now. I'm having some work done on my place."

"It's never felt like home, has it?"

"I've never felt the need to have a real home before. I'm feeling it now." He smiled at her. "It's probably the Knights Bridge effect." He glanced around at this favorite spot, appreciated Mark's skill as an architect, his own input with the house. He shifted back to Felicity. "I'm glad you're happy here."

"I didn't buy this place to get under your skin. I had no idea you'd owned it with Mark and had input into the design. I knew you'd loved it here growing up, but more as a place to be while you plotted your exit from Knights Bridge."

"That's not inaccurate." Gabe patted her thigh. "Go on. Get some sleep. You've had a long day, but it's been good talking. I have no regrets about keeping you up."

She hesitated, as if she couldn't decide what to do. "See you in the morning," she said finally, jumping lightly to her feet with more energy than Gabe would have expected.

He didn't let her energy put ideas in his head...for about two seconds.

She hadn't reached the deck before he envisioned taking her to bed with him. But they'd just become friends again, and he didn't want to do anything to risk or complicate that—at least not yet. He could exercise control tonight. As he stared at the dying flames, he knew somehow, someway, he'd have another opportunity.

Fourteen

$\sim\!\!\circ\!\!\Im\!\!\Theta\!\!\Im\!\!\circ\!\!\sim$

Even with his late night, Felicity heard Gabe's bedroom door open and shut early in the morning. *Back to life in the country*, she thought, amused. She gave up on sleep herself, pulled on shorts, a T-shirt and sandals and headed to the kitchen.

No sign of Gabe.

She noticed the door to the deck was cracked, but he wasn't there, either. She figured he must have slipped outside and gone for a walk. She could see why. It was a beautiful morning, probably the best part of what would be a hot summer day.

She went outside and listened to the birds and looked down through the trees to the river. The Jane Austen tea party was that afternoon, but she didn't have to rush around now. She took the stairs to the grass and made her way to the path that led to the swimming hole. She could see herself at seventeen, taking this same route. She'd ridden her bike to the campsite and left it by the fireplace before she set off down to the river.

Gabe had found her sitting on a boulder with her feet in the water as she read a book. It'd been mid-

June, just a few days left in the school year. He'd finished the bulk of his homework, but she had one more paper to write.

She could see him now, jumping down from the path. "What're you reading?" he'd asked her.

She'd held up her book. *"Portrait of the Artist as a Young Man."*

"James Joyce. Irish author. I think I faked reading that one."

"And here I was hoping you could help me with my paper."

She hadn't been hoping anything of the sort. Gabe had kept his nose above water in his classes, doing the minimal amount of work to pass. She didn't try to guess what he'd absorbed despite his middling grades. She, on the other hand, had been conscientious with her studies.

He'd stepped onto her boulder. "Did you know I'd be coming out here this afternoon?"

"No idea."

"Not sitting on a rock pretending to read while you wait for me?"

"No, Gabe, I'm actually reading. It's a beautiful day. I wanted to sit by the river in the shade. Somehow it makes James Joyce easier to understand." She'd shut the book and set it on her lap. "You're going for a swim?"

"Yep. Want to join me?"

"I'm not wearing a swimsuit under my clothes."

"Skinny-dipping could get you in trouble out here if someone drives by."

"I didn't mean I plan to skinny-dip, Gabe. I'd have

to swim in my clothes. Then I'd have to bike home in wet clothes. I'll just watch you swim."

He'd shrugged. "Suit yourself."

"I will," she'd said. "I promise I'll dive in clothes and all to save you if you start to drown or hit your head on a rock."

"Now there's a temptation," he'd said with a grin. "It's hot out, Felicity. Your clothes will dry in no time."

"If I go swimming, then how would I finish my book?"

"It's called a break."

"Hmm." She'd glanced at her book and then back at him, and smiled. "Maybe a break is a good idea."

Before she could change her mind, she'd handed him the book, and he set it on the boulder. In a flash, he'd scooped her up and tossed her into the river. She'd tucked her legs into a cannonball and landed, squealing, in the water.

She'd always told herself she was like a sister to him. That was the first time she'd felt it might be otherwise. Popping up, laughing, yelling at him for not giving her any warning, she'd noticed the way he'd looked at her.

Not so brotherly, that look, she thought now, years later, on another warm, sunny day. She knew she needed to put Gabe out of her mind and let him get back to his life without any further complications from her. She had her own life here in Knights Bridge. That was why they hadn't let things get too far between them last night. Sleeping with each other might be a natural temptation, but it was one they needed to resist.

She didn't think it was that big a leap to assume he'd been tempted. Being out here with her was a throwback to their past, if not to a simpler time, at least to one that had led to one wild night together.

Best to leave that thought there, she told herself as she reached the swimming hole. She didn't see Gabe. Just as that day back in high school, she didn't have a swimsuit under her shorts and T-shirt, but this time she didn't care or hesitate. She got a running start, grabbed the rope and flung herself as far out into the river as she could. She let go and went into the water feetfirst.

When she surfaced, Gabe had materialized, treading water next to her. "I eased in from the bank," he said. "I didn't use the rope. I was thinking I'd catch you skinny-dipping."

"Ha. Don't you wish."

"I remember when I found you out here reading a book. James Joyce, right? Did you ever finish it or did you skim it and wing the paper?"

"I read the whole thing and wrote the paper."

"And got an A."

"Of course."

She swam past him toward the middle of the river. He joined her, and they found a cluster of underwater boulders and stood on them, waist deep in the water instead of over their heads. She saw now he had on shorts, not a swimsuit. No one else was out on the river—no canoes, kayaks, fishermen. Just her and Gabe.

He was already going for the rope, and she followed him.

She could have spent the entire day out there, jumping into the river from the rope and rocks, diving, swimming, just floating on her back next to Gabe, looking up at the summer sky. But after thirty minutes, they climbed onto the boulder where she'd read James Joyce and sat in the sun. She noticed rivulets of water in the bumps and crevices in the granite from her dripping T-shirt and shorts.

"You have a good life here, Felicity," Gabe said.

She smiled. "I do."

As the river water dried on his bare skin, she noticed the well-formed muscles in his chest and legs. She also noticed her T-shirt wasn't as modest as she'd thought.

"You'll stay in touch after I leave Knights Bridge?" he asked her.

"Do you want me to?"

"Sure. Let me know how things go with the badger party."

"I will," she said. "You're getting an invitation, you know."

"Russ mentioned it. I didn't think he was serious."

"Boston's not far."

He caught the ends of her dripping hair by her chin between his fingers. "Ant," he said. "It's gone now. Your hair will take a while to dry in this humidity." He kept his hand close to her face. "Never have been fussy about your hair, have you?"

"I'm your classic wash-and-go type."

"It works," he said. "I've missed you, Felicity. Right now I realize how much I've missed, too, by letting you stalk out of my life. We were damn good friends."

"Best buds, huh?"

His eyes darkened. He'd shifted slightly and was catching some of the shade, maybe. But that wasn't it, or at least not all of it. It was his natural intensity, his laser-like focus—directed at her at the moment. Entirely at her.

She cleared her throat. "Gabe…"

"Is that what you want? To be buddies again, the way we were when you slept on my couch?"

"I missed you, too. I used my anger at you to motivate me, never thinking…" She took in a breath. "Never thinking it'd be three years before I saw or spoke to you again."

"More than three. It was in the teens that day. It's, what, eight-five now?"

"Getting there," she said.

He eased his hand to the back of her neck and lowered his mouth to hers. "Let's see where we go from here, okay? But I don't think we're ever going to be just 'best buds' again." He smiled. "What do you think?"

Her skin seemed sensitized, as if every inch of her were alive, crying out for his touch. Her lips parted slightly, and their mouths touched, tentative at first, then less so—definitely less so. She put a hand on his upper arm, balancing herself as their kiss deepened. This wasn't the chaste kiss of friends or the reckless kiss of their teenaged past but something more. She shut her eyes, giving herself up to the sensations coursing through her. The taste of him, the touch of his hand on her wet, bare skin, the feel of the warm breeze, the sounds of the river. They all mixed together, stirring her senses and her emotions.

Then Gabe swore and sat up straight.

Felicity gaped at him. "What? Did a mosquito bite you?"

"Kayakers." He pointed up the river. "It wouldn't do for them to catch us."

She followed his gesture and spotted two brightly colored kayaks headed their way. "I guess it wouldn't."

He sighed. "A kiss is one thing, but we were headed to more than that."

"Think so?"

He grinned at her. "Yeah. I think so."

"Did you see the kayakers before you started that kiss? So you'd have an out and wouldn't get carried away?"

"I never get carried away. I'm always in supreme control of myself."

She rolled her eyes. "Oh, sure."

He winked. "I'm going to need another dip in the river. How about you?"

"Take your time. I'll meet you up at the house. I'll make coffee." She stood up on the wet boulder, mindful of not slipping. "I can't believe we did all this before breakfast."

He gave her a look that suggested "all this" wasn't, in fact *all* he'd wanted to do, but he eased into the water without comment, or before she could comment.

"Gabe," she muttered to herself. "Oh, Gabe."

He'd always been her best friend, but as she watched him swim hard, smooth strokes into the deep water, Felicity realized he'd always been more, too. Only she'd never let herself take that idea too far. Even their night together before college, she hadn't examined her feelings too deeply. She hadn't wanted to risk their friendship by getting soppy.

And here she was, doing it again.

She slipped into her sandals and walked back up the path to her house. She put on coffee and ducked into her room for a shower and dry clothes. When she emerged, Gabe was in the kitchen. He'd poured himself coffee. "I can pour you some—"

"It's no trouble, thanks."

"I wasn't sure when you'd be out of the shower." He took a sip of coffee. "I'll get out of your way, let you work. I might grab a bite at Smith's. Felicity…" He sucked in a breath before he continued. "I have to leave today, and I want to and I don't want to. I can't pinpoint why, but I'm going to guess it has to do with you."

"It has to do with being back here, on your grandfather's old campsite. If I'd rented an apartment at Moss Hill, you wouldn't think your ambivalence about leaving had anything to do with me."

"Wrong."

"Wrong? You can't just tell me I'm wrong. I'm giving you an opinion."

"I disagree. Better?"

She poured coffee. "Marginally."

"I disagree because I'd have still gotten a rope and tied it to a tree and found a way to get you down to our old swimming hole, because it was meant to be." He set his mug on the counter and stood straight. "There. Chew on that while I'm at Smith's making my way through a stack of buttermilk pancakes."

He strutted off down the hall to the guest room.

Only word for it, Felicity thought, arms across her chest. *Strut.* As if he *knew* what she was thinking— knew the inner workings of her mind and heart, her deepest desires, what was *good* for her…

Which she realized she didn't find annoying, not the way she would have three years ago.

He wasn't telling her what to think or feel or what

she was thinking and feeling. For once, he was telling her what *he* thought and felt, at least in his Gabe way. He believed their kiss by the river was meant to be. That swimming, leaping from the rope, laughing and enjoying each other's company—all of it was meant to be. In saying so, she'd felt as if he'd reached deep into her mind and heart.

In two minutes, he returned to the kitchen with his duffel bag. "Thanks for putting me up."

"No problem. Safe trip."

"It's just to Boston. Come visit." He smiled as he kissed her on the cheek. "You won't have to sleep on the couch."

By the time she caught her breath, he was gone, the kitchen screen door slowly shutting behind him.

Fifteen

Gabe rapped on the open door to his grandfather's cozy apartment at Rivendell, Knights Bridge's only assisted-living facility. It was located down a quiet road on a ridge with glimpses of the reservoir in the distance. "Hey, Gramps, sorry I missed your hundred-and-twentieth birthday."

The old man grinned, rising from his lounger. "Good thing you didn't go into comedy. You never were funny."

They embraced, and Gabe could feel how thin and bony his grandfather had become since his last visit. One of Rivendell's few male residents, John Gabriel Flanagan had been born and raised in Knights Bridge. He'd lived away from home once, when he joined the army at the tail end of World War II and served in Europe for two years. When he returned, he'd married his high school sweetheart, who'd waited for him while working at the cafeteria at the elementary school. He'd gotten a job at a nearby factory, she'd quit her job and they'd raised four children together. Three girls and a boy. Two of Gabe's aunts still lived in the area but not in Knights Bridge itself. One had moved to Tennessee after high school and had never looked back, but she visited at least once a year. All were married with grown children and grandchildren.

Mickey Flanagan, Gabe's father, the youngest, liked to call himself the no-account Flanagan. He was the one who could never quite get his act together—the dream-chaser who was still, in his late fifties, ever hopeful of finding his proverbial pot of gold at the end of a rainbow. He'd graduated from high school at the top of his class and was accepted at every college he'd applied to, settling on UMass-Amherst because it was the most affordable. He hadn't lasted. He'd dropped out his sophomore year and hit the road, the start of a long history of unfulfilled dreams, restless optimism and disappointments, at least by his standards. To everyone else, Mickey Flanagan was a great guy, the life of the party.

He'd finally returned to Knights Bridge after a few years "seeing the country" and married a nursing student, another local, a woman who shared his optimism and believed in his dreams and had many of her own. They'd settled into life in their small town, raising their sons, making a living, having fun. His father in particular had been ever hopeful a better life—a different life—lay just ahead, if only he kept believing it would happen, never mind taking consistent action, seeing things through and having any kind of realistic plan.

Gabe was in college when his mother was diagnosed with cancer. At her funeral, he'd seen how much she'd meant to his father, despite his chronic dissatisfaction with his life—at least what had looked to Gabe like dissatisfaction. Maybe it hadn't been. Maybe it had just been his father's optimistic, restless nature. He never gave up.

His grandfather snapped his fingers in front of Gabe's face. "Lost in thought? Tune in. I've got cookies." He pointed at a tin of Danish butter cookies. "I keep a stash handy."

"Sorry, Gramps. Mind wandered. I'll skip cookies. I can't stay long, but are you up for a walk? It's hot—"

"Good. I'm always cold these days. Let me grab my cane. I don't need you to hold my hand. I can still get around on my own."

"Okay, good to know."

They walked down the hall to the sunroom and went out that way through sliding glass doors to a trim lawn and garden bursting with summer flowers. It was hot, but they edged onto a shaded, paved walkway, suitable for canes, walkers and wheelchairs. Gabe noticed his grandfather moved well, if more slowly than just a year ago. "How was California?" he asked.

"Sunny," Gabe said with a grin.

"You moving out there?"

"I toyed with the idea of relocating there."

They passed through pine-scented shade. "You could move me out with you. Sun shines all the time. I don't mind assisted living, but I knew every old lady in this place when we were kids. One more reminds me I wet my pants in first grade and I'm packing up and living in my car."

Gabe grinned at the old man. "Mark says you have a crush on Daisy Farrell."

"Wouldn't do me any good if I did. Daisy was and always will be Tom Farrell's gal."

Gabe remembered Tom Farrell, a longtime Knights

Bridge fire chief who'd died a couple of years ago. "At least you have friends here."

"A few old cranks, too, but not many. I'm not as hard on people as I was as a younger man. Getting old isn't for the faint-hearted, that's for sure. Thought I'd be in an urn by now."

Gabe wasn't surprised by his grandfather's blunt manner, but he hadn't had a dose of it in a while. "Instead you're here talking to me. Imagine that."

"Yeah. My hotshot grandson." He slowed his pace, then paused by a patch of daisies. "You're going to be an uncle. That change things for you?"

"It's a factor."

His grandfather peered at him. "A factor? It's not like you're buying a used car and its mileage is a 'factor.'"

"Well, it would be," Gabe said lightly. "I didn't get much sleep last night. Cut me some slack."

"Ha. You stayed with Felicity MacGregor." He waved a hand. "Not asking."

"I sat out by the fire in your old fireplace. Alone."

His grandfather raised an eyebrow, skeptical.

Gabe grinned. "Mostly alone, but it's not what you think." Time to change the subject. "I should stop and see Dad on the way out of town."

"He's on his way here. He got wind of a Jane Austen tea party this afternoon and wants to talk me into dressing up as a Regency guy. He doesn't fit into any of the tights or I swear he'd do it. Say what you will about your father, he's game for anything."

"Do you fit into the tights?" Gabe asked, amused.

"It doesn't matter. I'd never get them off and I'm not asking one of the aides to help me."

"The sight of you in tights would get all the old ladies excited."

"The sight of *you* in tights would."

Gabe let that comment slide past him. They resumed their walk, the path looping past empty birdfeeders, ready to be filled for winter, back toward the sunroom.

"Your father had a rough time after your mother died," his grandfather said, his gait steady as he walked next to Gabe. "He's got his act together these days. Well." He gave a slight, knowing grin. "As much as he ever will, Mickey being Mickey. He's got a new woman in his life, but he still misses your mother. They didn't always bring out the wisest in each other, but they were a pair."

"That they were," Gabe said with a rush of affection.

When they returned to his grandfather's apartment, Mickey Flanagan was just arriving.

"Hey, Pops, I thought I'd find you napping in the sunroom, and you're out plotting to take over the world with Gabe." He nodded to his younger son. "Hey, there."

"I was going to stop by after visiting Gramps."

"Yeah, yeah." His father grinned, deep lines at the corners of his eyes. His hair had turned gray but he was as rail thin as ever—no change there. "You never could lie worth a damn. That's a good thing, by the way."

Truth had rarely been a casualty in the Flanagan family, but frankness often had been, if only to avoid hurting someone's feelings. Gabe had overcompensated, perhaps, by being blunt—often more so than he needed to be. Hence, his fight with Felicity that wintry February morning. He'd learned to be more diplomatic since then. Oddly enough, one of his tactics to avoid saying too much was to say nothing at all, with romantic partners in particular. He wouldn't lie so much as avoid the truth when it was uncomfortable. He'd never had the urge to avoid and dissemble with Felicity, but look what'd happened when he'd blurted what had been on his mind? No brownies and three years of the cold shoulder.

Not that he'd done anything about it.

"Thanks, Dad," Gabe said. "You're looking good. Getting close to retiring, aren't you?"

"I'll never retire. I love working on cars and will as long as I can. I like working at home. I've fixed up the shed out back since you were there last. I'm restoring a couple of classic motorcycles."

"That's great," Gabe said.

His grandfather hung his cane on a hook by his favorite chair and sat down with a sigh. "Wear a helmet, Mickey. Your luck, you'll ram one of those motorcycles into a stone wall."

"I didn't say I'd be riding them."

"You will be. It's how you're wired."

Gabe didn't come between them. His father and grandfather had a relationship built on unconditional love but tested by their different takes on life. Both were devoted to family and friends, but for Johnny Flanagan, stability, duty and predictability mattered more than ambition, risk and crazy dreams. "Best to want what you have," he'd tell Gabe. For Mickey Flanagan, the grass was always greener doing what he wasn't doing at the moment. He'd settled down some in recent years, but it hadn't happened overnight.

They visited for a few minutes, but Gabe could see his grandfather was tired. His father leaned over and kissed the old man on the cheek. "I'll walk Gabe out. You take care, Pop, okay? I'll see you next week."

Gabe gave his grandfather a hug, realizing, as he had for the past few years, this visit could be their last. He hoped it wouldn't be. California suddenly seemed so damn far away when he'd tried telling himself it was just a plane ride, but Boston might as well have been the moon for his father and grandfather.

"You take care," Gabe said, hearing the catch in his voice.

"Call me anytime, Gabe. Grace Webster knows how to do video calls. Says it's easy. Skype or FaceTime or some damn thing."

"We'll set one up," Gabe promised.

His grandfather yawned. "I'll take a short nap. I've got to be ready for that tea."

"Not giving in on the tights?" Mickey asked, grinning.

"I don't want to give any of the girls a heart attack."

On that note, Gabe left with his father, neither speaking until they were outside. His father had parked his motorcycle next to Gabe's car. "Nice," his father said. He nodded back toward the building. "I visit at least once a week. It was his choice to move in here. He didn't want to come live with me."

"It was an option?"

"Yeah. I have a spare bedroom. You're welcome to it next visit. I'm on my own at the moment. I have a lady friend but we're not…you know. I don't live in a fancy town or a fancy neighborhood, but it suits me."

"Thanks for the offer," Gabe said, meaning it.

His father squinted at him in the hot sun. "I hear you stayed at the house you and Mark built out on the river. Does it bug you Felicity MacGregor owns it now?"

"It doesn't bug me, but I'd have bought it."

"Might have mentioned that to your brother."

Gabe shrugged, smiling. "Might have."

"It's just as well." His father held up a hand. "I know you, Gabe. I know how you think. I know you better than you give me credit for."

"Know what I'm thinking now?"

His father sighed. "Do I want to know?"

"Sure. I'm thinking I'd like to give that old motor-cycle of yours a spin when you get it restored."

"It's a beauty." His expression turned serious. "You'll stay in touch, won't you?"

"Sure, Dad. Always."

"You're doing okay?"

Gabe nodded. "Just fine. No worries."

"You're doing fine financially. What about the rest of your life?"

"We'll see," Gabe said, leaving it there.

His father hesitated. "All right, I won't go there. It's your life." He looked down at his feet—he had on old sport sandals—and then raised his eyes again to Gabe. "The woman I'm seeing is a nice gal, just retired early from the bank. Worked for Felicity's father."

"That's good, Dad. Do I know her?"

"Probably not." He cleared his throat, started for

his motorcycle. "I should get moving. Have a good trip home."

"Come see me sometime."

"I just might. Felicity told me I can stop by her place anytime. She appreciates that it was a special place for us. She always was a nice, pretty girl. Mark says you two went out to the swimming hole. Your mother used to worry you boys would split your heads open or drown. I didn't. I figured the worst that could happen was a few stitches or a broken wrist or toe or something. Nothing life-threatening. Kids need to take a few risks."

"The attentive dad," Gabe said with a grin.

"Mark already told me he's doing things different with his kids than I did with mine. Hell, I hope so, although you two came out all right, no thanks to me. Your mother…" He cleared his throat. "She did her best."

"She *was* the best, Dad," Gabe said. He winked at his father. "You provided Mark and me a certain level of motivation."

His father laughed. "You could say that. See you, son. Safe travels."

He put on his helmet and climbed onto his old motorcycle. In a moment, he eased out of his parking space and cruised onto the main road. Gabe sighed. Some saw Mickey Flanagan's unrealized potential. At that moment, Gabe saw a man in his late fifties who was enjoying his life and work. He couldn't find it in him to judge his father and the demons he'd fought. A by-product of time, his own success and what it meant—and didn't mean—or just being back in his hometown?

The Felicity MacGregor effect, maybe.

He'd have thought of her, anyway, but he recognized her Land Rover turning into the parking lot. She came to a stop in the spot his father had just vacated and hopped out, apparently unaware of his presence. She lifted the hem of what appeared to be a pretty, low-cut dress out of a Jane Austen novel. She had her hair pinned up, with corkscrew curls bouncing at her temples.

"Oh, Gabe," she said, stopping abruptly. "I didn't see you. I just passed your father. That was him on the motorcycle, wasn't it?"

"In all his glory. We were visiting my grandfather."

"I'm here to set up for the afternoon tea."

Gabe smiled. "That explains the dress."

"Mmm. Yes." Spots of color appeared in her cheeks. "It's not too revealing, is it? It's about a half size too small, I think."

"It's fine. Perfect."

She tugged at the bodice, hiking it up to cover more of the swell of her breasts. "I have a shawl I can put on when I'm in air-conditioning. Grace Webster hasn't talked your grandfather into wearing one of the gentlemen's Regency outfits, has she?"

"Not a chance."

"You wouldn't be interested—"

"No."

She grinned. "Not even the top hat?"

"Is there anything I can do to help you set up?"

She shook her head. "I did most of the work upstream since I had the boot camp yesterday, too. None of the men signed up for the tea, by the way."

"Imagine that," Gabe said. "I bet a few will change

their minds. Are all the women wearing Regency dresses?"

"I doubt it, but I brought dresses for anyone who wants to wear one. They're fun. I did my hair the best I could, but I've never been good with a curling iron and gels and wax and whatnot."

"You own a curling iron?"

"Present from my mother. She told me not to read any hints into it." Felicity motioned to her Rover. "I wouldn't mind a hand with some of the boxes if you have a minute."

Gabe carried the largest of the boxes to the sunroom where the tea was being held. Felicity had collected a mix of china teapots, cups and saucers and plates from various people she knew as well as her own collection of dishes featuring Peter Cottontail and other Beatrix Potter critters. "My grandmother gave them to me," she told Gabe. "She loved Beatrix Potter and got a kick out of sharing our name with Farmer McGregor. Not quite the same spelling and no one in my family's had a farm in the last hundred years."

"Details," Gabe said, smiling. "It'll be a great party."

She returned his smile, her left-side corkscrew curls already unwinding.

Grace Webster—Dylan McCaffrey's grandmother—rose from a rocking chair that faced the lawn and garden where Gabe had walked with his grandfather. In her nineties, Grace was frail but mentally sharp. She set a small pair of binoculars on a side table and started on about various birds she'd just spotted, but she quickly focused on the upcoming tea. As a former English teacher, she had more than a passing familiarity with Jane Austen.

Gabe decided to leave Felicity to her tea, but he didn't get out of the room before Grace tried to get him into tights. "I'm sure they'd fit you," she said.

He could just imagine. "Time for me to make my exit."

Grace's nonagenarian eyes twinkled. "What? It could be fun. We're old. We're not dead."

"You'd make a good Mr. Darcy," Felicity added.

"Rich, arrogant, damn good-looking. I could do that. Not doing the tights." In fact, he wasn't doing any of it. "Have fun at your tea. Goodbye again, Felicity."

She curtsied. "Farewell, Mr. Flanagan."

On his way out, he passed Maggie Sloan, who'd arrived with food. He offered her a hand, but she assured him she had everything under control. "You could look less relieved, Gabe," she said with a laugh.

"They need a Mr. Darcy."

"I've a surprise for that. Seize the moment, Gabe. Run."

"I don't need to be told twice. Good seeing you."

And he was out of there.

Sixteen

To Grace Webster's delight, her grandson surprised everyone at the tea—including Felicity—when he showed up in a partial Regency outfit, arranged by his wife and Maggie Sloan. Felicity thanked Dylan, who seemed to get a kick out of the entire experience. "I used to wear a hockey uniform," he whispered. "This isn't all that different."

It fit him well, too. It wouldn't have fit Gabe—not that he'd have acquiesced even if it had fit. But he had a grandfather in Rivendell, not a grandmother, and perhaps more to the point, he wasn't a part of the fabric of the town any longer. His life in Boston, or wherever, had beckoned.

Most of the residents—men and women alike—assembled in the sunroom for a mini fashion show. Grace Webster provided commentary on Jane Austen's life and works, with details on each of the dresses modeled by Felicity and a half-dozen various elderly women thoroughly enjoying themselves. Grace had done meticulous research, and she had good teacher's instincts and experience to know when her audience had had enough.

As Felicity cleaned up after the tea, she found herself wishing Gabe had stayed, but she hadn't asked him to. He might not have realized he could have stayed. Whenever she was at Rivendell, she appreciated the rich lives the residents had. She wasn't naive. Many of the men and women who'd enjoyed today's tea had chronic health issues, and they would be the first to say they had fewer days ahead of them than behind them. Felicity had known most of them her entire life. She liked being around them. Her own grandparents were gone. Her maternal grandmother, the last, had died a few months after she'd quit finance and started work as an event planner.

Several of the residents had pulled her aside, reminiscing about how her grandfather had helped them get mortgages when they were starting out in life. He knew them, and he knew they were good for it, they'd tell her. That had been a different world from the one she'd entered as a financial analyst, but she'd never wanted to follow her grandfather and father into local banking. That world, too, had changed since her grandfather's day.

By the time she returned home, she was dead on her feet. The house seemed so quiet. She peeled off her Regency dress—imagining Gabe was there—and forced herself to pull the sheets off the bed he'd used and throw them in the wash.

That was enough for now.

Tomorrow she'd turn her attention to Kylie's book launch and other events further out in her calendar. The work she did now, upstream, would make everything smoother later on.

She placed a slice of leftover tea cake on a plate and

poured a glass of champagne, walked out to the deck and sat on the most comfortable chair. It didn't have a footstool, but she put her feet up on the low coffee table and set her goodies on the side table. A cool breeze floated through the trees. She could smell the river, and she could hear ducks not too far in the distance. She thought she could smell ashes from Gabe's fires the past two nights, but she decided that was her imagination.

She picked up her champagne and held it up to the trees. "To me," she said with a smile.

She'd managed her biggest party in Knights Bridge to date, with its very own movers and shakers, and she'd segued right into a Jane Austen tea. She'd survived her odd encounters with Nadia Ainsworth. She'd developed a rough plan for Kylie's badgers.

Most of all, she'd gotten through having Gabe Flanagan as a houseguest.

They were friends again, weren't they?

Maybe. She thought so. He could also go back to Boston and she wouldn't hear from him for another three years. For sure any friendship wouldn't be the same as the one they'd had before she'd marched out of his apartment that cold February morning. It couldn't be. They weren't the same people they'd been then.

Felicity raised her glass a bit higher. "Cheers, Gabriel Flanagan, wherever you are, whatever is next for you—for us."

By noon the next day, Felicity was deep into the world of the clever, fictional Badgers of Middle Branch. She packed a rough version of two of the badgers in her tote bag and walked to the Mill at Moss Hill and met Kylie and Russ on their balcony.

"These are fantastic," Kylie said, grabbing one of the tiny stuffed badgers and holding it up. "Sherlock Badger is going to have friends. I hope he doesn't get jealous because they're cuter than he is."

Russ turned to Felicity. "Kylie thinks Sherlock is real," he half whispered. "Indulge her."

Kylie grinned. "I considered asking Sherlock to walk me down the aisle."

Her artistic imagination and sense of fun were somehow compatible with her ex-navy security consultant husband. Russ clearly appreciated his bride's talents as an illustrator and storyteller. The mysteries of love, Felicity thought as she picked up the second half-done badger. "I see this one as the mom badger and the one you're holding as the dad badger. We can dress them in outfits from the first book in the series. Does that work for you?"

"Love it," Kylie said. "I do okay with a needle and thread but best to farm out any real sewing. Do you have anyone in mind? Can I help find someone?"

"Still working on that. I can sew, but it'll be faster to get someone else to do it."

"I can help, but you'll know more people in town than Russ and I do. You grew up here. You'll never be a newcomer."

For whatever *that* was worth. Felicity wondered what it must be like for her new friends to look at her hometown through fresh eyes. They wouldn't see the pre-renovation boarded up windows at Moss Hill, or remember Mark and Gabe as teenagers plotting their exit from Knights Bridge. It wasn't a positive or a negative, just a different relationship with their new home.

They reviewed the guest list, the schedule for the

evening and everything that needed to happen between now and Friday. As events went, the book-launch party wasn't complicated, but Kylie, Felicity had discovered, was afraid no one would come. Even with RSVPs, she was convinced everyone who'd promised to be there would bail at the last minute and she'd be there at the library, alone with Russ, Felicity and her badger friends. Despite her success as Morwenna Mills, Kylie Shaw had some stubborn insecurities.

Kylie set the dad badger next to his wife on the table. "I spoke with my sister, Lila, this morning, and she says she'll be there. I asked what she'd do if a veterinarian emergency came up, and she assured me she'll have backup. Our parents are on a trip, so it won't be them. They'd have gone at a different time, but they planned the trip before I set a date for the party. I don't want them flying in from Tuscany early." She brushed at her fair hair, the heat and humidity already frizzing it up. "Even if it's just Lila and us, we'll have a great time."

"I look forward to meeting your sister," Felicity said.

"She's amazing." Kylie smiled at her husband. "You don't have to be there if work comes up, especially in California—"

"It won't," Russ said. "I tied up all those loose ends when I was out there last week. Work won't interfere. I'll be at the party. I wouldn't miss it."

"I'm an introvert. I have to angst about these things." She spoke without any undertone of self-criticism. She turned again to Felicity. "Russ has a few things he wants to discuss with you. I'll go inside and look over the work-back schedule. I can access it on my phone. You emailed it to me, right?"

Felicity nodded, and Kylie thanked her, jumped to her feet and dashed inside.

"It's not as cloak-and-dagger as it sounds," Russ said with a smile. "Kylie's working on a new badger who does security at tall buildings in the city and visits Middle Branch to unwind. Her head's in that world right now. He's younger than Sherlock. Apparently they don't get along at first."

"Do you get approval on this new character?"

"Input, not approval." Clearly that was fine with him. He sat forward, folding his hands on the table. "I wanted to talk to you about Nadia Ainsworth. She's back in California. I checked. I don't think she's an immediate concern, and she might not be one at all."

"But?"

"I did some digging on her."

Felicity tried to ignore the twist of tension in her stomach. "Anything I need to know?"

"Maybe. Her history isn't that different from what she told you and Gabe. She worked with him on an early start-up that didn't go well and then continued with him on this latest one, which did go well. She put her heart and soul into the company, but she wasn't in senior management or even an employee. Gabe then sold it to her husband, David Ainsworth, just as he— David—bailed on Nadia."

"I know that much," Felicity said. "Most of it, anyway."

Russ nodded. "Bear with me. David's new team brought in their own customer development specialist, so Nadia was out of a major client as well as a husband. Meanwhile her grandmother back East died. She told me she's taking some time off to settle her grandmother's affairs, regroup and figure out what's next."

Felicity welcomed a slight, cool breeze off the water. "What about event planning?"

"She oversaw several corporate events Gabe held to get everyone together. He did them at least twice a year given that his people all worked remotely, whether they were employees or freelancers. The last retreat was at a resort in Aspen."

"Nadia probably coordinated with the resort's staff planner who did most of the work." Felicity frowned, considering Russ's words. "She stretched the truth a bit on that one, didn't she?"

"That's correct," Russ said, nothing light about his tone. "She has no business relationship or any other kind of relationship with Gabe at the moment. There was no logical reason for her to have contacted you the way she did."

"I see."

"My guess is Gabe was taken off guard by her sudden appearance here," Russ added. "He strikes me as a decent guy, and it didn't occur to him she'd try to get information from you, maybe get under your skin."

"What does she want from him? Can you say?"

Russ sighed. "A bad divorce, the loss of a major client, not having Gabe in her life day-to-day—whatever her feelings toward him—and her grandmother's death all at once is a lot. Then she finds out Gabe is presenting at Dylan McCaffrey's first boot camp, and his childhood friend Felicity is organizing the day. I'm not sounding the alarm, but my guess is this woman is a bit jealous of you because you have what she wants."

"Which is what? I'm not planning Gabe's company retreats, I'm not a customer development specialist, I'm not married and my grandmothers are gone, too."

"But you have Gabe's attention and interest," Russ said without skipping a beat.

Felicity grabbed the two badgers and tossed them into her tote. "Gabe and I grew up together. That's it. There's nothing else there. I organized the boot camp party for him because Mark asked me to—which made perfect sense since I was the planner for the rest of the day." She sat up straight. "End of story."

Russ's eyebrows went up.

Felicity crossed her arms on her chest. "What? Go ahead, Russ. Say it."

"All right," he said, clearly reluctant. "You two might not realize it, but everyone else can see the connection you and Gabe have with each other. You two have known each other since nursery school. That's something Nadia doesn't have and never will have with him."

"We weren't speaking for a few years."

Russ nodded. "Reconnecting could fuel her bitterness. Gabe's happy. Nadia's miserable. She doesn't have to have a romantic interest in him herself to be obsessed with you."

"Gabe and I were never romantically involved." Felicity all but squirmed at her near-lie, but she would argue their one night together hadn't been about romance. She wasn't sure if Russ noticed her discomfort. Probably, she thought. "We were never a couple or anything like that. You know."

"Yeah. I think I do."

Felicity suspected he did know, but she shuddered,

thinking about what might be running through Nadia Ainsworth's head. "Jealousy and envy are bitter emotions to have take hold of you," she said. "They can make a person irrational. I haven't experienced that myself, but I've seen others who have—on both sides. Maybe Nadia's looking for a distraction from her grief over her job, her marriage and her grandmother, or she's creating drama because she's bored. If she's in California, we don't need to worry about her, though, do we?"

"Just let me know if she contacts you," Russ said. "If she does, ignore her. Don't answer the phone, don't respond to texts, emails or voice mails. Tell me. Let me handle her."

"If she shows up on my doorstep again or leaves me a bottle of wine?"

"Call me. I'm right here down the road. Or call the police. Don't take chances."

"I often leave my doors unlocked—"

"Don't." He smiled then, as if deliberately toning down some of his intensity. "You shouldn't be doing that, anyway. I know it's a small town, but still."

"An ounce of prevention and all that."

"Exactly."

That off Russ's chest, Kylie rejoined them, and they shared lunch with Felicity on the balcony. She'd brought a few leftovers from the Jane Austen tea that were a huge hit. "We'll take a walk along the river after lunch," Kylie said as she finished the last of the Victorian sponge cake. "We can burn off the extra calories."

Felicity laughed. "No calories in Maggie Sloan's cooking."

Russ and Kylie refused to let her help with cleanup.

She had badgers to deal with, after all. Felicity thanked them and headed home along the river, content with her life—but wishing she'd find Gabe sitting on her deck or down at their swimming hole. Even without Russ's take on Nadia, Felicity felt she and Gabe had unfinished business. Plus, she thought, she just wanted to see him, talk to him, laugh with him.

She groaned, blaming the hot, hazy early summer afternoon for her emotions.

There was no Gabe, of course, when she arrived back at her house, just tiny black ants that had discovered a gooey crumb on her kitchen floor.

She threw her hands on her hips. "How'd you guys get here so fast?"

She dealt with the ant mess, welcoming the sense of normalcy that came with it. Ants weren't unusual this time of year.

Dealing with a potential stalker *was* unusual.

Felicity took her laptop out to a shaded spot on the deck and checked her messages. No texts, emails or voice mails from anyone, never mind Nadia Ainsworth.

As she worked, Felicity noticed dark clouds gathering to the west, adding a gray cast to the river. The air was still, oppressively hot and humid. She welcomed the cold front that the dark clouds signaled was moving in, but she'd happily skinny-dip in an isolated spot in the river right now. Probably not a good idea to be swimming when lightning struck.

She went inside and sat in front of a fan in the living room. It was one of those rare days when she wished Mark had installed air-conditioning.

A text came through. She glanced at her screen. "Gabe," she whispered as she read it.

Made it to Boston. Thanks again for everything. What are you up to?

She typed her answer: Resisting our swimming hole.

Not good to swim alone.

Who says I'm alone?

But you are.

She smiled, surprised she wasn't annoyed. I am. Storm's coming. No swimming for me. Working. You?

Always working. TTYL

Should she bring up Nadia? Felicity shook her head, but she'd known she wouldn't before she'd posed the question to herself. She typed a quick response: Talk soon.

Two minutes later, Gabe sent her a short video of bulldog puppies, a throwback to their pre-fight friendship. She watched the video twice, smiling even as she warned herself not to get sucked in by Gabriel Flanagan. He liked to have things his way, and she wasn't going to twist herself into knots to please him. That didn't mean she knew what they were to each other after the past few days, but if she wanted a man in her life, Gabe was a distraction if not an outright impediment—not because she couldn't have male friends but because of their history, because they'd kissed at the swimming hole.

Because they *weren't* just friends and maybe never had been.

If he were here, what would they be doing now, with a storm moving in on a hot, sweaty day?

Not a question that needed an answer, Felicity decided as she got back to work on Kylie's badgers. It wasn't long before she heard thunder rumbling in the distance. The storm hit soon after, bringing high winds, heavy rain, thunder and lightning and flickering power but no damage on Felicity's stretch of the river. She took advantage of the weather to put away her laptop and add a few finishing touches to her badger couple. She'd never been particularly crafty, but she wanted a decent prototype for whomever she found to sew them.

A needle prick that drew blood convinced her to start making calls.

She grabbed a bandage out of her first-aid kit in the kitchen, managing not to drip blood on her badgers. She flashed back to her life before returning to Knights Bridge and moving into her house on the river. She loved Boston. She'd never tired of it—it was close enough she could slip into the city for the day. She had friends she could stay with overnight now that she was no longer living and working there. Like Mark Flanagan, Olivia McCaffrey and Maggie and Brandon Sloan, Felicity had done her bit in the city. She didn't know about the others, but she'd moved back to Knights Bridge because she'd *wanted* to.

Gabe, she knew, would never want to move back to his hometown.

She dug out a name for a local seamstress, but she held off on making the call. Instead she called Olivia and Jess, and by dinnertime, Felicity, with Kylie's permission, had a plan. Audrey Frost, Olivia and Jess's grandmother, would get together a group of her friends at Rivendell who loved to sew and they would take on the badgers. Audrey, one of the younger residents, loved the idea. Felicity drove out to the assisted-living facility and spoke with her, and in minutes, they had enough volunteers to do the job.

A former school bookkeeper in town, Audrey was matter-of-fact. "What can go wrong? If a few of them end up looking more like pigs than badgers, there's no harm. But they won't. We have some brilliant crafty types here."

Felicity was both pleased and relieved to leave the project in Audrey's capable hands.

The badgers settled, she returned home, enjoying the cooler, dryer air as she grabbed a bottle of wine and went out to the deck, taking one last look at Gabe's puppy video.

In the morning, Felicity drove into Amherst for supplies for her badger seamstresses. Although not that far from Knights Bridge, the busy, upscale college town and her smaller, quieter hometown were in many ways a world apart. She dropped the supplies off at Audrey Frost's apartment at Rivendell. "Don't you worry about a thing," Audrey said. "We have hundreds of years of sewing experience in this place. Go on, now. Leave the Badgers of Middle Branch to us."

Felicity headed out, relieved that Audrey was in charge of the badgers. She made a detour to Carriage Hill on her way home. Jessica and Olivia were sitting in chairs outside on the terrace and were comparing their experiences with morning sickness. They reiterated their confidence in their grandmother and her abilities to sew and organize the making of the badgers. "Grace has arthritis in her hands and can't hand-sew," Olivia added, referring to Dylan's grandmother. "But she's game to do whatever she can. They'll have a blast."

When Felicity headed home after a quick stop at the country store in the village, she found herself restless and out of sorts. She couldn't explain why—or maybe she didn't want to delve into why.

She peeked into the room where Gabe had stayed and sighed. "Yeah," she whispered. "He's why you can't sit still."

She headed out to the deck, the cool, dry breeze seeming to bring with it an urge to tell Gabe about her day. This restlessness, nostalgia, loneliness—whatever it was—had to pass.

She was relieved when her phone rang, and she saw Kylie's number on her screen. A distraction. *Good.* She assumed it was about the upcoming party, but Kylie started by assuring her it wasn't about work. "Russ and I are heading to Smith's for a quick bite," she said. "Join us?"

Felicity seized the chance to get out with friends. "I'd love to. I'll be ready."

Fifteen minutes later, they picked her up. As they drove along the river into the village, Felicity sensed herself beginning to relax, feeling more at ease in Knights Bridge now than she had growing up here. She'd made the right decision in returning. It was home.

Felicity invited Russ and Kylie in when they dropped her off at her house after a friendly, largely work-free dinner. She and Kylie had wine, but Russ stuck to water. He wanted to take a look at her "security setup."

"I just want to do due diligence," he said.

Felicity pointed to the doors to her deck. "I did lock them. My 'security setup' consists of regular locks, no alarm system, no weapons outside of the knife drawer and things like my old softball bat. I did have my badgers couple, but I gave them to Audrey Frost as prototypes."

Russ didn't laugh at her remark about badgers, but Kylie smiled.

"Good cell service?" Russ asked.

"Most of the time. I don't have a panic room or anything like that, either."

"Any windowless room where you could lock yourself against an intruder while you waited for police?"

"No, except for a closet."

"Does it lock?"

"I never noticed. Probably not." Felicity shook her head. "Russ, this is Knights Bridge."

"I'd ask the same questions anywhere. It's just an assessment. I'm not saying you need a panic room. You just need a plan. Your closest neighbor isn't exactly within shouting distance."

"A mile," Felicity said. "I'm in good shape. I can run if necessary."

"Stay close to the road if you ever do need to run. Don't head down to the river. It's too isolated, and if you're caught down there—" He stopped midsentence. "Never mind. The place has decent passive security. You might consider an active alarm system."

"Are you and Kylie installing one at your house?"

"No," Kylie said. "No Kevlar vests in the front closet, either."

Russ went out through the sliders to check the deck and the approach to the house from the river. Felicity stood by the slider and watched him. "He's thorough," she said to Kylie.

"It's not you or this Nadia woman," Kylie said. "It's just the way he operates."

"I hope he doesn't feel as if he needs to be my protector or bodyguard or anything. I'm fine, but if I do run into trouble, I know what to do. Please don't worry about me."

Kylie nodded. "Of course. It's good practice for Russ, too. Things are usually so quiet around here, he can keep his skills sharp."

Felicity doubted Russ's skills had dulled, but she appreciated Kylie's gesture. He rejoined them, and they went outside to the driveway together. "I'm more likely to run into trouble with an exposed tree root or an irritated red squirrel than a crazed stalker," Felicity said. "But thanks for taking a look."

Russ smiled as he pulled open the passenger door. "Suspicious tree root on the path down to the river."

Felicity laughed. "Have to mind those tree roots."

She waited for him and Kylie to pull out of the driveway and start down the country road toward Moss Hill before she went back inside.

She checked her voice mail, texts, email and social media sites, but all was well. Nothing from Nadia, or from Gabe for that matter. Felicity debated texting him but resisted. Instead she walked down to the river and watched the ducks swimming on the opposite bank. When a handful of mosquitoes found her, she went back up to the house. She'd left the place unlocked. This paranoia thing was going to take some getting used to. She dug out her softball bat, checked the house for any sign of an intruder and then leaned the bat against the wall next to her bed.

Take a picture of her bat and send it to Gabe?

Not one of her better ideas.

She did a bit more work before finally retiring with a book, feeling both unnerved and comforted at the presence of the softball bat and the concern of friends.

Seventeen

Gabe sat on a couch covered in drop cloths in his living room while Shannon paced in front of the windows. She stopped abruptly and faced him, studying him. "You're going to need a few more days to get your bearings," she said. "You've got that 'I need more mosquitoes and black ice in my life' look. It's the Knights Bridge effect. Happens every time you go home."

More like the Felicity MacGregor effect, but Gabe smiled without comment.

"Nadia Ainsworth stopped by this morning, Gabe. She's a problem. I'm telling you."

"I thought she went back to California."

"She did—for forty-eight hours. She took the red-eye last night and landed in Boston early this morning. She was on the same flight as Marty Colton."

"Who is Marty Colton? Any relation to Russ Colton?"

"Marty is Russ's older brother. He's an aspiring screenwriter who makes his living tending bar in Hollywood. Several people with Knights Bridge connections are regulars. Marty was severely injured in a helicopter crash. His and Russ's father was killed in the crash."

"That's awful," Gabe said. "I had no idea."

"Not the sort of thing that comes up in casual conversation, I imagine. Marty recovered from his injuries, but he has scars and he doesn't like to fly."

"How do you know all this?"

Shannon flicked her fingers. "I got it from Nadia."

Gabe frowned. "Marty told her his life story?"

"People do things like that when they don't want to think about how much they hate to fly. It's a long flight to Boston from Los Angeles. Talking probably helped, and Nadia's easy to talk to."

"Got it."

Gabe reached for his cold-brew coffee on the side table. Nadia. Damn.

What was she up to?

He drank some of his coffee and set the glass back on the table. "What did Nadia want to talk to you about?"

"Nothing. She wants to talk to you. She's obsessed with you, Gabe." Shannon spoke matter-of-factly, as if Gabe must have seen this for himself by now. She adjusted a drop cloth on the back of a chair. "It's not romantic—she wants to manipulate you into doing something for her. My guess is it's money related. Work, ex-husband, new start-up idea she has. Something. She told me how you give her credit for your success, she's been with you from early on, loves working with start-ups—how you two have a special bond given your history. She laid it on heavy."

"Did she mention Knights Bridge?" Gabe asked.

Shannon nodded. "Nadia found out that Marty was Russ's brother while she was in Knights Bridge. She said Russ misinterpreted her interest in the boot camp.

Isn't holding it against him." Shannon rolled her eyes. "Good of her, don't you think?"

"Did she say why she came back here so soon?"

"Her grandmother's estate. That was it. She said she hadn't expected being back at her grandmother's house to affect her as much as it had. I guess she's got an offer on it. It's actually not that far from Knights Bridge."

Gabe ignored a tightening in his gut. "Did she tell you her plans?"

Shannon shook her head. "Didn't say."

"Did she mention anyone in Knights Bridge besides Russ?"

"Morwenna Mills—Kylie Shaw Colton. Nadia said she's reading the Badgers of Middle Branch series and hopes the launch party goes well. My kids love those books, by the way." Shannon paused, standing back from the chair. "Nadia reminded me she's an expert in customer development and its importance to start-up entrepreneurs. She noted she wasn't invited to speak at the boot camp."

"Why would she have been invited to speak?" Gabe asked, mystified.

"You got me."

It had been a good lineup of speakers, with a diversity of backgrounds and experience. Nadia would have fit in and had a lot to offer given her experience both working for him and as a solo entrepreneur herself, but he couldn't fathom why she would have been on Dylan McCaffrey's radar to invite. It certainly hadn't been a slight.

"Did you invite her to your boot camp party?" Shannon asked.

Gabe shook his head. "It was for people at the boot camp. I had no reason to personally invite her. She shouldn't read anything into it. She lives in California. The McCaffreys don't know her." He stopped himself. "I can't believe this is even an issue."

"Nadia's overstating her relationship with you. You've had that happen before, Gabe. People sometimes convince themselves they're essential to a successful person when they're not. Nadia did good work for you and contributed to the success of your company, but she wasn't indispensable." Shannon beamed a smile at him. "Even I'm not indispensable."

Gabe glanced around him. He'd done well in a short time. He had decades ahead of him. Nadia had always seemed rooted in reality, if caught up, at least to a degree, by her fantasies of her life with her hard-driving narcissist of a husband.

Acting out a fantasy could be harmless, but whatever Nadia was up to, that wasn't it.

"Anything else?" Gabe asked.

Shannon shrugged. "Nadia said she was more taken with Knights Bridge than she'd expected to be. I can understand that, to be honest, but I thought it'd be a hellhole. I had really low expectations. It didn't have far to go to beat them."

Not entirely Gabe's doing, either. He got to his feet, grabbing his cold brew. "Where is she now, do you know?"

"No idea. I asked her what her plans were. She said she wasn't sure what she was doing after heading to her grandmother's house."

"Marty Colton?"

"On his way to Knights Bridge, according to Nadia. It's a surprise visit."

Russ didn't strike Gabe as a guy who liked surprises, but a visit from his brother to his new home, to celebrate his wife's latest book, might be an exception.

Gabe didn't much like surprises, either.

He hoped Nadia was sleeping off jet lag and getting her head screwed on straight.

Shannon greeted two electricians and showed them to whatever they needed to do. Gabe finished his cold-brew coffee, but after that, he didn't know what to do with himself. Drive out to find Nadia at her grandmother's house and have a word with her? Call her? Was she trying to provoke him into contacting her? At this point was negative attention better than no attention?

A lot of questions for which he had no answers. He had no playbook for her behavior.

He took the elevator down to the garage and got in his car.

Out on the street, traffic whizzed past him. A knot of middle-aged men and women—obviously tourists—stood at a crosswalk, waiting for the light to change. The sky was clear, the air still and dry, in the upper seventies. In truth, he had a thousand things he could do. *Needed* to do. Why was he letting Nadia get under his skin?

Who was he kidding? That was an easy one. "It's because of Felicity," he said under his breath.

He called Shannon, who picked up on the first ring. "Where are you?" she asked.

"Heading to Storrow Drive in two minutes. You haven't heard from Nadia, have you?"

"Not since you left here. What's that been, ten minutes? Do you want me to check?"

"Yes."

A few seconds elapsed while, presumably, Shannon checked her messages. "Nothing. Why, do you think she's watching you?"

"No, but I don't like her behavior." He left it at that. "I got an invitation to the party for a new badger book, didn't I?"

"A what? Oh, right. The Badgers of Middle Branch series. Yes, as a matter of fact, you did. It's a lovely paper invitation. It arrived yesterday. The party is on Friday at the Knights Bridge public library. You were just in Knights Bridge. I assume you want me to decline on your behalf?"

"No. Accept."

"Okay." She sounded dubious. "I thought you were going to travel, do something fun. Go to… I don't know. Wyoming, right? Isn't that next?"

"Maybe. It'll keep for now."

"Okay, it's your life. Do you want me to book lodging for you in Knights Bridge, or will you be back here by nightfall—"

"I'll take care of lodging," he said, doing his best to dismiss an image of Felicity sitting next to him on the blanket in front of the fire, the river coursing down through the trees on a warm summer night.

"Gabe?"

"All set, Shannon. Thanks."

He returned to the parking garage and headed back up to his condo.

Shannon eyed him dubiously. "I'm heading home. You're not leaving tonight, are you? You have an appointment with your accountant in the morning. I've postponed it twice."

He'd forgotten. Of course. "Right. I'll be there."

"Do you need me to make you dinner reservations for tonight?"

"I'll go for a walk later and grab something."

She smiled. "It's a beautiful evening. Enjoy."

"Thanks. You, too."

She left, and a few minutes later, the electricians took off. Gabe ducked into his bedroom to pack. It was his second-least favorite part of traveling. Least favorite was unpacking. He got out his duffel bag and set it on his bed. Should he tell Felicity he was on his way? Just show up? She was organizing the book-launch party. Shannon was sending an RSVP on his behalf. Felicity would put two and two together.

Would she let him stay with her again? Did he want to?

He stood straight, taking a breath as he tried to quiet the questions his mind was throwing at him. He wouldn't be staying with his brother. That much he knew. Jess might be over the worst of her morning sickness, but he'd still be underfoot. They'd told him they'd love to have him stay with them anytime—"My barfing isn't *that* bad," Jess had told him before he'd left, not getting that he didn't want to disturb her, not the other way around.

Olivia's inn wasn't open to drop-in overnight guests—it wasn't that kind of inn—but she and Dylan would put him up if he asked. But he wouldn't ask. They had a baby on the way, too.

One of the Sloans?

Justin Sloan and his new wife, Samantha, were in the process of renovating Red Clover Inn, a sprawling, traditional inn located just down the street from Smith's. Once it reopened in a few months, it would be a great place to stay while in the area. Gabe didn't know Samantha, but he and Justin had always gotten along. Even if the inn wasn't open to the public yet, they'd probably let him stay in one of the rooms.

Eric Sloan would let him sleep on his couch. Mark had an unoccupied apartment at Moss Hill that Gabe could borrow.

Hell, he could stay with his father and help him tinker with his vintage motorcycles.

Gabe walked over to the windows and looked out at the city he loved. He wasn't fooling himself. He had many options but only one place he wanted to stay. He got out his phone and texted Felicity: Okay if I camp out in your guest room again tomorrow night?

I just heard from your assistant. You're coming to Kylie's party. Why?

Sounds like fun.

You were just here. Fast turnaround. When do you arrive?

Afternoon.

There was nothing more for a full two minutes. Finally her response popped up on his screen: I'll leave the key by the gutter on the deck if I'm not here. Russ has me locking up.

Because of Nadia, he thought. But it was a good idea in general.

Thanks. See you tomorrow.

I put clean sheets on the bed.

Setting boundaries? Gabe decided not to go there. Great.

Safe travels.

Gabe didn't have a detailed plan—he didn't have much of a plan at all—but he had no second thoughts about going back to Knights Bridge when he returned to his condo after his meeting with his accountants. He'd then had lunch with a friend who had extensive experience with venture capital and angel investing, an area of interest to Gabe since selling his company.

He grabbed his bag and headed to his car. He'd skipped countless parties and other events in Knights Bridge over the years given his schedule, priorities and, when he was on the road, the distance involved.

Always a reason.

He'd send a gift if called for, usually through Shannon. After a while, he assumed no one seriously expected him to attend anything short of something like his brother's wedding, and invitations were a courtesy. He never took offense when he discovered he hadn't been invited to something. More and more, even when he was fairly close, living in Boston, his hometown and his friends there were in his past, not a part of his current life. It'd been beyond him when he'd heard Felicity had returned to Knights Bridge, but she'd always been happier there than he had.

Gabe got in his car but didn't start the engine right away. What if he did decide to move to California or somewhere else far from New England? Did Felicity ever consider a radical move? Did she ever dream of such a dramatic change in her life, or was she rooted now in Knights Bridge?

He'd traveled to countless places but never to Wyoming. Before Felicity had marched out of his life, he hadn't wanted to go without her. Afterward, he hadn't wanted to remind himself of her. He was only in his early thirties, though. He had time to travel to Wyoming and loads of other places he wanted to see.

He started his car, trying to ease the grip nostalgia—memories—had on him. Felicity used to run up her credit cards between jobs to take trips. "Might as well take advantage of the time off," she'd tell him, despite knowing—she'd *had* to know, given her background as a financial analyst, even a failed one—that made no sense. Classic fight-or-flight. If she truly had gotten her financial house in order in the past three years, Gabe didn't see how she would have had much money for trips. Paying down debt, managing living expenses, putting together an emergency fund, transitioning to being a solo entrepreneur, saving to buy a house—paying property taxes and upkeep, buying furnishings, saving for any upgrades. It was a wonder she'd managed all that in three years, given the hole she'd been in. But this was Felicity MacGregor. She usually managed to figure out how to get what she wanted.

As he started out of the parking garage, Knights Bridge might as well have been on another planet. It was definitely in a different world than the one he now knew.

Felicity belonged there, Gabe reminded himself. She wanted to be there. He had no business interfering with her life. He'd done that once before, and she'd bolted. It didn't matter that she'd heeded his advice. He'd lost her as a result of his meddling, and she'd been figuring out that finance wasn't right for her. She hadn't needed him to cut into her process and tell her.

But he didn't turn around and go up to his condo and talk to painters and figure out his life. He continued onto Storrow Drive and headed west, toward Knights Bridge.

Eighteen

E very morning, Felicity liked to identify three things for which she was grateful. She'd made it a habit after the second time she'd been fired. That morning, drinking coffee on the deck, her mind on Gabe's impending arrival, sleep having eluded her most of the night, she'd written her three things in her journal.

I'm thankful Gabe let me know he's on his way, and his visit isn't a surprise.

I'm thankful he won't have time to go swimming, and I therefore won't be tempted to join him.

I'm thankful I put clean sheets on the bed in the guest room.

She glanced at her notes, still open on her coffee table. *Thankful* struck her as not quite the right word. *Relieved* better described her emotions. "I'm thankful I have enough work to keep me solvent," she said with a smile, leaving it at that.

She took a shower, got dressed and headed into town. She parked on South Main and walked down the shaded, picturesque street to the library. With its dark wood, elegant fireplace in a cozy reading nook and small stage, the library had a distinct late-nineteenth century feel to it, but it was also modern, a place for patrons of all ages to come. The space lent itself beautifully to Kylie's book party. She often led the children's reading hour. Somewhat shy and reclusive by nature, she would come to life reading a story, whether a classic like *Winnie-the-Pooh* or a book by one of her writer friends. From what Felicity had heard, the kids loved her.

Clare Morgan, Phoebe O'Dunn's capable successor as library director, greeted Felicity and took her into her office at the back of the main floor. Since arriving in town last fall, Clare, a widow, had made a place for herself and her young son. Over the winter, she'd met and fallen in love with Daisy Farrell's grandson, Logan, an ER doctor. They were now married and had moved into his grandparents' former house down the street from the library.

Clare sat at her oversize oak desk, probably original to the building. She and Felicity went over everything for tonight's party and reviewed the library's policies and guidelines for outside events. "A woman was just in and asked if Kylie's talk is open to the public," Clare said. "I told her it is and it's free but she'll need a ticket."

"That's right," Felicity said. "Would you like me to speak with her?"

"No, I think I answered her questions. I explained we need an approximate head count because Morwenna Mills is so popular and she could attract quite a crowd, even here in out-of-the-way Knights Bridge."

Clare frowned. "This woman actually had a ticket, so I'm not sure what confused her."

The evening agenda consisted of Kylie's talk followed by refreshments. "We can handle a few last-minute arrivals. Russ will see to that. He and Kylie are having a few family and friends over to their place at Moss Hill afterward. Will you be joining us?" Felicity asked.

"No, I'll make sure everything's all set here and head home. Logan has a rare night off." She smiled at Felicity, seated in an old captain's chair on the other side of the desk. "Did you organize the post-party party, too?"

"It didn't take much organizing," she said with a laugh.

"Well, everyone's excited about tonight. Don't hesitate to get in touch with me if there's anything I can do or if you have any questions."

"Same here."

Felicity thanked Clare and returned to the library's main room. As she headed to the entrance, she glanced into the alcove at the front of the library where the children's section was located. All the Badgers of Middle Branch books were on display on a table. Kylie had kept her pseudonymous identity secret for months, but Knights Bridge had taken to her with appreciation but not so much fanfare that she felt awkward or out of place. This was her home now. Townspeople understood that, since it was their home, too.

Our home, Felicity amended to herself.

She stiffened when a woman moved from farther into the children's nook and peered at the books on the badger table.

Nadia Ainsworth.

Felicity didn't know what to do first. Alert Clare? Text Russ? March over to Nadia and demand to know what she was doing here? She couldn't just leave without doing *something.*

She reached into her tote bag for her phone as she simultaneously turned to head back through the main room to find Clare, but Nadia spotted her, smiled and waved. "Felicity!" She winced, touching her hand to her mouth. "Sorry," she said in a loud whisper. "Library."

She scooted out of the nook and joined Felicity at the door. "I didn't realize you were in town," Felicity said.

"I never would have left if I'd known I'd have to turn around and come back so soon. I need to deal with some issues with my grandmother's house before we can finalize the sale." Nadia gave a self-deprecating roll of the eyes that struck Felicity as insincere. "Bad planning on my part, but some things you can't plan, really. I'm sure you understand. Um…chat outside? I feel like I'm going to be shushed any moment."

"Here's fine."

"Oh. I'm getting the stalker treatment. I don't blame you. I know it's my own fault for being weird when Gabe was here." She made a face, then smiled. "Sorry. Are you parked nearby? Why don't I walk to your car with you, or do you have errands to run? I see you aren't borrowing any books."

"I was here for a meeting."

"To discuss tonight's party, right? I asked the librarian about the party earlier. I'm coming, by the way. I understand you sent out invitations and offered some tickets to the public since there's limited space." She spoke fast, clearly self-conscious if not nervous. "I got my hands on a ticket at the front desk when I was here a few days ago. I was going to give it up since I was on the other side of the country, but it's a good thing I didn't, isn't it?"

"Nadia…"

"It's fine, Felicity. Promise. I'm just doing my best to take my mind off giving up my grandmother's house. I know I'll never have the chance again to make chocolate-chip cookies with her, since she's gone, but the house—it's filled with memories. It's like she's there." She paused, biting down on her lower lip, her eyes filling with tears. She sniffled, smiling. "Anyway, I'd never heard of the badgers until recently. A friend with kids informed me how much fun they are. Do you have any nieces and nephews, Felicity?"

"I do. Look, I should go—"

"No children of your own, though. You're still young, but I'm starting to feel the tick-tock of my biological clock." Nadia stood straight, pushing back her hair. "I'll be on my way. I can see I'm making you uncomfortable."

She yanked open the heavy door and bolted.

Felicity had a quick, internal debate with herself about her options even as she followed Nadia outside, running down the steps and intercepting her on the sidewalk in front of the library. "I'm sorry," Felicity said. "I was a bit taken aback just now. I have a few errands I need to run in town. Where's your car? I can walk with you."

Nadia smiled, cool. "Do you want to find out what kind of car I'm driving and report back to—hmm. To whom, I wonder? Russ Colton? He has me pegged as a problem, and he's Kylie-slash-Morwenna's husband. Well, I've done nothing wrong. He can't bar me from attending tonight without a good reason."

"Nadia, I don't think anyone intends to bar you."

"No?" She sighed, her smile warmer now. "I'm just being paranoid, then. I know I didn't make a good first impression, and I'm probably not doing that great right now. I'm emotional because of my personal issues. Nothing to do with Knights Bridge, or Gabe—or you, certainly."

"Are you in Knights Bridge for any other reason besides tonight's party?"

"Smith's pie of the day?" Her smile reached her eyes now. "Sorry. I'm just distracting myself from memories. My grandmother's death hit me harder than I ever would have expected. I didn't realize it until I got out here. My father's been a complete ass about her estate, too. That doesn't help. Here, let's walk. It's such a beautiful day."

Nadia was visibly calmer as she and Felicity walked to her car, parked around the corner on Thistle Lane. Felicity couldn't get any further details from her. "Will we see you tonight?"

"Maybe. I don't know for sure." Nadia pulled open her car door. "I haven't been able to make plans for several months. I'm such a planner, too. I try, but something comes up. It's like the universe sets off a flash-bang in my face every time I commit to something." She smiled. "Best to remain flexible."

"I'm sorry you're going through a tough time."

"It has been difficult, I admit. Is Gabe coming for the book-launch party? He and Russ Colton hit it off, and his brother lives in Knights Bridge, too. And you're here, of course."

Felicity decided to dodge Nadia's question. "The party will be fun, whoever is there."

"Yes. I'm sure." Nadia smiled, as if to take the edge off her clipped response. "I'll see you later, then."

She yanked the door shut before Felicity could respond and quickly got the car started and pulled onto South Main Street. Felicity gave the departing car a slight wave, but she hoped Nadia would change her mind and not return for tonight's party. In the meantime, Felicity knew, she needed to let Gabe and Russ know about Nadia's visit.

Felicity wasn't surprised when Russ Colton fell in next to her as she returned to her car. He shook his head and sighed. "You walked Nadia Ainsworth to her car? Felicity…"

"What was she going to do, throw a bag over my head and shove me in the trunk?"

"I can give you a long list of things unbalanced, obsessed people can do before they even know they're going to do it—never mind the stuff they plan."

"I was about to text you. Nadia was here for a change of scenery. She's in the midst of selling her grandmother's house and needed a break from the emotions."

"That's at best a white lie," Russ said.

"What?"

"Her grandmother's house is under contract. Nadia's father accepted the offer. She has no say. She came out for one last look at the house before the new owners took possession, but she and her grandmother weren't that close. Nadia's parents moved to California when she was in high school. She's forty-two now, so it's been a while. Her mother died five years ago. Her father remarried two years ago. He retired to Whidbey Island near Seattle."

Felicity blew out a breath. "Why would she mislead me about something like that?"

"To get empathy and rationalize her behavior."

"She doesn't need to save face with me. I don't have any relationship with her. Maybe the offer on the house fell through."

Russ shook his head. "It didn't. I spoke with her father, Felicity. Gabe told me she was back East. I felt that was enough to justify checking in with the father. He said he saw her a month ago. They had a pleasant visit at his place. He said she's taking it easy, enjoying her freedom from a bad marriage and not pushing herself so hard. He approves. He did say she's wanted to come back here to visit and now has the time."

They came to Felicity's Land Rover. "Nadia could have exaggerated her situation to create a sympathetic cover story—to make things easier for everyone, including herself."

Russ nodded. "Now she's stuck with it. Point is, we don't know. Gabe, Dylan McCaffrey, Noah Kendrick and Kylie are all people she could want to curry favor with, or at least find out what they're up to."

"She didn't need to lie."

"Most people don't, but that doesn't stop them."

Felicity glanced across the street at the common, as if she might see Nadia sneaking through the shade trees. She turned back to Russ. "You got here fast."

"I was at the country store." He smiled. "Words I assure you I never thought I'd say."

More relaxed, he asked Felicity to repeat her conversation with Nadia. He'd obviously dealt with worse than a wealthy entrepreneur at a loose end, inserting herself into a small New England town.

"Gabe says he's staying at your place again," Russ said. "Is that right?"

Felicity shrugged. "As far as I know."

"Tell him to lock up, too."

She made no comment. Russ started across the street to the common, but not before she saw his knowing grin. Given that he was relatively new to Knights Bridge, he could have misinterpreted her relationship with Gabe.

"You kissed Gabe at the swimming hole," she muttered, climbing into her Rover.

But their kisses hadn't meant anything, any more so than their night together as teenagers. Friends going too far with each other. Hormones. Didn't matter. It was done. It wasn't happening again.

When she arrived at her house, Felicity brought a carafe and water glass into the guest room. She debated picking a few wildflowers and putting them in a vase on the bedside table, but she decided that was going too far. Gabe would know he'd gotten to her and she hadn't put his last visit behind her.

So. No flowers.

She fixed herself a glass of iced coffee and took it out to the deck to go through her checklist for the party. She couldn't wait, really. If Nadia behaved and Gabe wasn't a huge distraction, it would be a fun evening.

* * *

"That's a lot of badgers," Gabe said, stepping onto Felicity's deck. He pointed at the lineup of mini stuffed badgers on the table. "Mark said the ladies at Rivendell sewed them for tonight."

She nodded. She'd heard his car in her driveway but hadn't gotten up, figuring he'd find her. She'd just gotten back from picking up the badgers at Rivendell. "I should have gotten them started sooner, but they dove right in. Audrey Frost said some of the men helped, but they'd never admit it."

"Different generation. I'd admit it."

"Audrey said they did the manly things. Her words."

Gabe pulled out a chair and sat in the shade of the umbrella. "My grandfather didn't try to sew private parts onto the guy badgers, did he?"

Felicity bit back a laugh. "No, he did not. He and the rest of the men there were perfect gentlemen. They helped staple and glue and fetch things, and they provided moral support."

"They're invited to the party?"

"Absolutely. We've got tickets and arranged transportation for anyone who wants to attend, and we'll bring goodies to those who aren't up to it."

Felicity leaned back in her chair, a pleasant breeze blowing through the trees. Gabe looked relaxed, dressed casually in a dark polo shirt and khakis. If anything, he was better-looking than three years ago when she'd slept on his couch. She tried not to let herself notice details when he'd been out for the entrepreneurial boot camp, but she had, anyway. Now it was worse. Everything she noticed about him was mixed up with all sorts of emotions.

"Felicity?"

She cleared her throat and sat up straight. "Sorry. Mind's on tonight. Did you bring your bag in yet? Need any help?"

He shook his head. "No and no. Thanks. Anything I can do to help you?"

"I skipped lunch." She decided to postpone telling him about her encounter with Nadia, the primary reason she hadn't felt like eating. "I could have pie and call it lunch."

"I didn't get to Smith's when I was out here last weekend. Why don't I fetch my bag and then we'll drive into town? I'm in the mood for pie. As I recall, you're always in the mood for pie."

"You know me well," she said, laughing as she got to her feet.

"Yes," he said, leaving it at that.

They took his car to town. "It's a sleepy summer day in Knights Bridge," Gabe said as they drove along the river.

"Feel free to take a nap out on the deck when we get back. Justin and Samantha have a hammock at Red Clover Inn. I'm sure they'd let you use it."

"You could hang a hammock at your place."

"I don't have two trees at the right distance apart, and I'd never get in it. Have you met Samantha yet? She and Justin got married in England in June. Scottish honeymoon." Felicity sighed. "Sounds so romantic, doesn't it?"

"No, I haven't met Samantha yet, and, yes, an English wedding and Scottish honeymoon sound romantic. You didn't go?"

Felicity shook her head. "I was invited, but I'd just

bought the house—I couldn't swing a trip to England, too. Samantha's an expert on pirates. Not the kind of pirates in the movies. Real pirates. She and Justin are trying to get the inn in shape for her cousin to have her wedding there at Thanksgiving."

"Her cousin being—"

"Charlotte Bennett. Samantha's a Bennett, too. Their grandfathers were brothers. Long story, but Charlotte stayed at the inn while Samantha and Justin were on their honeymoon—only unbeknownst to her, so did Greg Rawlings. Greg's a Diplomatic Security Service agent, one of Brody Hancock's colleagues. You remember Brody, don't you?"

"Hell-raiser."

"That's Brody. Or it was. Did you help the Sloan boys run him out of town after his high school graduation?"

"I wasn't involved, and 'run out of town' is somewhat of an exaggeration from what I've heard. Still, I bet it was a shock when he and Heather got together."

"Mmm. See what you miss when you don't come round often?"

Gabe grinned. "Yeah, I see. What's Heather doing in London?"

"She's studying interior design. She plans to come home and work with the family business again. She and Brody want to build a house out where he grew up on Echo Lake."

"Another of Knights Bridge's pretty spots," Gabe said, no trace of sarcasm in his tone.

"Heather had it rough with five older brothers," Felicity said.

Gabe laughed. "Tell that to her brothers. They'll tell you she had it easy. Spoiled rotten."

"Didn't get her name in the family business."

"Sloan & Sons was named before she was born, when her folks had given up on having a girl—not that it would have mattered, because her parents never would have envisioned her going into the family construction business."

"But she did, and she's good at it. Simple as that."

"It's never simple as that, is it?" Gabe said.

Felicity wasn't positive he'd absorbed everything she'd said. She'd probably rattled on a bit. Nerves, maybe. Not nervous-oriented nerves. Awareness-oriented nerves. She was feeling self-conscious and exposed with him so close to her, even if he was driving.

They parked on the street in front of Smith's. The small restaurant was crowded, but they got a table by a side window. Russ Colton was at the counter next to Eric Sloan. From their glances at her, Felicity guessed Russ had filled Eric in on Nadia's library visit. Russ wasn't one to overreact, but he was thorough.

Gabe narrowed his eyes on Felicity as they took their seats. "What's going on?"

She told him, sticking to the facts and not inserting any of her personal reaction to Nadia. She noticed Gabe's jaw tighten as she finished with Russ's caution to her. "It's okay, Gabe. I'm fine."

"I'm sorry, Felicity. I heard Nadia was back East again but I had no idea she'd beelined here."

"I've told you before, you're not responsible for her. It wasn't a big deal. Russ read me the riot act, but he was nice about it."

"He got his point across?"

"Oh, yes."

"Good. I don't know what Nadia's got in mind—"

"She wants your attention. That's my guess, anyway. Does she know you're here?"

"No doubt."

"Nothing happened. Nadia's behavior might be inappropriate, but she hasn't crossed any serious lines. Russ would turn the matter over to the police if she had—or if she does. So would I."

"I'll speak with her."

Felicity shook her head. "I wouldn't do that, Gabe. Just let it be. She's moved into crazy-maker status. Best thing is for us to go about our business and let Russ know if she gets in touch."

"Don't participate in her compulsion to create drama," Gabe said with a sigh. "Yeah. I know."

"It's hard not to feel some sympathy toward her, but she's got to sort out her own life and look for support from her own family and friends. You made it clear you're not available for that kind of thing." Felicity tilted her head back, eyeing Gabe. "Right?"

He nodded. "Right. In no uncertain terms."

"You're not counting on her to read between the lines. I know you're straightforward with me to a fault—"

"That's because you're Felicity MacGregor who mooned me in kindergarten."

"I did no such thing."

"Oh, yeah, you did. I remember."

"That was some other kindergartener. I was a model student."

He laughed, relaxing visibly as their pie orders arrived. Chocolate cream for him, fresh raspberry for her. "I'm sorry about Nadia," Gabe said again. "I can't explain her. She's never behaved this way before."

"She'll say she's just curious about Knights Bridge and means no harm. She told me she hadn't realized Knights Bridge existed when she lived in Massachusetts."

"That I can understand," Gabe said with a slight grin.

"One of its charms," Felicity said. "I suppose it's more on the map these days with the new ventures and various goings-on. Kylie had mixed feelings about having her book party here, but I think it's a great choice."

"It'll be fine," Gabe said, if only to reassure her. He pointed his fork at her pie. "Local raspberries?"

Felicity nodded. "From out by the Sloan farm."

"No wonder you skipped lunch. You were planning ahead."

She grinned at him. "Imagine that."

"No offense intended."

"None taken."

"You haven't lost your spontaneous spirit, have you?"

"I work hard but I'm not a grind. What about you?"

"What do you think?"

"A challenge." He dipped into his chocolate cream pie. "As perfect as I remember. It's been years since I had Smith's chocolate cream pie."

"A good thing you were in the mood for chocolate. This was the last piece of raspberry pie. I'd have hated to have to fight you for it."

"I'd have let you have it," Gabe said.

Felicity raised an eyebrow. "Without a struggle, huh?"

"Smith's chocolate cream pie after a day that included a meeting with my accountant and Nadia sneaking into town isn't a bad thing."

"Barring dietary restrictions, Smith's chocolate cream pie is never a bad thing."

Gabe looked downright nostalgic as he sampled the pie. "I picked the right day to spirit you off to lunch," he said. "It's been a long time since I had simple homemade pie with an old friend."

"Longtime friend," Felicity said. "Not old."

He laughed. "I stand corrected."

"Remember when we thought thirty was ancient?"

"I still might think that."

"Is there anything you haven't accomplished that you set out to accomplish at thirteen?" she asked him.

"Not at thirteen. Then I was all about getting out of Knights Bridge and making a fortune. Later, though." He paused, swirling his fork into more of the creamy chocolate. "I have a number of things I haven't accomplished by now that I set out to. What about you?"

"My train jumped the tracks, remember?"

"You just needed to make a course correction."

"I never saw a party with little stuffed badgers in my future, but I'm glad there is one. You shifted to me too fast. What else is on your revised list? Besides making your next million."

"Marrying you."

"Ha. Funny. On your *current* revised list, not on the guilt-ridden list the morning after you seduced me at eighteen."

"I could argue who seduced whom, but I won't." He

pointed his fork at her. "You have a raspberry hiding under your whipped cream."

"I'm saving it for last." She smiled at him. "See? I've learned to save."

"I never doubted you."

"There are actually two raspberries hiding under the cream. Do you want one? I'll share."

"I'm good, thanks."

Felicity saw he wasn't oblivious to the undercurrents of their conversation. Not that either of them had taken any pains to be subtle. He insisted on paying for lunch. "Least I can do since you're putting me up," he said.

"For how long?"

"Let's see what happens, shall we?" He smiled in that heart-stopping, sexy Gabe way. "One of the perks of having sold my business. I'm not on a tight schedule. I have time."

Nineteen

~~~~~∞∞~~~~~

Gabe sat in the shade on Felicity's deck while she got ready for tonight's party. He had misgivings about his abrupt return to Knights Bridge but, so far, no regrets. It might not be the easiest attitude to explain, but he was good with it.

He'd feel better if he had a true fix on what Nadia was up to. He considered checking with her ex-husband, but he doubted that would get him anywhere—and it would be inappropriate. David Ainsworth was brilliant and could be incredibly charming, but the guy was a soul-sucking narcissist who'd dropped Nadia when he no longer needed her. He'd made sure she believed it was her fault he was gone. He'd had her convinced she hadn't been supportive enough. She'd been too preoccupied with her own career. She didn't share his interests.

All nonsense.

Gabe had never gotten involved with their personal lives, but he'd worked with Nadia long enough and knew David well enough to have seen what was going on.

Felicity joined him on the deck. She'd put on a simple dress for the evening in the same shade of green as her eyes. "You look comfortable," she said.

He smiled. "I'm getting lazy. I haven't worked a full schedule in weeks."

"It's good to relax."

"I thought I might stop by Mark and Jess's before the party, but I'll see them tomorrow."

"It's nice she and Olivia are having babies so close to each other," Felicity said. "Marriage, babies, Knights Bridge. Does that thought give you hives?"

Gabe grinned at her. "Only a few. You? Not Knights Bridge, obviously."

"Marriage, babies?" She sat across from him at the table. "Haven't thought too much about them."

He gave her a skeptical look.

She snorted. "It's true!"

"Been too busy, huh?"

"As a matter of fact, yes. I have a lot going on with the house and work."

Gabe stretched out his legs, enjoying the breeze and the sounds of the river. "You didn't buy the house because you've given up on marriage?"

"I don't see how there's a cause and effect there. You've bought multiple properties. Have you given up on marriage?"

"They were investments."

"But you lived in them," she said. "That makes them homes, doesn't it?"

"I don't know. Does it?"

"Now you're getting serious," she said lightly. "I suppose there's a difference between a place to live and a true home. This place was special for you and your family when you were growing up. I always felt that when I was here as a kid. It's different now."

"It's a wonder my happy-go-lucky parents didn't accidentally set fire to the woods."

"They were great together."

"Yeah," Gabe said. "We did all right as a family, all considered. It was tough losing my mother. I can see her out here yelling at Mark and me to leave a bees' nest alone."

Felicity laughed softly. "I bet it wasn't you boys she was worried about."

"Oh, definitely it was the bees. What about your family? You still all get along well?"

"We do. My parents are enjoying retirement and being grandparents. I thought they might move to a warm climate full-time, but they'd miss the kids."

"Would they miss Knights Bridge?"

"They would, but it was never home the way it is for the Frosts and the Sloans."

"And the way it was for my grandfather," Gabe said. "Mark and I never hated it here. We just wanted out, a chance to do something with our lives that we felt we couldn't do in Knights Bridge."

"You didn't see a life here for yourselves. Mark does now, obviously." Felicity narrowed her eyes. "And you never will."

He pointed at her. "We're talking about you."

"I like being back here. It's not as expensive as Boston, for one thing. Anyway, I need to pack up for the party." She started to her feet. "Take a nap if you'd like."

"I can help."

"Great. You can carry the badgers."

"Well, why not?"

Gabe swung to his feet, reenergized as he followed Felicity inside. The badger box wasn't heavy, but it was awkward to carry and fit into the back of Felicity's Land Rover. She'd have managed on her own. He had no doubts about that, but it had to be easier with his help—not that she'd ever admit it. She told him as much when she handed him another box.

He made no comment. It wasn't just that she was independent and self-reliant—traits he admired. She was also stubborn, defensive and determined not to show any weakness—at least to him. He noticed it more than he had last weekend, or she was more that way now after having had a few days to consider what had gone on between them. Gabe found himself wanting to break down her reserve—penetrate the protective shell she'd put up around her—and get her to be herself around him, without reservation, without fear that he might criticize or lecture her. He didn't want her hiding behind her defenses. He wanted her to feel free to tell him anything, not just here and there but all the time.

He needed to tell her that, he decided. But not now, when she was on the job.

"I'm not having dinner," she said as they went inside. "I'll sneak a few hors d'oeuvres tonight. There's stuff in the fridge if you're hungry."

"I'm still working off that chocolate cream pie. I can wait until the party."

She glanced at her phone and then looked up. "We still have some time. Want to take a quick walk?"

It struck Gabe as an excellent idea. "Smarter than taking a nap," he said.

"Napping isn't the best way to burn off pie."

He hadn't necessarily been thinking about napping. Something in his expression must have given him away because Felicity turned red and bolted down the hall, muttering something about changing her shoes. Probably didn't think he'd noticed her outsize reaction, but he had. And it was good. In fact, it was very good. He preferred to have her thinking about whiling away a few hours in bed with him instead of reading a book on the deck while he took a nap.

Maybe that explained her defenses. Maybe it wasn't about stirring up their past. Maybe it was about stirring up their ideas about the future. There'd always been a certain amount of sexual tension between them, but, except for that one night as teenagers, it had never dominated their relationship. It'd never been the one thing they'd thought of. Their friendship had taken precedence. They'd accepted without question they weren't right for each other as romantic partners and hadn't wanted to impede each other in that department.

What if some guy picked her up tonight for the party? Met her at the library?

Gabe put the thought out of his mind. He wasn't one for wasting time ruminating about something he couldn't control or influence, particularly when it was something that likely wouldn't happen. Every vibe he got from Felicity told him she didn't have a man in her life. He hadn't gone so far as to ask his brother, but Mark would have said something by now, if only to keep his younger brother from messing up her romantic life with his presence.

Gabe went to his room and dug a pair of trail shoes out of his bag.

Five minutes later, he and Felicity were walking along the river in a comfortable but pointed silence. They paused on the covered bridge and leaned against the rail, looking down at the water. "I often come out here to think," she said. "Something about the sounds of the water and the walking itself anchors my mind. I don't necessarily stew on a problem, but when I get back home, I often have a breakthrough. Things sorted themselves out while I was looking at ferns or listening to chickadees. If I stayed at my desk and tried to force a solution, everything would just dam up and I wouldn't get anything done."

"Have to know when not to force something, I guess," Gabe said.

"True. Sometimes I need to muscle through a problem, and coming out here would be a form of resistance."

"Where does this walk fit?"

She squinted up at him. "It's purely social."

"Not chewing on a problem?"

"I'm relaxing and enjoying the company of an old friend. How's that?"

"Did you think up that line just now, or was it simmering while we were walking?"

She smiled knowingly. "I had a feeling you'd ask. You're in that mood."

"What mood is that?"

"The 'ask Felicity questions' mood." She turned around, leaning back against the rail. "I remember walking out here when I was a senior in high school, and you interrogated me about my plans for college."

"*Interrogate* is a loaded word. I was interested."

"Oh, was that it? You were dubious about what I

had in mind. You already knew I wouldn't last in finance, didn't you?"

"I had no idea," he said without hesitation. "I had a feeling you were doing what you thought you should do, not what you wanted to do."

"That's not unusual at eighteen, at least for a lot of people. Not for a Flanagan. You and Mark never did what you thought you should do. You did what you wanted to do."

He grinned at her. "Calling us selfish bastards?"

"Driven."

Gabe stared down at the water, aware of her eyes on him.

"That's not a bad thing," she added.

"I did have a sense of duty. Mark, too. We thought we should be here for our parents. Our mom especially, after she got sick. They never asked anything of us. Sometimes I wish they had." He cleared his throat, surprised at the emotion he felt. "I know Mark and I didn't abandon her, but sometimes it feels as if we did—at least that I did."

"She was a good soul, Gabe."

"A flake but a good soul." He smiled, pulling his gaze from the water. "Do you want to go farther or turn around now?"

"Let's go farther. Have you seen Kylie and Russ's house since they bought it?"

He shook his head, and they continued up the road, more houses cropping up as they got closer to the intersection with the main highway.

"Kylie says she doesn't see Russ's brother, Marty, moving East," Felicity said. "Knights Bridge is developing quite a Southern California contingency. Dylan and Noah are from San Diego, obviously. His personal attorney lives there. She's not going anywhere, but she's married now for the first time, thanks to Knights Bridge."

Gabe nodded, familiar with the people Felicity referenced. "Loretta Wrentham and Julius Hartley, Russ's former colleague with a Beverly Hills law firm."

"You've met them?"

"When I was out in California," he said, without elaborating.

"Did you meet Daphne Stewart, too?"

"Not yet, but Mark told me about her."

"Her real name is Debbie Sanderson. She's the great-granddaughter of George Sanderson, founder of the Knights Bridge Free Public Library and investor in the hat factory Mark has now renovated. She secretly sewed copies of movie stars' dresses in the library attic before she ran away to Hollywood forty years ago. Now she's a respected Hollywood costume designer."

"I understand she's quite a character."

"She's a total diva," Felicity said with obvious affection. "I only met her briefly when she came back here in the spring to do a master class. I heard she considered moving back part-time, but she decided against it. Hollywood is home for her now. She's a regular at Marty Colton's bar. Ruby O'Dunn is staying with her while she's out there."

"I don't think I've seen Ruby since she was in braces."

Felicity smiled. "Our hometown is small, but its reach is wide."

"The Knights Bridge effect?"

"I hope so. I'd hate to think we spread misery—Christopher and Ruby aside. Who knows, maybe you'll meet someone because of Knights Bridge. I imagine the entrepreneurial boot camp could attract your type."

"What's my type?"

"Not for me to say—"

"Sure it is. You obviously have ideas."

"Okay." She considered for a moment, a twinkle of amusement in her pretty eyes. "In the spirit of not minding my own business, I would say your type is smart and accomplished but not as driven as you are. Someone who doesn't work nine-to-five and can drop everything to accompany you when you're indulging your wanderlust. She'd have money but not too much money, not because of your ego but because it'd be too complicated. How's that?"

Gabe leaned in close to her. "You didn't mention if my 'type' would be good in bed."

She didn't skip a beat. "No need. You'd see to it, wouldn't you?"

Felicity was quick. Gabe would give her that. "Hair color, eye color, West Coast, East coast?"

"Doesn't matter. You're mobile. You cut your roots to Knights Bridge a long time ago."

If he'd ever truly had roots. They came to Russ and Kylie's house, gray shingles with black shutters, old stone walls, lilacs and maple trees. It was tucked up on a hill across from the river and oozed New England charm. Gabe doubted anyone would have put Kylie and Russ together a year ago, but now they were married, moving into a house on the river—and plainly in love with each other.

"Gabe?"

He yanked himself out of his thoughts. "Any other qualities to my type?"

Felicity screwed up her face, exaggerating how much thought she was giving her answer. "Hmm. She'd have to get my approval, of course. As your friend, someone who looks out for you. I couldn't have you marrying just anyone." She grinned, tugging on his hand. "Kidding."

He swooped his arm over her shoulders. "What if you're my type?"

"I do sort of fit the profile. Scary, isn't it?"

"You didn't have yourself in mind?"

"Definitely not. I doubt I'd ever be as indulgent of you as the woman of your dreams would be."

He laughed. "That's for damn sure." They turned back down the road. When they came to a path to their swimming hole, he couldn't resist. "Jump in the river in our clothes?"

"That would be indulging you."

"Yeah, it would be, but I bet the idea crossed your mind, too."

"It always does on a warm summer day."

"Do you have time for a dip?"

"No, but—" She smiled. "If we make it quick."

He took her hand into his. "Then let's go."

Felicity made Gabe turn around and stand behind a tree while she slipped off her dress and eased into the water in her bra and underpants. Gabe followed suit, diving into the river in just his underwear. She stayed underwater from the neck down, but it was patently obvious she was all but skinny-dipping.

"If anyone paddles by in a kayak or canoe, I'm done for," she said.

"No one will."

Probably true. The shallow, rocky river was popular with paddlers in spring with the winter runoff but less popular in the dead of summer. "Don't touch me," she warned him. "If you do…" She considered her next words. "Things are complicated enough between us."

He smiled. "As you wish."

What did he wish? Did she even want to ask?

No, she didn't.

She swam toward the large boulder on the edge of the river and placed a hand on the rough granite. She didn't climb onto it or rise up out of the water. She felt the cool river water coursing over her bare skin. "Just as well I have a lot to do the rest of the day," she said half to herself.

"You go on," Gabe said, closer to her than she realized. "You've got a job to do. I'll turn my head while you get dressed."

He materialized by the boulder. Felicity noticed river water creating rivulets on the well-developed muscles in his chest. She ignored the dryness in her throat, the awareness in every part of her body. "Then I'll do the same for you."

"No worries."

All went according to plan. Felicity didn't know if she was disappointed or pleased, but she did accept that she had a party to get to. She'd have died of embarrassment if she and Gabe got seriously physical and someone happened upon them.

"Best to check for ticks," she said as they returned to the road.

"Will do."

She heard a faint but unmistakable note of amusement in his voice. "I mean it, Gabe," she said. "I don't want you getting Lyme disease."

"Me, either. Are ticks the reason you jumped into your clothes so fast?"

"They could be *in* our clothes."

"How to take any romance out of the moment." He slung an arm around her and kissed her on the top of her head. "You smell like a trout."

"Speaking of romance-killing comments."

He laughed, dropping his arm from her as they started down the road. "Now I keep feeling ticks in my shorts."

"I keep sharp-pointed tweezers in the bathroom."

"Ah. Good to know."

He disappeared into the bathroom when they got back to her house. Felicity went into her bedroom. Her soaked underwear had dampened her dress. She peeled off everything and left it all in a heap on the floor while she checked for ticks, spiders, mosquitoes and anything else she didn't want crawling on or stuck to her. She didn't find anything, just bits of leaf debris and bark. It was her usual post-swim routine, but it felt different today.

She jumped in the shower, and when she emerged, she presumed she no longer smelled like a trout.

When she returned to the kitchen, Gabe greeted her with a glass of iced tea. "No ticks?"

She shook her head. "You?"

"None. I found a spider and escorted him outside where he belongs. Don't know his chances, but he's on his own." He made a face. "Something to be said for swimming pools."

"Is that what you want in your next house?"

"If I move to California, for sure, but I doubt I'd get in it much."

"Not the same charm as our swimming hole."

"I generally hit the treadmill for exercise, and I don't have a lot of time for things like hanging out at the pool or walking along the beach. Hanging out in general."

"You don't take the time, you mean. You'd rather do other things. Work. Do you hang out with friends?"

"More than I used to. What about you? What's your life in Knights Bridge like these days?"

"Other than skinny-dipping in the river?" Not waiting for an answer, Felicity sat at the kitchen table with her tea. A few more minutes and she'd have to leave for the library. "Work, house, more work, more house, some friends, some family. I hope to establish a more normal work schedule and get things done on the house and have more time for friends and family. I was away from Knights Bridge for a long time. Some old friends and I don't have anything in common anymore. I've made new friends—people I didn't necessarily have much to do with in high school, like Olivia and Jess, and new people, like Russ and Kylie."

"Then being here is a fresh start more than a re-start."

"I hadn't thought of it that way, but it really is."

"I'm glad you've made a place for yourself here," Gabe said. "Need to get going?"

She nodded. "You're welcome to ride into town with me, but I have to be there early and leave late."

He shrugged. "I don't mind."

"Do you plan to contact Nadia?"

"It's best I don't," he said. "That's my instinct, and Russ agrees."

"Makes sense." Felicity held up her glass, suddenly feeling awkward, self-conscious. "Thanks for the tea." She pushed back her chair. "Time for our badger book party."

Twenty

❧━❧❀❧━❧

Felicity's first stop was Rivendell. Gabe saw that he hadn't thrown her off schedule with their walk and quick swim, and the fresh dress she'd put on looked as good as the one that had gotten wet. The women attending tonight's party were dressed up, waiting for the car Felicity had arranged to take them into the village. Audrey Frost was driving herself and Daisy Farrell. In the two years since his grandfather had moved to assisted living, Gabe had learned not to make assumptions about the elderly residents and their motives, capabilities or health.

Of course, party-planner extraordinaire Felicity MacGregor had arranged with the staff to make sure she had a little something for those who weren't attending, including anyone on restricted diets.

While Felicity saw to her craftspeople, Gabe checked in with his grandfather at his small apartment. "I always liked Felicity," his grandfather said after Gabe explained why he was there. "Thought you two would be married by now, but you never did like to do what anyone thought you'd do."

"Saying I was a difficult teenager?"

"Difficult, period." The old man grinned. "I was blunt even before I hit eighty."

"Plain-spoken," Gabe amended.

"And maybe unpredictable is a better way to think of you. Do you still like to be unpredictable?"

"I don't know if I ever liked it. These days I like to think I'm spontaneous and flexible, able to maneuver after a setback and capitalize after a coup."

"You're not set in your ways." His grandfather sank deeper into the worn cushions of his well-used chair. "I thought I'd die at home. To be honest, I never thought I'd see seventy-five, never mind eighty-five, and here I am."

"For a while, I hope. I have to run, Gramps. Be good."

He winked. "No fun in that. See you, Gabe. Enjoy your party. The girls had a good time doing up those critters. The writer and artist—what's her friend's name again?"

"Kylie Shaw, but she writes under the name Morwenna Mills."

"I wouldn't have kept that straight at forty. She's talented. She and Felicity both are."

"That they are," Gabe said. "Want me to bring you your slippers or something before I go?"

His grandfather eyed him as if trying to gauge if Gabe was teasing him. Finally he shook his head. "All set. G'night, and you be good, too."

Gabe met Felicity in the parking lot, and they continued into the village. He watched the scenery out his window, appreciating how little had changed since he'd moved away. No ex-urban sprawl here. The air was clear and dry. The stars would be bright again tonight.

When they arrived at the library, he helped carry things in. Kylie and Russ arrived, but Felicity shooed them inside. "This is my job," she told Kylie. "Yours is to be Morwenna Mills."

Kylie smiled, obviously ambivalent about the evening ahead. "I love seeing people, but an event like this—it does take a lot out of me."

"You've got Russ this time," Felicity said.

"And a bunch of your badger buddies," Gabe said, lifting the box out of the back of Felicity's Land Rover. "Did you bring Sherlock?"

Russ grinned. "Always."

Kylie smiled, too, looking less jittery. "Sherlock, Russ and friends. Can't go wrong."

If she was worried about Nadia, she didn't say as she headed up the steps into the library. Maggie Sloan arrived in her van with the food for the evening. She burst out of the van with her usual energy, her red hair coming out of its pins and clips. She'd been like that in high school, too. Gabe grinned at her. She seemed to read his mind and put him to work.

"Brandon still hiking?" he asked, grabbing a covered tray.

"Home tomorrow. He loves it. Sloan & Sons has tons of work with all the construction going on around here, but he needs these excursions. They keep him from getting restless. We were separated for a while, did you know?"

"I heard something about that."

She nodded. "I'm not surprised. We've been together since the beginning of time, I swear. We got married and had kids young, but we both wanted to see what was beyond Knights Bridge."

"That's not unusual for those of us from small towns," Gabe said.

"We're both happy being back here. It's a great place to live and to raise our boys. We've made a place for ourselves with the work we do. Brandon's a damn good carpenter, and we'll see how he does with his first adventure travel excursion."

"Are you worried he'll like it too much?"

"Not worried at all. I used to think Knights Bridge wasn't a great place to be young and single, but that hasn't been the case lately, that's for sure."

"Is that a hint?"

"You're a tumbleweed, Gabe, but one of these days you'll get swept somewhere and stick, don't you think?"

"See me back in Knights Bridge?"

"I didn't see Brandon and me returning, but we did, and now we're having the best time of our lives. Our work, our boys, our extended families, life here. It's all good, Gabe. It's not without problems, of course, but that's life."

He smiled at her. "I'm glad to hear it, Maggie. Really."

"Excellent. That tray is holding delicate tarts. Don't go bull-in-a-china-shop on me, okay?"

He promised he wouldn't and managed to get the tray up the stairs, into the library and on the food table without incident. At that moment, nothing seemed more important. Maybe it was true—maybe nothing *was* more important.

As he headed back outside, he glanced at his phone in case he'd missed a message from Nadia, but there was nothing. He paused and looked up and down South

Main and across the common, but he didn't see her. There were no obvious rentals or out-of-town cars parked yet on the street or in the parking lot, but he knew that would be happening soon. Security wasn't his job tonight, but he did feel responsible for Nadia.

Felicity eased in next to him. "Nadia's not in the library. I checked with Russ. He made sure she's not hiding in a bathroom or one of the library's nooks and crannies—although it'd be hard to check every single one of them. That's why Daphne Stewart's secret sewing room in the attic went undetected for so many years."

"Decades," Gabe said.

"She loved creating a mystery. Nadia's more straightforward, I think. I'm sorry she's had it rough lately."

"I'm sorry, too, but there's no reason for her to take her troubles out on anyone else."

A black town car pulled up to the library. Gabe tensed, but when the back door opened, a man in his mid- to late-thirties got out, thanked the driver and shut the door and turned to Gabe with a grin. "Relax. I'm Marty Colton, Russ's big brother."

Gabe introduced himself and Felicity.

Marty glanced at the retreating car. "Man, I wish I had a picture of my arrival. I've always wanted to make a grand entrance." He turned back to Gabe. "If we want to call arriving at the Knights Bridge public library an entrance."

"Point taken."

"But, hey, it counts. The car wasn't as expensive as I thought. I got in early yesterday and took a day in Boston to get my feet under me."

"Is Russ expecting you?" Gabe asked.

Marty shook his head. "I'm surprising him. I figured this is as good a time as any to see his new town. Good Lord, it's cute, isn't it? I'm such a desert rat. Daphne's told me about this place in bits and pieces over countless French martinis."

"I can imagine," Gabe said. "You were on the same flight as Nadia Ainsworth. Do you happen to know where she is now?"

Marty shook his head. "No, I don't. She seemed nice. Any problem with her?"

"We used to work together." Gabe decided that was enough. He motioned to the library entrance. "Russ and Kylie are inside if you want to surprise them."

"Russ isn't easy to surprise. He'll know I'm here by now. Probably knew the minute my car crossed into Knights Bridge." Marty sighed as his younger brother emerged from the library. "See?"

Gabe stepped aside as the two Coltons greeted each other. Russ seemed genuinely pleased that Marty had made the trip East for the party, but he'd obviously had an eye on the hired car and whoever was in it. The pair went inside, and Gabe resumed helping Felicity get the evening festivities set up.

"Kylie told me Marty didn't make it to the wedding. Hates to fly," Felicity said.

Gabe nodded. "He was severely injured in a helicopter crash in which his father died."

"That's terrible. I knew there was a reason, but it wasn't the moment to ask for details. How did you find out? Did Russ tell you?"

"Shannon."

"Ah. She could work security herself. Well, Russ

seems thrilled Marty's here now, and I know Kylie will be."

Kylie's sister arrived. She introduced Lila to Felicity and Gabe, no one awkward at the intermingling of personal and professional relationships, given Felicity's role that evening. Gabe didn't think he'd ever seen her so comfortable in her own skin—at ease with her work, herself, her place in her hometown. No way was he messing with that.

"Feeling cocky?" she asked him during a moment's lull, after they'd finished setting up.

"About what?"

"That you were right about me. Aren't you taking a little credit for my new life as an event manager?"

He grinned at her. "Let's see if the badgers behave first."

"A few aren't tightly sewn. I hope their stuffing holds through the night."

"I know the feeling."

She laughed. "Don't we all."

"You don't seem as nervous tonight as you did at the boot camp. Kylie's well-known."

"She is, but she's not you, is she? She's a friend. Not that you aren't, but I hadn't seen you in such a long time, and we'd had quite a parting of ways. I mean, it involved brownies."

"It involved deception about brownies," Gabe said lightly.

"I'm ignoring you. The boot camp was a first, too. A lot was at stake, not just for me but for people I care about—Dylan, Olivia, Maggie, Brandon, Noah, even Phoebe. Russ, too. And you."

"You didn't want to screw up."

"Especially in front of you," she added pointedly.

"I guess I can understand that." He tilted his head sideways, eyeing her. "I could make an argument that skinny-dipping in the river helped relax you for to-night."

"Oh, sure. That was very relaxing. Technically I wasn't skinny-dipping, but it was madness."

"But fun?"

She smiled. "Maybe."

"You have to cut loose once in a while, Felicity."

"I hear you, but you don't have to tell me what I need to do or don't need to do. I'm not looking to you for that, Gabe."

"As if you ever did."

Her smiled broadened. "Now you're getting the idea."

A stream of guests came through the main library doors, and she was off to do her thing.

Gabe went into fly-on-the-wall mode, but it didn't last. The Sloan brothers in attendance spotted him. Eric, Justin and Christopher. Adam, a stonemason and the quietest of the lot, wasn't there, and Brandon was still in the White Mountains with his adventure travelers. Justin was with Samantha, his pirate-expert bride and one of Kylie's first friends in town.

"How's it going, Gabe?" Justin asked.

"Just fine," he said, meaning it as he watched Felicity direct guests. "Just fine."

As far as Gabe could tell, the evening was a smashing success. He'd never been to a party for a children's book author and illustrator. To any kind of book party, in fact.

He wandered outside while Felicity wrapped up

with the last of the guests. He'd help her clean up and load the Rover. Nadia, thankfully, hadn't turned up.

Justin and Samantha Sloan trotted down the library steps. Eric and Christopher had left already for their shifts as police officer and firefighter. Justin was a volunteer firefighter—he and Samantha had met when she'd ducked into an old cider mill he owned and it caught fire in a lightning strike. It occurred to Gabe that as little time as he spent in Knights Bridge, he did know a fair amount about its goings-on, mostly thanks to his brother—but he could have told Mark he wasn't interested, and he never had.

Justin and Samantha said good-night and headed off, hand in hand, across South Main and the common, toward their rambling, ramshackle inn. If anyone could renovate Red Clover Inn and make it better than it ever had been, they and the rest of the Sloans could—and would.

Gabe stiffened, noticing the silhouette of a woman on the common.

Nadia.

He glanced behind him. A few stragglers chatted in front of the library. He debated alerting Russ, who was inside, but decided there was no need. Let Russ enjoy the rest of the celebration with his wife and his brother. Gabe had no reason to believe Nadia would cause trouble, at least any he couldn't handle.

He crossed the quiet street and walked through the lush grass on the common. Nadia stood in front of a World War II monument. She didn't glance at him as he approached her. "Imagine all the dead and maimed during those terrible years," she said, staring at the names carved into the polished stone. "It seems like such a long time ago, but my grandfather served in the Pacific. He seldom talked about it. I found pictures after my grandmother died of the two of them. He was in his uniform. They were so young." She turned to Gabe, her skin pale, colorless, in the dim light. "The march of time, huh?"

"What are you doing here, Nadia?"

"Resisting temptation. I had a ticket for tonight's celebration. I talked myself out of going. I realized today that I've upset people here. I didn't want to be the skunk at the picnic." She bit on her lower lip, her eyes shining with unshed tears. "I'm sorry, Gabe. I hate that I've made your friends here nervous."

"Then take a different approach, Nadia."

"Like what?"

She sounded helpless, at a loss. "Go home," Gabe said gently. "Change course. You're dealing with big changes in your life. Talk to your family and friends. Get professional help if you need to."

She sniffled and attempted a smile, but there was no hint of it in her eyes. "Yes, well, you make it sound so easy."

"I know it's not easy. Being truthful with yourself and others is a place to start."

"That's a polite way to call me a liar." She held up a hand. "It's okay. I'm not mad. I know I haven't been entirely truthful, but sometimes everyone is best served by a social lie that doesn't hurt anyone."

"I'm not here to tell you how to live your life."

"Good." She shifted back to the monument. "I loved David, Gabe. His energy, his can-do approach to life, his charm. His laugh—he has a great laugh. I was devastated when he left me. I never saw it coming. I blamed myself for the failure of our marriage. Part of me still does."

"I'm sorry, Nadia."

"He'll do right by the company we—you built. He's not why I'm here. Not directly, anyway. I'm here because I've been so lost. I didn't have a relationship with my grandmother in her last years because I always put David first, and now she's gone. It's over. I can't undo the past and have a relationship with her." She looked back toward the library, lit up against the dark night. "Seeing the people here—your family and friends—has made me realize what I gave up and can never, ever get back."

"You have family and friends," Gabe said.

"Yeah. Yeah, I do." She turned back to him, her expression less strained. "I know my relationship with David has nothing to do with you, but did he tell you he planned to leave me? Did you guess?"

"Nadia…"

"Unfair question, sorry. It's not your fault my marriage dissolved. The signs were there. I just didn't see them."

"Nadia, don't take on what he did. Why don't I walk you to your car—"

"I can't help but have regrets. You're young, Gabe. You're very young for what you've accomplished. Don't isolate yourself the way I did. You have friends and family here in Knights Bridge. You matter to them. They matter to you."

"I know that, Nadia."

"Do you?" She crossed her arms on her chest, as if she needed to hug herself. "I'm parked in front of the country store. I don't need you to walk me over there."

"Where are you staying tonight?" Gabe asked.

"My grandmother's house. The buyers are talking about turning it into a bed-and-breakfast. They shared some of their ideas with me. It'll be a sweet place if they can pull it off. This has been difficult emotionally, but it's also been…" She paused, sighing. "Cathartic, you know? In a good way. Has being back here been good for you?"

He didn't want to talk about himself. "You'll get through this, Nadia." He motioned toward South Main. "I need to go. I'm chief box hauler tonight."

She laughed, or tried to. "I can think of a dozen people off the top of my head who'd love to see you right now, playing the Knights Bridge hometown boy. Enjoy your box hauling, Gabe."

"Take care, Nadia."

He watched her walk across the common toward Main Street and the country store. He could see a car parked there. He waited until its headlights came on. Then he let out a breath and returned to the library. When Gabe crossed South Main, Felicity was shoving an empty box into the back of her car. She glanced at him with a measure of sympathy. "Nadia?"

"Yes."

"Fun way to end the evening. You okay?"

He nodded. "I'm fine. Come on. I'll help pack up."

No *way* was Felicity going into her house first. Gabe could see that thought take root as she pulled into her driveway and turned off the engine. "What if Nadia booby-trapped the place?" she asked, hands still on the wheel.

"Do you believe that?"

She sighed, loosening her grip on the wheel. "No. That's why it's a *what-if* question. She doesn't strike me as dangerous. That said…" She turned to Gabe in the dark. "I'd have felt better if she'd come inside tonight and enjoyed herself instead of lurking out on the common, but all this talk about locking my doors has me a bit on edge. She's your friend."

He felt his jaw tighten. "Friend is a stretch."

"Yes, well—you go first. Reconnoiter and come back and tell me she didn't short-sheet my bed or spread dog poo on the kitchen counters."

"What if she's hiding in the bushes by the driveway and jumps you while I'm inside?"

"Good point." She let go of the wheel and reached for the door handle. "I'll go with you and stand outside the screen door until you give me the all clear."

They got out of the Rover, and, leaving everything they'd brought back from the library in the car, they headed across the driveway to the house. Gabe understood Felicity's humor and intentional exaggeration were in response to his somber mood since they'd left the village. Nadia's troubled state of mind didn't automatically make her a danger to anyone. But wasn't that often the way? People would see signs and ignore, downplay or dismiss them, only later to wish they'd done something when the unacceptable behavior first arose. At the same time, Gabe knew he'd done what he could to steer Nadia onto a better course for herself. Russ Colton had agreed they had no reason to do more. So had Marty, who'd spent hours on a plane with her the night before. Her family knew she was struggling. She knew she was struggling.

If she showed up in Knights Bridge again, that could change things.

Felicity did as promised and stayed just outside as Gabe made quick work of a search of her house. He was convinced no one had been inside. It wasn't just drama on Felicity's part, he knew. Nadia had behaved badly, lying and sneaking around, justifying her intrusiveness because of her own emotional pain. Her misplaced actions would only get her into real trouble if she didn't come to terms with the big changes in her life.

"All clear," Gabe said as he opened the door for Felicity. "Anything we need to get out of your car?"

"Nothing that can't wait until morning, but we might as well get it over with."

He followed her back to the Rover. All the badgers had gone home with guests, leaving just the empty box. There were a few other items to deal with—her laptop, binder, decorations and posters. Three trips and they were done.

"What's your next event?" Gabe asked, opening the refrigerator.

Felicity plopped onto a chair at the table. "Let me enjoy pulling this one off before I think about the next one. Not that I haven't been thinking about it. I mean now."

"Good to take time to celebrate a great night."

"It wasn't my night. It was Kylie's night."

"Celebrate a job well done, then."

She opened her mouth but shut it again before speaking. He pulled a bottle of champagne out of the fridge. "Where did that come from?" she asked.

"Imagine."

"You sneaked it in here? That's an expensive label. Did you buy it in town?"

"Boston," he said, setting the bottle on the counter.

"In anticipation of a reason to celebrate?"

"Champagne is always correct."

He got two glasses out of a cupboard and set them on the counter before opening the champagne. He filled the glasses and handed one to Felicity. She rose with it, nodded toward the living room. "Sit outside and drink champagne to the stars?"

"I was about to suggest that myself."

"Uh-oh. We're thinking alike."

But he heard an odd note in her voice that he couldn't pinpoint—whether she was being sarcastic, frank, funny, hopeful. He let it go and followed her out to the deck.

"Let's not light any candles or turn on any lights," she said softly next to him.

He slipped into the living room and kitchen and turned off any interior lights. He went back out to the deck and stood next to Felicity, turned to her to click glasses with a simple "cheers." They leaned on the rail, his eyes adjusting to the darkness. The stars were out, spread across the night sky in sharp relief, as bright as he'd anticipated they'd be.

"No moon tonight," he said. "It's beautiful out here at night."

"You don't do much stargazing these days?"

"Even if I took the time for it, the stars wouldn't be as amazing in Boston or San Diego as they are here."

"It's a good spot," Felicity said, picking up her champagne again.

"I didn't pay much attention to the stars when I was growing up here."

"Neither did I. We didn't know what we were missing."

"We didn't know what we had," he said.

She let out a deep breath. "Heavy, Gabe. Damn."

"Stars and bubbly bring out the Yoda in me."

But he couldn't quite make his attempt at humor sound genuine or stick, and he settled for drinking his champagne in silence next to Felicity.

"Will you go back to Boston in the morning?" she asked after a while.

"I don't have a set schedule. I didn't expect to be back here so soon. Justin Sloan offered me a room at Red Clover Inn if I end up staying longer. They haven't started renovations. They're still working on the plans. He says the rooms are in good working order." He paused, finished the last of his champagne. "I don't want to be underfoot here."

"Whisking me off to swim in my undies isn't conducive to getting work done."

"Can't beat it for a break on a summer day."

"Not unless you get me arrested. Well, since you don't have a plan, we can worry about tonight. I say we plan on pancakes and sausage at Smith's in the morning."

"Works for me."

She yawned. "Champagne and post-event winddown are taking their toll. I'm turning in. Thanks for the help with the party." She angled a smile at him. "Swimming today was fun. A little well-chosen rulebreaking once in a while is good for the soul."

Gabe let her go without a word. He didn't know

why, except that he hadn't the vaguest idea what to say—which also troubled him. He might say the wrong thing but he always said *something*.

He walked down to the river in the dark, without the benefit of a flashlight. The stars helped but not as much as a full moon would have. He jumped onto a boulder that jutted into the water. He used to come out here as a boy. His parents never noticed, or if they had, they'd never said anything. Normal in their world, a kid slipping down to the river in the dark.

A different time if not a different place, he thought, watching bats swoop in the sky above the river, against the stars. If he had any sense, he'd head to Red Clover Inn now, before it got too late and he risked waking Justin and Samantha.

But when had he ever had any sense, at least here on the river?

He dipped a toe in the water, the river swifter and colder here than at the swimming hole. He could feel the air turning, a front moving in that would lead to cooler, dryer air. In Boston, he'd be—doing what? He didn't even know. Having drinks with friends, maybe. Flirting with pretty women. Thinking about life back in Knights Bridge. His grandfather in assisted living, his brother and his wife looking forward to their new baby. His father, working on his old motorcycles. Friends. Family. Where did Felicity fit in?

He looked behind him, up the steep bank toward the house. *Her* house. But wasn't that as he'd always seen it?

Aggravated with himself for overthinking, he headed back up the footpath to the deck. Felicity had left her glass on the rail. He grabbed it, and his, and headed inside. He thought he'd wash them, but he left them in the sink.

He walked down the hall and raised his hand to knock on her door, but she opened it before he could make contact. She was in her nightgown, hair down, face washed of makeup, eyes wide and soft as they connected with his. "Gabe, what are we doing?"

"I have a feeling you know."

"I have a feeling I do, too."

There would be no Red Clover Inn tonight. No guest room across the hall from Felicity, and no couch.

Twenty-One

Felicity slipped out of bed early, without waking Gabe—or maybe he was pretending to be asleep, giving her a moment to process last night. He lay on his side, facing the window. They'd kicked off the covers hours ago, but sometime during the night he'd pulled the top sheet over them. It was now just over his hips, leaving his torso exposed in the milky light. She inhaled at the sight of the muscles in his arms and shoulders, his smooth skin, his tawny hair. Her own skin tingled, and her fingers twitched at the memory of touching him, holding him, feeling him inside her.

With no neighbors to worry about hearing them, they'd both cried out, more than once.

"Oh, Gabe," she whispered now, still loose and warm from their lovemaking.

She grabbed a robe and slipped into it as she tiptoed down the hall to the kitchen. She put on coffee, standing by the counter while she waited for it to drip through the filter. Her entire body felt raw, exposed, satiated, as if he'd touched every inch her. Of course, he pretty much had. And she'd done the same with him. Neither of them had held back, as if they'd been building up to this moment for the past thirteen years and all the pent-up longing and need had burst, and they'd known exactly what they wanted. He'd pulled off her nightgown without a hint of tentativeness. She'd reached for him, pulled him to her with the same abandon, the same urgency.

"I want you inside me," she'd whispered. "Now, Gabe."

Even as she'd spoken those words, he'd thrust into her. She'd been ready. So ready.

They'd exploded in seconds, clawing at each other, crying out shamelessly.

Later, when they made love again, they'd taken time to explore each other's bodies, to kiss, to nip, to lick, to tantalize. She still could feel his tongue between her legs. Her tongue on him. The way he'd parted her legs, entering her again, slowly, as if to make sure she felt every inch of him and would never forget that moment.

"No chance of that," she whispered to herself, grabbing a mug and pouring coffee.

She took her coffee and a notepad and pen out to the deck and jotted a note for him:

Help yourself to breakfast. I'm off to pick wild blueberries. Taking today off (sort of).
Felicity

She didn't specify where she'd be picking blueberries. Would he remember their favorite spot? Maybe, maybe not, but it wasn't a test. She could very well be back before he got up. They could make blueberry pancakes together. That thought—the images that came with it—made her throat feel tight with emotions she didn't want to explore, or didn't dare to.

She finished her coffee, took her mug inside, left it in the sink and tiptoed back down the hall. She grabbed clothes, making as little noise as possible, and got dressed in the guest bathroom. Gabe hadn't stirred by the time she emerged. She returned to the kitchen for insect repellent, a water bottle and a container with a cover. She left the note on the table where he couldn't miss it and headed outside.

It was a gorgeous morning, the sort she'd be thinking about in a few months, on a cold winter day. In a few minutes, she parked at the Quabbin gate at the end of Carriage Hill Road. She took an old pre-reservoir road, or what was left of it, into the woods. She hadn't been out this way since moving back to Knights Bridge, but she knew this part of the protected wilderness well. After about a hundred yards, she veered off the road onto a footpath that cut back toward the McCaffreys' land. She could have parked at Dylan and Olivia's new place or at the Farm at Carriage Hill, but it was so early—she didn't want to disturb them.

She took in the early-morning sights and sounds. Birds, dew-soaked leaves, ferns and grasses, a cool breeze in the trees.

"I do love it here," she said aloud.

Finally she came to the field behind Olivia's antique house and made her way to a section by a stone wall where low wild blueberry bushes spread out before her, laden with their ripe and ripening fruit. She'd have no trouble filling her container. All she had to do was stay at it.

She started with the bushes in the sunlight, figuring

she could switch to shade as the morning progressed and the sun grew hotter. She stepped past an anthill in the sandy soil and relished the sound of the first tiny berries plopping into the bottom of her container. As a kid, she'd use a coffee can, but she couldn't remember the last time she'd bought coffee in a can.

After a while, she heard a rustling sound behind her. Not a squirrel. Bigger. A deer?

"The best spot in Knights Bridge for blueberry picking," Gabe said, his shadow falling across her.

Felicity stood, feeling a pull in her lower back from her crouching. "I've been at it forever, and I only have half my container filled. Did it always take this long?"

"Wild blueberries are small."

She laughed. "Thanks for that tidbit."

"Goes faster with help."

"Another useful tidbit."

He grinned at her, the sun on his face now. He'd obviously showered. He wore shorts and a faded Red Sox T-shirt. "I brought my own container," he said, holding up a quart-size freezer container. "We can combine what we pick and have a blueberry feast."

"Your favorite is cobbler, as I recall."

"Now my mouth is watering." He pointed his container toward the shade. "Why don't I take a look over there and see how ripe the berries are? You haven't been there yet, have you?"

"Not yet."

He set off, picking his way through the low bushes, skirting the anthill. Felicity watched him, wondering if she looked as at ease out here as he did. It was familiar territory, but it had been years since either of them had picked wild blueberries.

"Do you know what to do?" she called to him.

He glanced up at her as he crouched by a cluster of low bushes. "Nothing to it."

"I have bug spray if you need it."

"So far, so good."

But in five minutes, he'd attracted a mosquito, and she tossed him the repellent. The weather turned hot quickly, but they managed to get a quart and a half of ripe blueberries between the two of them. "Enough for cobbler, muffins and a small batch of pancakes," she said.

"Can't go wrong."

He stood straight, stretching out his lower back and surveying the field. "It's easy to forget how pretty it is out here. I haven't hiked up Carriage Hill since high school."

"You can see Quabbin from the top."

"I remember. Have you hiked to the summit since you moved back here?"

She shook her head. "Not since high school, either. Want to go?"

"Sure, why not? Did you bring water?"

"I did. I noticed you didn't, but I'll share."

They left the blueberries on a rock in the shade and headed across the field to a trail that would lead them up the hill, all the way to the top with its spectacular views. They'd done the hike many times as teenagers, and she'd done it with her parents and brother. There'd been times she'd wondered—hoped—there was more to life than a hike up a hill, but her attitude had softened since then. She knew it was being here with Gabe, too. For now, she wanted to let herself enjoy his company without propelling herself into the past or the future.

"I parked at Olivia's place," he said as they paused at a steep section of the trail. "Maggie was there. She's waiting for Brandon to get back from the White Mountains with his adventure travel clients. She's preparing lunch for everyone. She invited us."

"You told her I was here?"

"She saw you pass by. She was already at the house."

"I didn't notice her vehicle."

"She walked down from the barn. Olivia and Dylan are waiting there for the adventurers." Gabe's gaze settled on Felicity. "I'm seeing Dylan later on."

"About what?"

He gave a slight grin. "I knew you'd ask."

"Saying I'm nosey?"

"Interested. He and I have business to discuss."

"Ah. Intriguing."

"We'll see."

She thought he might continue with more information, but he didn't. "You're figuring out what's next for you. You're ready."

"I am ready. You're good at what you do, Felicity."

"But it's what I do," she said. "It's not who I am."

He took a drink from her water bottle and handed it back to her. "Let's go."

They reached the top of Carriage Hill in another ten minutes. Breathing hard, sweating, Felicity stood atop a rounded boulder and looked out at the view of the valley, flooded decades ago to create the reservoir. The waters continued for miles out of sight, behind more hills.

"Hard to believe we're supposed to get rain later today."

"Perfect weather to make blueberry cobbler," Gabe said next to her.

She glanced at him and noticed he didn't look winded. Whatever he did day-to-day, his schedule had to include exercise. She wasn't particularly winded, either, but she could feel the lack of sleep in her muscles.

They didn't linger on the summit. For one thing, lunch beckoned. For another—Felicity couldn't explain it. She wanted to be around him and didn't want to. She knew he'd leave. She knew they couldn't be friends the way they'd once been friends, not just because of last night. Because of everything. Swimming, talking, sitting by the fire, their families and friends, Knights Bridge itself, their memories of growing up there. She embraced all of it, without any of the anger and hurt of three years ago.

Gabe was quiet on the hike back down the hill. They fetched their blueberries, but he nodded toward the inn. "Shall we join Maggie and company for lunch?"

"I should get back."

"You said in your note you're taking today off."

"Sort of. I added that in parentheses. Plus there's cleaning and laundry and errands."

"All right. I'll meet you there and help."

She tilted her head back and eyed him. "When's the last time you cleaned and did laundry?"

He grinned. "Doesn't mean I've forgotten how."

But he'd called her bluff, and he knew it. Felicity smiled. "Lunch at Carriage Hill sounds great."

* * *

Brandon Sloan arrived at the Farm at Carriage Hill in time for lunch. He looked sweaty, rugged and happy—not just to see his wife and their sons, Felicity knew, but because he'd been off doing something he loved. He'd walked down to the antique house after seeing his adventure travelers off, on their way back home to their jobs and lives.

"How are the White Mountains?" Maggie asked him as she set out a simple meal of salads, cold meat, rolls and ginger cookies.

"Gorgeous. I found a great spot to take you and the boys."

"Oh, my favorite thing, climbing tall mountains with my food spoiling and my clothes sticking to my back, no bathroom, no—"

"It's an inn we can use as a base for day hikes."

She grinned at her husband. "Now you're talking. But I'd hike with you. You know that."

"Only because you know I'd carry your pack," Brandon said, clearly amused. "The inn's nice, but it's not as grand as where I stayed with Noah and Dylan after our big hike last summer."

"It doesn't have to be grand if it has running water and a flush toilet," Maggie said.

Her husband winked at her. "That's my roughing-it Maggie." He turned to Gabe and Felicity. "How 'bout you two?"

"We just hiked up Carriage Hill," Felicity said.

"You could always pitch a tent up there," Brandon said. "It's not on Quabbin land."

Gabe sat at the terrace table. "Mark and I used to camp out in the woods out here. He liked sleeping under the stars better than I did, which is funny considering he became an architect. We never noticed mosquitoes. I probably would now."

"Spoiled by life in the city," Maggie said with a grin.

Gabe laughed. "I'd at least want a tent now."

"What about you, Felicity?" Brandon asked. "Tempted by adventure travel?"

"When you do inn-to-inn tours, let me know."

"We're planning one in Scotland. Newfoundland's up next later this summer. I'm leaving that one to someone else. We're getting started on construction at Red Clover Inn, and I want to take Aidan and Tyler camping. They'll be happy pitching a tent out at Heather and Brody's land on Echo Lake."

"They'd love it," Maggie said.

Felicity was aware Maggie and Brandon had been separated last summer but had worked out the problems in their marriage after he, Dylan and Noah had hiked up Mount Washington together. She didn't know what had precipitated their near breakup or what compromises had been involved in their reunion, just that they were renovating a house off Knights Bridge common and clearly happy with each other and their lives, separately and together.

After lunch, Aidan and Tyler whisked Brandon off to show him some discovery in the backyard.

"He's never happier than when he's slept on rocks and roots," Maggie said with a laugh, watching her husband. She turned to Felicity. "Kylie's book launch worked out well. She'll be happy to return to her routines. The fairy-tale books she's doing are amazing. I'm glad there were no incidents."

Meaning Nadia. Felicity nodded. "Everything worked out great."

If Maggie wanted to ask about Nadia, she didn't. "Well, you deserve a quiet day."

Gray clouds to the west and a rumble of thunder reminded Felicity of the impending turn in the weather. "My Rover's down the road," she said. "I'll get going. Thanks for lunch."

"Anytime," Maggie said.

Felicity thanked her and headed out with her wild blueberries. Gabe stayed to meet with Dylan, whatever that was about. She'd resisted asking. Dylan likely still had more connections in San Diego, even now, than he did to Knights Bridge, and Gabe had just spent two months in Southern California.

When she reached the isolated spot where she'd parked, Felicity was surprised when she spotted another car. Nadia was shutting the driver's door. "I didn't expect to find you here," she said. "I'm off for a walk to clear my head."

"Alone?"

"Mmm. I left a note on the windshield in case I get lost or trip on a rock or something, but I'm not worried. I'm not going far. I have a cell phone, but I know coverage can be spotty." She pointed at Felicity's container. "Blueberries?"

"Wild ones," she said.

"Yummy. What are you making?"

"Cobbler, I think."

"Gabe's favorite." She held up a hand. "Just something I know by accident. It's not some crazy stalker comment. I'm really sorry I've been acting weird—I went overboard trying *not* to look like a stalker. Look, enjoy your blueberries. I'm off. It looks as if it's a pretty good walk to reach the water. My dad used to love to fish on the reservoir, before we moved West. I went with him once or twice—I couldn't have been more than five or six. He told me about the lost towns. I remember thinking there were houses and people under our boat. Little kid logic, huh?"

"It's understandable."

"Your grandfather was from one of the towns, wasn't he?"

Felicity nodded. "Prescott."

"It was a small farming community. What a hard-scrabble existence for most people, but your family—the MacGregors were bankers even then, weren't they?"

"A family tradition. I should get these blueberries home. We're getting bad weather. You know that, right?"

"That's how Justin Sloan and Samantha Bennett met. In a thunderstorm. Maybe I'll get lucky and meet some hunky guy. My weather app says I've got about ninety minutes before any real weather gets here. That's plenty of time for this city girl to take a walk in the woods."

Feeling somewhat hesitant and ill at ease, Felicity wished Nadia well and got in her car. She had lousy cell coverage and waited to text Gabe when she turned off Carriage Hill Road toward town. Nadia on walk in Quabbin by gate.

You saw her?

Just now. On my way home.

Good.

She's alone.

Thanks for letting me know.

By the time Felicity reached her house, the sky had darkened with ominous-looking clouds. The radar on Felicity's phone showed storms approaching but not overhead. She took her blueberries inside and set them on the kitchen counter. Had Nadia spotted her Land Rover and decided on the Quabbin walk? Had she followed Gabe? Whatever she was up to, Felicity didn't like the idea of her being out in unfamiliar woods with severe weather on the way.

But wasn't that the whole point? Nadia *wanted* people thinking about her.

Specifically, Gabe.

It might not be romantic jealousy at work, but it wasn't anything good.

She let Russ know and wasn't surprised Gabe hadn't been in touch. Maybe he was leaving Nadia to her own devices—not getting sucked into her drama—or was handling her on his own. Either way, Russ promised to investigate.

"I hope I'm not meddling," Felicity said.

"You're not, but meddling makes sense when you're dealing with someone off her stride like this woman is."

"Russ, if she went on this hike with the idea of hurting herself—"

"You said she left a note on her windshield?"

"That's what she told me."

"I'll take a look. Kylie's deep into her work, but you can save me some cobbler."

"This is what happens when you tell people you're making blueberry cobbler."

But her attempt at levity was short-lived, and when she hung up, Felicity had to work at focusing on cobbler. She started by picking over the blueberries, getting rid of stems, bits of leaves and two tiny ants. She washed them and spread them on towels to dry. She could have worked on the dry ingredients, but she took her laptop out to the deck. Thunder rumbled in the distance but she took a few minutes to check her email. It wasn't too bad, considering she'd been off-line all day.

A text came in from Russ Colton: All clear. She found a tick crawling on her and beelined to her car. Off to her grandmother's house.

A tick would do the trick for most of us.

Yep.

Felicity debated a moment but decided not to ask if Gabe was with him. Felicity put Nadia out of her mind and dove into answering her emails. She hadn't anticipated making cobbler alone, but there was no going back now that she had a taste for it. If Gabe didn't return before she finished her email dash, she'd get started.

Gabe saw Nadia on her way and was grateful for Russ's intervention with her. Russ had the patience and professional distance Gabe was having increasing difficulty summoning, given Nadia's intrusions.

Fortunately he had his meeting with Dylan, following up a preliminary meeting in San Diego. This one took them into Knights Bridge village. They stood outside the old Sanderson house, a sprawling Victorian built by George Sanderson about the same time he spearheaded the construction of the library where his portrait hung above the mantel. The grand house abutted the small cottage where Phoebe O'Dunn—soon to be married to Noah Kendrick—had lived when she was the library director. The quietest and eldest of the four O'Dunn sisters, Phoebe had discounted marriage for herself. Then she'd met Noah at a costume charity ball in Boston, and both of their lives changed. Gabe had gotten the story from his sister-in-law. He'd been surprised at his growing interest in townspeople, whether ones he'd grown up with, like the O'Dunns, or newcomers, like Dylan, Noah, Samantha, Russ and Kylie.

"The house needs work," Dylan said. "That's not uncommon in this town."

"A lot of old buildings here," Gabe said.

"No shortage of them, that's for sure."

Gabe ran his toe across overgrown grass. "Knights Bridge has its charms. You grew up in Southern California. Miss it?"

"The weather sometimes but Olivia and I still have a place in Coronado. I bought it before I knew her. She's added color. She says everything can't be cappuccino. Her word. I just say it's neutral."

Gabe grinned. "That's what you get, marrying a graphic designer." And if he married a party planner? He put the thought aside.

"No more flying for me until the baby's here."

Gabe noticed the same about-to-be-a-dad tone in

Dylan's voice that he'd heard in his brother's voice. He wondered if he'd ever hear it in his own voice. He pushed that thought aside and nodded to the house. "It'd make good offices. No problem with zoning?"

"None. We checked."

We meant some combination of Dylan, Noah, the Frosts, the Sloans, probably Mark. The entrepreneurial boot camps, the adventure travel and the destination inn would keep Dylan and Olivia busy, but they needed office space. Olivia had a small office at her antique-house-turned-inn, but she planned to give it up when she and Maggie hired an innkeeper. Certainly there was space for her to work out of their new home, but Dylan and Noah wanted to get into venture capital. They needed to hire more staff and needed proper offices. They didn't have enough office space at the barn. Knights Bridge was home base for Dylan and Olivia, but they would be on the go even after the baby. Noah and Phoebe planned to be part-time residents of Knights Bridge, dividing their time between the East Coast, the Kendrick winery on the Central California Coast and his home in San Diego. At eighteen, Gabe would never have predicted Olivia Frost and Phoebe O'Dunn would be married to two such men, but that didn't mean it didn't feel right—it absolutely did.

"You, Noah and I have had a lot of success at a relatively young age," Dylan said. "There's so much opportunity here. So much more to do."

"Anyone else in mind to join us?"

"Yeah. We're just getting started. We're talking to a woman who just left the NAK board. She has more experience in this area than we do. We'd love to recruit her."

"Will she be interested in life in Knights Bridge?"

Dylan grinned. "Not happening but she can work with us from wherever she wants. You can, too, Gabe, but…" He shrugged. "Your choice. Knights Bridge is your hometown."

"Thanks, Dylan. I used to mow the yard here. Looks as if it could use me again."

"You'll think about joining us?"

"I will, very seriously."

"Great. You look as if you're in a hurry."

"I've been thinking about wild blueberry cobbler for the past few hours."

"Any kind of cobbler is irresistible as far as I'm concerned. Enjoy yourself."

Gabe stopped at Moss Hill on his way to Felicity and cobbler. Russ met him in the main lobby. "Nadia called me earlier," Russ said. "She knows she went too far and put people on alert, especially you and Felicity. She's been in a self-destructive mode. She doesn't want to end up getting a restraining order slapped on her. She said she knows feeling sorry for herself doesn't justify acting out inappropriately."

"She needs to pick up the pieces of her life and move on."

"You're not the one to help her do that. You know that, right?"

"Oh, yeah. I know."

"I told her not to try to make amends to you and Felicity."

"Do you think she'll take your advice?"

Russ didn't answer at once. Finally he shook his head. "No, I don't, and I wouldn't be surprised if her route to making amends will be inappropriate if not illegal. She's got work to do to get her head screwed on straight."

"Then again, don't we all."

But Russ didn't smile. "When are you putting your place in Boston on the market?"

"I don't know yet." Gabe felt his hesitation and suspected Russ noticed. "I didn't have a solid plan once I sold my company. That was a mistake, but I have options."

"Including in Knights Bridge?"

Gabe hesitated but nodded without going further.

"I swear this town has a tractor beam," Russ said. "It keeps pulling people in. I feel it. So does Kylie, and we aren't from here. I can't imagine what the pull would be with family in town."

As if to emphasize that point, Mark came out of his office. Gabe chatted with him for a few minutes after Russ excused himself. Jess was feeling better today, hoping she was over the worst of her morning sickness. Mark, too, queried his brother about how long he'd be in town this trip. Gabe didn't have an answer.

"The beauty of not having a nine-to-five job," Mark said. "Heading back to Felicity's place? Tell her hi for me." He paused, eyes narrowed. "And behave, Gabe. Breaking her heart twice is two times too many."

Twice? Felicity?

"I've never broken her heart at all."

His brother didn't bother to hide his skepticism, but he said nothing further.

Gabe, truly mystified, headed to his car. He saw a flash of lightning and heard a crack of thunder as he jumped behind the wheel.

Twenty-Two

❧❧❧

There was nothing like the smell of freshly picked wild blueberries bubbling in the oven, Felicity decided as she pulled the cobbler from the oven. The tart-sweet scent permeated the kitchen and living room, making her house feel homey and welcoming. It'd started to rain, but the worst of the storm had slid to the south. She'd pulled out the dry ingredients for the cobbler and measured the flour, sugar and butter, so everything was ready when Gabe walked through the door.

He'd looked preoccupied but insisted he didn't want to talk about whatever was on his mind, not with a cobbler to get in the oven. Felicity assumed the "whatever" involved his meeting with Dylan McCaffrey and Nadia turning up again, but she didn't press him for details.

"We can't eat a whole cobbler by ourselves," she said.

"We can't?"

"Correction. We shouldn't eat a whole cobbler by ourselves."

"I promised to stop by Red Clover Inn. I don't know about Samantha, but I don't see Justin turning down blueberry cobbler."

"We shouldn't dig in first. That would be rude."

"I'll call them."

While he made the call, Felicity covered the cobbler with foil and wrapped it in a towel. Gabe rejoined her. "That was quick," she said.

He grinned. "It didn't take much convincing." He lifted the cobbler but stood still. "Felicity…"

"What's on your mind, Gabe? Besides wild blueberry cobbler."

"I can't have it both ways," he said. "I can't stay in town for a few days *and* bunk with you. We need space—not just because of town gossip but because of us." He steadied his gaze on her. "I want to get this right."

She nodded. "I do, too, Gabe." She left it at that. "Where will you stay?"

"I've accepted Justin and Samantha's offer to stay at Red Clover Inn."

"Okay. Good. Makes sense." Felicity cleared her throat and pointed at the cobbler. "I'll limit myself to one helping of cobbler. You guys can polish off the rest and bring me back the pan."

He winked at her. "We'll wash it first."

The next days were a whirl of work, walks and getting to know Gabriel Flanagan again. Felicity wondered if it was the same for him in getting to know her again. They drove out to her parents' house for a picnic with her brother and his wife and two small children. Gabe visited his father on his own, met his father's new girlfriend, worked on old motorcycles with him. He called Felicity one evening, and they played Clue with Justin and Samantha in the musty, charming library at Red Clover Inn.

She and Gabe made love, too—sweet and intense

and wonderful, Felicity thought as she walked to the covered bridge, clearing her head after a packed work day. Last heard from, Gabe was reading a book in the hammock at the inn. He was definitely ready to get back to work, but he was taking his time, not plunging in with his usual impatience.

She didn't linger at the covered bridge. As she approached her house, she smelled smoke and assumed Gabe was there, but she didn't see another vehicle in the driveway. She went down to the fireplace. The fire was dying down on its own and posed no danger. An expensive handbag was plopped next to an Adirondack chair. Felicity recognized it as Nadia's and bit back her irritation. Nadia had promised she was going home to Malibu to hit the reset button on her life.

Felicity headed onto the deck and saw the doors were open. She poked her head inside and saw the living room was a mess, as if someone had started searching for something and then decided just to grab decorative pillows and throws and heave them onto the floor in frustration.

She ran back outside.

Where was Nadia now?

Felicity spotted footprints in the muddy path that led down to the river. She and Gabe had slipped off to the swimming hole twice since he'd moved into Red Clover Inn. They'd stuck to leaping into the river from the rope, swimming, sunning themselves on the rocks like a couple of happy seals. It was as if by unspoken agreement they'd decided to be friends only while at the swimming hole, test out what that was like. As far as she was concerned, it was great but not enough. Not that she had any plans to skinny-dip.

When she reached the swimming hole, the rope was

dangling from its branch, out of reach from the riverbank. The river was high, muddy from yesterday's
rain. She didn't see more footprints but noticed a towel
floating in shallow water by the rocks. She got closer
and realized it was hung up on a branch in the water.
She didn't recognize the towel as one of hers. Had
Nadia come down here with her own towel?

She jumped onto the boulder and peered up and
down the river, but she didn't see or hear anyone.

She started to turn but spotted a sandal in the water,
poking out from under a jutting section of the boulder.

Had Nadia fallen? Gone for a walk barefoot?

Felicity dug out her phone. She didn't know what
was going on with Nadia—why she was in Knights
Bridge, if she was in danger, wanted to cause trouble.

Time to get some help out here.

Gabe had vacated the hammock for Red Clover
Inn's sprawling front porch and was on the phone with
Shannon. "Nadia called looking for you," Shannon
said. "She's a mess, Gabe. I warned her against negative self-talk. That sort of thing isn't helpful. You don't
say, *My life sucks.* You say something like, *I've gone
through a rough time, but I've come out of it stronger
and happier.* Have you ever read a self-help book?
Visited a self-help website?"

"No."

"I'm not surprised."

"Shannon—where is Nadia now, do you know?"

"No idea. She said she wants to move on, but she
knows she needs to resist a fight-or-flight reaction.
She'll take her time deciding what's next. She came
out of the divorce okay financially. She doesn't need to
rush into things. She'll get her head sorted out first."

Gabe got to his feet and stood at the top of the porch steps. "Can you find out if she's in Malibu or out here?"

"I'll do my best. My guess is she never went home, and she's still out here."

"Are you concerned she's going to cause trouble?" Gabe asked.

"Fifty-fifty," Shannon said without hesitation. "More like she's going to cause trouble for herself. I'm keeping an eye out as best I can, but I'm not her keeper. Neither are you."

"Understood."

"I just wanted you to know she called and she's a mess. In case she shows up there again."

"Thanks, Shannon."

As he disconnected, Felicity called. "Have you seen Nadia?" she asked before he could say a word. He said no, and she quickly explained the situation. "It's wet out here, Gabe. The rocks are slippery. The water's high. If she fell and hit her head…"

"On my way."

Gabe grabbed Justin, but they decided not to take any chances and alerted his firefighter and police-officer brothers. They took Justin's truck out to Felicity's house and met her down at the swimming hole. The blustery wind stirred up the river, creating white caps in the fast-moving, mud-brown water.

Felicity waved to them from the rocks. She'd scooped a towel and woman's sandal out of the water and set them on the boulder next to her. She pointed down-river. "I think I just heard someone call for help. It must be Nadia."

"Wait here," Justin said. "More help's on the way."

But he and Gabe found Nadia about a hundred yards

downriver, clinging to a tree branch on a treacherous section of the tree-lined bank. She was terrified and shivering but otherwise unharmed. They got her back to the swimming hole. Justin called his brothers and canceled the search party.

"I was waiting for you and Felicity," Nadia said, clinging to Gabe. "I thought a fire would be fun. Welcoming. I wanted to tell you I'm going back to California in the morning. I'm making a fresh start, without David. Then everything got away from me. I threw a royal fit. I tore up your living room, Felicity. I told myself I was looking for proof Gabe and my ex-husband had colluded against me. Then I realized that was nuts."

"Just get warm," Gabe said. "Leave the rest for later."

"No, no—I have to say this. When I realized you and Felicity were happy and I was miserable—that you'd found someone and I'd lost someone—I wanted to blame you. I wanted to blame Felicity, too. Misery loves company, right?"

Gabe was at a loss. "Nadia—"

"Everything exploded inside me. It was cathartic, and yet I felt so out of control. I ran down here. I stood on the rocks and realized the life I could have had if I'd set better boundaries for myself with David. I've been so absorbed in regret, anger, venting, blaming—myself most of all—and I started to cry. Then I slipped. I couldn't get control of myself in the water." She stood back from Gabe, allowing Justin to put his overshirt around her shoulders. "I could have died, and everyone would have thought it was suicide. That's not me. That's not what I want. But part of me just wanted to float down the river and be done with it all. Then I knew I needed to let the past float down the river, but by then I was drowning."

"You didn't drown," Gabe said. "You're here, Nadia."

"Yeah. I am. I have work to do on myself, but I have plenty of money—not as much as if I'd stayed with David and done a better job of protecting myself, but enough."

"One step at a time."

"I didn't mean to end up in the river. I promise I didn't mean it." She sniffled, tightening the shirt around her. "This is proof I don't belong here."

Justin eased in on her right side, Gabe on her left, and they helped her up the steep trail. Felicity led the way back to her house. She assured Justin she didn't want to press charges against Nadia for throwing a few pillows and blankets, and he went on his way.

Nadia borrowed a set of flannel pajamas from Felicity and wrapped up in a blanket on the deck, her shivering easing as she warmed up and calmed down. "Is there anyone you want me to call?" Felicity asked.

Nadia shook her head. "Not on the East Coast, anyway, now that my grandmother's gone. If I'd drowned, I suppose my ex-husband would want to know, if only because of the paperwork." She managed a weak smile. "Sorry. That was a bad attempt at humor." Her voice caught. "It's time I went home once and for all. California is home for me."

"Stay here as long as you like," Felicity said.

"It must be hard sometimes not just to sit out here for hours and hours. It's so quiet and peaceful." Nadia was silent for a moment as she stared down through the trees. Finally she looked up at Gabe. "I never pictured you growing up in such a spot. I guess you and Felicity both grew up here, in a way. I'll never have that kind of shared history with anyone. It really is special."

He nodded. "It is."

"I've been such an idiot. How close was I to getting arrested?"

"Not that close," he said with a smile.

She grinned at Felicity. "You see? He's not like the SOB I married. David would have had me arrested in a heartbeat." Before Felicity could respond, Nadia sighed deeply, looking up at the clearing sky. "I need to stop thinking about him, talking about him—letting him control my life. Trust me, he's not thinking about me. I know that. I know what I need to do. Thank you."

Once Nadia was warmed up, she handed Gabe her key fob. "I parked down the road a bit and took a different trail to the swimming hole."

"I know the spot," he said.

He fetched her car and brought in her suitcase. She changed into her own clothes, thanking Felicity for letting her borrow her pajamas. "No problem," Felicity said.

"I don't think I own any flannel. I probably wouldn't even if I lived out here."

Felicity laughed. "Tell me that when it's ten degrees out."

"Ha."

"Where are you off to now?"

"The airport. I'll stay at a hotel there overnight and catch an early flight back to LA. I promise."

"Are you sure you don't want someone to drive you?" Gabe asked her.

She shook her head. "I'm okay, Gabe. Really. Nothing like a near-death experience to get one's head screwed on straight—well, straighter than it was." She kissed Gabe on the cheek. "Be well. Good luck with whatever's next for you."

"You, too, Nadia."

He walked with her to her car. She turned to him before she climbed in. "I've never had any romantic interest in you. You know that, right? It's been hard to let go of David. Harder than I ever would have imagined. Losing him left a big hole in my life, and it shattered my self-confidence. I'm sorry, Gabe. I've been so self-absorbed." She tilted her head back and smiled. "You know you're head over heels in love with Felicity, don't you?"

He wasn't going there. "Felicity and I have been friends for a long time."

"Noah Kendrick and Dylan McCaffrey have been friends a long time. You and Felicity? There's something else there. But that's for you two to work out." Nadia inhaled deeply. "It's a great little town but I'll be glad to be back in LA. I'll take the best of my old life with me and leave the rest behind." She bit her lip. "And therapy. I'll be in therapy for a while, I think."

"Good luck, Nadia."

"Thank you," she said, and she got in the car, blowing him a kiss before she started the engine.

The scare with Nadia had affected Felicity more than she wanted to admit—or even realized at first. She drove Gabe back to Red Clover Inn. Mark, Russ, Kylie, Justin and Samantha had all gathered on the front porch. Felicity watched Gabe as he explained what had happened, not that he had to. Felicity felt her throat tighten. She had an urge to pull him aside and tell him she didn't need to stay in Knights Bridge.

She could be an event manager in Boston or San Diego or just about anywhere else as easily as she could in Knights Bridge. Maybe more easily, or at least more successfully monetarily. But she resisted, instead choosing to enjoy the company of friends.

Gabe decided to drive to Boston. He had things he'd been putting off, he told everyone. Felicity walked with him to his car. "I'll be back soon," he said, pulling open the door.

"Sure thing." She forced a smile and blew him a quick kiss.

He blew a kiss back, and as he drove off, she realized he'd been affected by the scare with Nadia, too.

When she went home, it was as if nothing had happened. She and Gabe had tidied up after Nadia's fit.

Felicity poured herself a glass of wine and took it and a book out to the deck. Reading would help calm her after Nadia's near-drowning.

This was home for her.

After a few pages of Hercule Poirot on a train, she couldn't concentrate and gave up on her book. She stood at the deck rail and gazed down at the river. The water wasn't as high as it'd been earlier. She heard birds, watched a squirrel race up a pine tree.

Would she really give up her life here for Gabe's high-flying life?

Could he be happy here?

There were too many questions for tonight, all of them without answers.

Twenty-Three

~∽⟨⟨⟩⟩∾~

Shannon proudly showed off the finished living room in Gabe's condo. He was pleased with how it had turned out. With Nadia back home in Malibu, everyone was calmer.

"One more thing," Shannon said. "Felicity is in town."

"Boston?"

"Only town in my world. She's stopping by in—" Shannon glanced at her phone "—twenty-two minutes if she's on time."

"And she called you instead of me?"

"So it appears."

Felicity arrived on time. Apparently she'd meant to surprise Gabe, but Shannon had missed that cue. He gave her a tour of the condo.

"It's quite a place, Gabe," Felicity said when they returned to the living room. She stood at the windows overlooking Back Bay. "You've done well. You work hard. You take risks. You're smart. You treat your free-lancers and employees well. I'm not surprised, you know."

"Figured I'd be a successful start-up entrepreneur when we were in second grade?"

She grinned at him. "Kindergarten."

They both laughed, but he could sense something was on her mind. "What's up, Felicity?"

She turned from the windows. "I was just thinking about how different my life is from yours. How different Knights Bridge is from Boston. I mean, here I am, thinking about making my annual ratatouille when I get home."

Shannon frowned as she joined them from the kitchen. "What's ratatouille?"

Felicity explained. "I make enough to freeze for the winter."

"That's what people do in small-town New England, Shannon," Gabe said.

She shuddered. "I can see freezing tomatoes and applesauce, but the only eggplant I like is fried and covered with mozzarella, parmesan and tomato sauce."

"Ratatouille in the dead of winter reminds me of summer," Felicity said.

"Sitting on the beach in Fort Lauderdale for a week reminds me of summer," Shannon countered.

"Gabe's grandmother taught me how to make ratatouille," Felicity said. "She's gone now."

"But her ratatouille recipe lives on," Gabe said. "She'd like that. I think she was the first person in Knights Bridge to make it."

"There are all sorts of versions," Felicity said.

"I would like the kind that doesn't really taste like ratatouille," Shannon said. "Are you using vegetables from your own garden?"

"I don't have a vegetable garden yet," Felicity said. "That'll come in time. I get fresh veggies from friends with gardens and from the farmers' market."

"It's still every Wednesday on the common?" Gabe asked.

She smiled. "Some things don't change. Anyway, I postponed my ratatouille. I had some business in Boston I needed to tend to."

Gabe noticed Shannon make a discreet detour to talk with the painters, now working in the kitchen.

He turned to Felicity. "Need a place to stay?"

She glanced again out at the view. "It's a great location. This place is great, but it's—I don't know. It feels temporary."

"It is temporary."

"That's how you live your life, isn't it?"

"It has been, but I'm still young. So are you." He smiled. "You can always travel while the ratatouille is in the freezer or on the vine."

"I love to travel. I missed going places when I was digging myself out of debt."

"Do you think you got stuck in being hyper-responsible?"

"After being hyper-irresponsible? Maybe."

"You have to leave some room in your life for a little fun. If you could go anywhere, where would it be? Home doesn't count."

Her eyes sparked. She didn't hesitate. "Wyoming."

Felicity went to her meetings in town and met Gabe for dinner at a quiet restaurant in the North End. As much as she was enjoying her time in Boston, she knew it wasn't for her anymore. Knights Bridge, friendship, family. They were on her mind, even on a beautiful summer evening in the city.

"I never felt part of Knights Bridge growing up, not

the way you did," she said, seated across from Gabe at their cozy table. "I was always the banker's daughter."

"In your head. It was how you saw yourself."

"The way Nadia saw herself as her ex-husband's victim."

"Not that bad. You were just a kid."

"I feel a part of things now," she said.

"You made that happen by moving back to Knights Bridge, being yourself."

"Accepting I didn't want to be a financial analyst, never mind wasn't any good at it. What about you? How do you feel about Knights Bridge these days?"

"I've spent a lot of time telling myself I didn't belong there—convincing myself that success and happiness lay anywhere but Knights Bridge."

"But that's not true?"

"No," he said quietly. "It's not true."

She picked up her wineglass. "What's on your mind, Gabe?"

He told her about Dylan's invitation to join him, Noah Kendrick and a former colleague in a new venture capital business.

He studied her, his eyes narrowed in the candlelight. "You know about venture capital, don't you?"

"One of the jobs I was fired from. I lasted eight months. I learned a lot."

"Wasn't eight months your record?"

She smiled. "See?"

"I'll continue to do start-ups. I don't need to be in Boston to do that. Dylan's opening offices in the old George Sanderson house."

"I heard a rumor about that, but I didn't realize you two had been talking about working together." Felicity drank some wine and set down her glass, absorbing Gabe's words—taking in his mood. Focused, certain. He'd made up his mind since he'd arrived at her house ahead of the boot camp, wanting to sleep on her couch. "I've never been inside the Sanderson house. Can you see yourself with an office in the turret or something?"

"The octagon room," he said with a grin.

"People say the house is haunted. Evelyn Sloan insists it has more ghosts than the library, if you believe in that sort of thing."

"Is old George's ghost one of them?"

"Evelyn didn't say."

"Well, I guess we'll find out."

"We, huh?" She noticed her heartbeat had quickened. "You want me in on your ghost hunts, do you?"

"You'll love a good ghost hunt. Felicity, back after our night…the summer before college…" Gabe took a breath and leaned across the table, the candlelight flickering in his eyes. "I wanted to propose to you."

"Gabe…"

"I talked myself out of it. I knew it was crazy. We were too young, and I was afraid I'd lose you as a friend. And I was driven."

"You had places to go, things to do and money to make."

"I did, and so did you."

"Even if it brought me full circle back to Knights Bridge."

"Me, too. Us." He reached across the table and took her hand. "I memorized my proposal. I rehearsed it for days. I haven't forgotten the words. I love you with all my heart, Felicity. I want to be with you for the rest of our lives. You're my best friend, and you're the love of my life. Will you marry me?"

"Pretty good words, Gabe," she said.

He smiled. "They are. I'm not quoting them to you, Felicity. I'm saying them to you now, all this time later. It's been staring me in the face. Why I haven't settled with a woman. Why I'm so driven. Why I've never found a real home." He paused, his gaze riveted on her. "It's because you're my life. You're the woman I love and have loved since we were teenagers. I didn't want to risk losing you, and I almost lost you, anyway."

"Gabe…" She almost couldn't speak. "You've always been the one. Always. You always cared about me and just about me—not that I was the banker's daughter or the hotshot financial analyst, or now, whether I'm a success at event planning or just want to pick blueberries and make ratatouille. I see that now. I didn't want to disappoint anyone, but you least of all."

"You never could disappoint me, Felicity."

"I see that now."

"Do you want me to say them again?" he asked her.

"The words you memorized?" She smiled, squeezing his hand. "Yes."

"I love you with all my heart—"

"I mean *yes* to your proposal. I love you, Gabe. I've loved you for so long, and I'll love you forever. Yes, I'll marry you."

They walked back to his condo, hand in hand, enjoying the summer evening, talking about vegetable gardens and blueberry-picking and stacking cordwood for the winter…and their wedding. Felicity smiled as Gabe pulled her close.

"Another Knights Bridge wedding," he said.

"This time it'll be our wedding. It'll be a fun one to plan."

"I thought you don't do weddings."

She looked up at the city lights, imagined the stars at her house—*their* house—on the river. "I don't do many weddings, but ours?" She slipped her arm around his waist. "I can't wait."

Twenty-Four

~⟨⟨⟩⟩~

Gabe had tickets to Jackson Hole. A glamping tent reserved. Hiking routes mapped out. For now, though, he and Felicity sat in front of the fire on a cool evening on the river. She couldn't have been happier. It was just them, beautiful scenery and enough cordwood to last as long as they wanted to stay out here.

They'd set a date for their wedding. They'd have it at Moss Hill, and they'd spend their honeymoon in Wyoming.

Finally.

"Wyoming will be great," Gabe said. "But I love being here."

"It's perfect."

For a small town, Knights Bridge was as filled with news as ever. Olivia and Dylan had announced they were having a girl. Jess's morning sickness had eased. Justin and Samantha were hosting her cousin's wedding on the day after Thanksgiving at Red Clover Inn. Heather and Brody would fly in from London and take Heather's plucky grandmother back with them to see as much of England as she could manage at eighty-plus.

Christopher Sloan had flown out to LA to visit

Ruby O'Dunn. No report yet on that visit, except that he'd gone for a drink at Marty Colton's Hollywood bar. Nadia had been in a few times and was getting her head screwed on straight, talking to Marty about launching her own film production company.

Hammers and saws continued to fly in Knights Bridge, with all the new ventures and newcomers, but some things—the best things—didn't change.

The real things, Felicity thought.

"Are we going to let our kids in on our swimming hole?" Gabe asked, stretched out next to her on the quilt.

"Not without supervision—especially as teenagers."

"Ha. We'll see how that goes."

"We'll have a lifetime of grand adventures, whether it's at the swimming hole, picking blueberries or scooting off to Wyoming."

He smiled. "Making ratatouille doesn't count."

She laughed. "But it was good ratatouille, wasn't it? Don't lie to me, Gabriel Flanagan."

"It's the eggplant. I'm with Shannon on that one. Make ratatouille without eggplant, and I'm in."

"There's yet time."

"Or…we could do other things."

"Yes, we could," she said.

His mouth found hers as the fire crackled and the night turned dark, the river flowing gently down the steep bank through the woods.

* * * * *

Dear Reader,

Thank you for reading *The River House*. I hope you enjoyed your visit to little Knights Bridge. If it's your first visit, you can find a list of all the books in the Swift River Valley series and their reading order on my website.

For me, diving into a Swift River Valley novel is like returning home. I grew up on the western edge of the Quabbin Reservoir and its protected wilderness. How to fire a budding writer's imagination! Our family homestead is still there, and I visit often.

Summer in New England is a special time, and as kids, my six siblings and I had our favorite swimming holes. On my runs at home in Vermont, I often pass a popular swimming hole that reminds me of Felicity and Gabe's more private swimming hole. I've posted a few photos on my blog if you'd like to take a look.

I continue to add Swift River Valley recipes to my website. Unlike Gabe and Shannon, I love eggplant in my ratatouille! And you just can't go wrong with brownies…or oatmeal bread fresh out of the oven…or anything Maggie Sloan puts together. Blueberry cobbler is one of my favorites. Turn the page for a recipe!

Thanks again, and happy reading,

Carla
CarlaNeggers.com

A Recipe from Carla Neggers:
Blueberry Cobbler

Ingredients

3 cups blueberries
(fresh or frozen, wild or cultivated)
12 tablespoons butter
½ teaspoon salt
2 teaspoons baking powder
¾ cup sugar (reduce for less sweet cobbler)
½ cup whole milk
1 large egg
1½ cups all-purpose flour

Directions

Preheat oven to 375°F (190°C).

Spread 4 tablespoons of the butter, melted, in an 8-inch square pan. Top with the blueberries. Sprinkle ¼ cup of sugar over the berries.

Add milk and egg to remaining 8 tablespoons of butter, melted. Beat well. Mix flour, salt, baking powder and ½ cup sugar together in a medium bowl. Stir in the milk, butter and egg mixture. Pour or add by dollops to the top of the berries.

Bake for about 30 minutes, until dough is cooked through and berries are bubbling with the sugar melted. Serve plain or with whipped cream or vanilla ice cream.